Trouble in Paradise
Trophy Wives Club Series Book 4

Annette Mori & Ali Spooner

Also by Annette Mori

Single Books

Georgetown Glen
Disconnected
The Others
Sculpting Her Heart
One Shot at Love
The Panty Thief
Pleasure Workers
A Window to Love
The Book Witch
The Book Addict
The Dream Catcher
Unconventional Lovers
Captivated
The Termination
The Review
The Ultimate Betrayal
Locked Inside
Out of This World
Asset Management
The Incredibly True Adventure of Two Elves in Love
(Affinity 2014 Christmas Collection)
Love Forever, Live Forever
The True Story of Valentine's Day
Vampire Pussy...Cat
Nicky's Christmas Miracle X3
(It's in Her Kiss, Affinity's Charity Anthology)
Donner Junior Saves the Day

Co-authored
The Organization with Erin O'Reilly

Also by Ali Spooner

Trouble in Paradise
Trophy Wives Club Series Book 4

Annette Mori & Ali Spooner

Affinity
Rainbow Publications

2022

Trouble in Paradise
Trophy Wives Club Series Book 4
© 2022 by Annette Mori & Ali Spooner

Affinity E-Book Press NZ LTD.
Canterbury, New Zealand

1st Edition

ISBN: 978-1-99-004980-4 (paperback)
ISBN: 978-1-99-004977-4 (EPUB)
ISBN: 978-1-99-004978-1 (PDF)
ISBN: 978-1-99-004979-8 (KINDLE)

Editor: Angela Koenig
Proof Editor: Alexis Smith
Cover Design: Irish Dragon Designs
Production Design: Affinity Publication Services

ACKNOWLEDGMENTS

Annette's

A huge thank you to Ali Spooner who lets me wiggle my way into her brilliance by agreeing to co-write yet another in the TWC series. I would also like to express my gratitude to Affinity Rainbow Publications who continue to provide feedback to tighten up manuscripts that need help and publish my unconventional work. I am eternally grateful for the opportunities they give me to let my stories see the light of day. Thanks to Nancy Kaufman for her beta edit. Thanks to Angie for her magic as the final editor to further tighten the story. She is a delight to work with. Inevitably, those pesky errors slip through, and I am thankful that Alexis Smith, the final proof editor, caught those before the book went to print. Thanks to Nancy Kaufman for the final cover. A huge thank you to all the other readers and fellow writers who have sent personal emails, written reviews, and posted nice things on Facebook (you know who you are). The Affinity authors are an incredibly supportive group and often share posts or send words of encouragement. Finally, my wife, Jody, continues her support even when it interferes with our time.

Ali's

I would like to thank my fans for following my stories, providing great feedback, and encouragement. Writing wouldn't be so much fun without you. Thanks to Affinity, Irish Dragon for the cover art and the team of editors, readers, and publishers who continue to help me grow as a writer.

DEDICATION

*To Erin O'Reilly who was our mentor and friend.
We will miss her gentle spirit and wise advice.*

TABLE OF CONTENTS

CHAPTER ONE

Marley looked at her lover, Luna. "I wonder what the urgent staff meeting is about?"

"It does seem a bit odd for Lindy to give us an hour to prepare," Luna said.

"That barely gives me enough time to get everyone in early." Marley groaned.

Luna's phone pinged with a text, then Marley's. Luna looked at hers first. "Alex wants to know about the meeting. She got a text from Lindy to be here by eight."

"Same with Elise," Marley reported. "I hope it's not bad news."

"Me too," Luna said. "It's a heck of a time of the year to be looking for a job."

Marley shook her head. "Lindy and the others have too much invested. They would lose big time if they shut this place down. Still, I can't figure out what is so important we have to have an emergency staff meeting."

"I guess we'll know in less than an hour. We better get a move on if we are going to shower and eat some breakfast," Luna pointed out.

"I don't think I can eat right now, but a shower is much needed. You gave me a heck of a workout last night." Marley smiled at her lover.

"We consumed a lot of carbs last night with that pasta. I promised I would work them off of you." Luna returned her smile. "I enjoyed burning every one of them, too."

"You didn't hear me complaining either," Marley reminded her. "Let's hit the shower, and I'll head downstairs while you eat."

†

Lindy and Remy were finishing up breakfast. Remy looked over at Lindy. "You know how cruel this must feel to them, calling an emergency meeting and not telling them why?"

"I know but, hopefully, after we give them the news, they will forgive me," Lindy said as she handed the server a credit card. "I didn't want someone to let our little secret out of the bag. You didn't tell Chancy yet, did you?"

Remy laughed and shook her head. "Goodness, no. She's not capable of withstanding the pressure from Alex or Luna if they grilled her."

"Good call then. I think the group will all be pleasantly surprised. When are you going to tell Chancy?" Lindy asked.

"Today, when I buy you a burger at Sisters. Unless the grapevine has gotten to her first, should we warn them about tipping her off?"

Lindy laughed. "If you want it to be a surprise, we'd better ask them not to tell Chancy. Does Danna know yet?"

Remy shook her head vigorously. "Hell no, she's worse than Chancy. It would have been all over Atlanta this morning if she knew. I think we'll let Alex have that pleasure."

Lindy smiled at her best friend. "I do like how you think." Lindy signed the check. "Are you ready to go break some news?"

"I am going to have a hard time keeping a straight face, but I'll do my best," Remy replied.

"That's all I could ask. Let's roll." Lindy stood and led them out of the restaurant.

†

"I can't believe you have no idea what is going on," Alex grumbled. "You're our manager, after all. You should know everything."

"Well, I'm sorry I don't. I'm just as much in the dark as you all," Marley admitted. "I have no clue what Lindy is going to drop on us."

"I guess we will know in just a few minutes," Luna said as she pointed to the security monitor showing Lindy's car pulling up.

"No matter what it is, we'll make it through this, ladies." Marley attempted to cheer everyone around the table, but the sad looks she was receiving let her know they weren't buying the story.

†

Lindy walked through the front door and saw the worried looks on the faces of her employees, and she felt remorseful for a few seconds.

"Thank you all for meeting with us this early and on such short notice," Lindy said as she and Remy took a seat around the table.

"You've certainly got our attention this morning, boss. What's up?" Marley asked.

Lindy looked at Remy, who nodded. "We have news we wanted to share with you this morning before any more time goes by," Lindy reported. "Remy and I have come to a decision. We are closing the club."

"You're what?" Luna cried out.

"Wait and hear me out before you jump to any conclusions," Lindy said, but Luna was already out of her chair and pacing.

"You should know that we would never leave you in the lurch," Remy said.

"I would hope not. We have bills to pay and would need a new place to live," Luna retorted.

"You better give them the Paul Harvey before Luna pops a muscle," Remy told Lindy.

"Luna, please come sit back down," Lindy requested. Once Luna returned to her seat, she continued. "We are closing the club, but only for two weeks to do some deep cleaning and routine maintenance."

"Thank goodness," Marley said.

"It was a bit cruel to tell you like this, but I hope after our next bit of news, you'll forgive me," Lindy said. "Oh, and before I forget, it does not leave this room until all parties, a.k.a. Chancy and Danna, are notified. Got it?"

"Yes, ma'am," Marley answered.

"Remy and I have decided it's time for a TWC family vacation. We are preparing to fly everyone to St. Kitts in the eastern Caribbean to stay at one of her resorts for two weeks."

"Did I hear that correctly? The Caribbean, for two weeks?" Marley asked.

Remy nodded. "That's right, the week before and after Christmas, if that's good with everyone. We'll fly home after the New Year."

"Holy cow. That's so much better than being fired," Alex said.

"That's only two weeks away," Marley replied. She punched Luna in the arm. "We've got to get busy shopping. I've got nothing suitable to wear."

Remy smiled at Marley's comment. "I will send you the website address to the resort later this morning. You will have access to every amenity at the resort, free of charge. Snorkeling, surfing, ATV tours, you name it, and it will be available to you."

"Pinch me, so I know I'm not dreaming," Marley said. "This is the best Christmas ever. Thank you. I'm still not sure you'll be completely forgiven today for being so cruel, but that's a damned good start, boss."

Lindy smiled. "I couldn't resist, but I'll promise never to do it again if that helps."

"You almost gave me a heart attack, boss," Luna replied.

5

"That's another thing. When we get to the island, I'm strictly Lindy, and no work is permitted. Only fun and pleasure for you and your partners."

Marley's eyes had filled with tears. "Thank you both for this wonderful gift."

"You all have worked so hard to build this club into something special for the other members and us, and we wanted to be able to give you something in return." Lindy smiled. "Besides, a little fun in the sun never hurt anyone, right?"

"Do I need to send an email to the members regarding the maintenance shut down?" Marley asked.

"Yes, go ahead, Marley. With all the holiday parties and activities, I don't think anyone will be too disappointed," Lindy replied.

"Should I go ahead and schedule the maintenance and cleaning, too?" Marley asked.

"Yes, we will need to store the upstairs equipment somewhere so the cleaners won't be able to determine the special services rendered there," Lindy said, making air quotes with her fingers.

"We could get footlockers for storage and then put them in our flat, which we could seal off from cleaning or maintenance," Luna suggested.

"That's a great solution," Lindy said.

"I can help you, and we'll get a few today," Alex offered. "They will fit easier in the bed of my truck."

Remy chuckled. "I love it when a plan comes together."

"Okay, so now that everyone's blood is pumping, let's get to work. Marley, you and I need to go over the financials," Lindy said.

Remy looked at Lindy. "See you at Sisters at eleven?"

"I'll meet you there," Lindy replied.

"I don't have an appointment until ten. Do you want to go get the footlockers?" Alex asked Luna.

"Yes, we can do that," Luna said.

"Come back to the office, and I'll get you a credit card," Marley told Luna.

"I'll be right back," Luna said and followed Marley to the office. "That was some great news, but that was mean of Lindy to do that to us."

"It was all in good fun. I don't think Lindy realized the effect it would have on us, so maybe that was a good lesson for her, too," Marley replied. She opened a small safe and handed Luna the credit card. "I can't wait to go shopping with you."

"Maybe tonight?" Luna asked. "It may be hard to find swimsuits this time of the year, so the earlier we start, the better."

"I hadn't thought of that. If we can't find something here, I'm sure we can find swimwear once we arrive in St. Kitts," Marley replied.

"That's a definite yes, but I want to see you modeling them." Luna laughed. She bent down to kiss Marley. "I'll see you soon."

"See ya, boss," Luna called to Lindy as they passed in the hall.

"Sorry about almost giving you a heart attack," Lindy said.

"It's all good," Luna said.

"That was pretty mean of you," Marley said. "We had already been going through doomsday scenarios while we waited for you, and then you dropped the bombshell."

"Not my best effort at humor. I realize that now, and I hope to make it up to you all soon," Lindy admitted.

"I'm sure by the end of the day, we'll have forgiven you." Marley smiled. "It's hard to stay upset with you."

"That's good to know," Lindy replied.

"You normally treat us very well," Marley said.

"I promise that won't change. I hope everyone is as excited about the trip as Remy and I."

"Once reality sets in, I think everyone will be busting at the seams to go," Marley told her. "Once Remy sends me the link to the resort, I'll share it with everyone."

"Very well. Let's get down to business," Lindy said.

†

Marley and Lindy reviewed the financial spreadsheets for over an hour. Over all, Lindy was pleased with the performance of the club. Marley had proven to be a quick study with the financial software and understood the report well. She and Lindy discussed areas where the club could improve and put an action plan together to reach the new goals.

†

Luna and Alex went to one of the local sporting goods stores to purchase the footlockers. Several heads turned to look at the two bronzed Amazons as they walked down the aisles.

"Can I help you ladies find something?"

Luna turned to see a petite blond approaching.

"We're looking for footlockers," Luna said.

"Follow me," the young woman said. She led them to the section for storage containers. "Do you have a preference for size?"

Luna looked at Alex. "Something big enough for a body?" she asked.

"Yeah, she's not much bigger than this young lady." Alex played along.

Luna saw the woman's face contort in horror. "We're just teasing. I think two of these smaller ones would work."

"Especially if we cut her in half," Alex said with a wink to Luna.

"You two better stop before I'm obliged to call the police," the woman said.

"We need it to store some equipment," Luna explained. "I'm a personal trainer, and this one, lugs power tools around all day."

"I see," the young woman said, but she was careful to keep a safe distance from them.

"Blue or black?" Luna asked.

"One of each, so we can keep them separate. Do these come with locks?" Alex asked.

"No, but we have a wide selection of locks. Do you need me to get a cart?"

"No, ma'am. We've got these," Luna said and picked up a container.

"I wonder if they float?" Alex asked.

The young woman spun on her heels. "Stop it," she said with a grin. "No, they won't float."

"Hey, do you still carry swimsuits and beachwear?" Luna asked.

"We have some on a clearance rack, but the sizes are pretty limited. I, uh, don't think we have any that would fit either of you," the woman answered.

"Not for me. For my girlfriend. We're going to the Caribbean for Christmas," Luna explained.

"Lucky you. The Speedo shop in the mall may still carry a selection," she offered.

"Thank you. You've been a great help and a good sport," Luna said.

"That's the most excitement I've had in here for days. Have fun on vacation," the woman said and walked deeper into the store as Luna and Alex stepped into the checkout line.

"That was fun," Luna said. "Does that make us as bad as Lindy?"

Alex nodded. "Yep, pretty much."

Luna slid the credit card through the machine and waited for the receipt. She picked up the bag holding the locks and followed Alex from the store.

Alex looked at Luna. "I still can't believe we are going on such a lavish vacation," Alex said.

"We're going to have so much fun," Luna replied.

"Do you have Marley's Christmas gifts taken care of yet?" Alex asked.

"No, not yet. I'm still struggling with ideas," Luna admitted.

"I know that feeling. What do you buy someone who already has everything?" Alex asked.

"I believe we are both overthinking this. Danna and Marley may have everything, so I think they would appreciate something genuine from us. Just don't ask me what."

"You're not much help, my friend." Alex groaned.

"Hey, if you come up with something better, let me know," Luna said.

"Maybe we should talk to Lindy. She's pretty creative, and she owes us after that stunt this morning." Alex grinned.

Luna climbed inside Alex's truck. "Yeah, she does. Maybe she'll still be there when we get back."

†

"Are you all set for Christmas?" Lindy asked Marley.

"Ha! Not even close. I'm struggling with gift ideas for Luna. Any suggestions?"

"Let me think about it," Lindy said. "You may want to wait until we reach the islands. I'm sure there will be some unique gift ideas there."

"That's a thought," Marley agreed. "The only thing I've gotten her so far is one of those super smartwatches that tell you everything but the number of teeth you have."

"Oh, she'll love that," Lindy said.

"I think so, too," Marley said. "Are you sticking around for a massage today?"

"I'll be back after my lunch with Remy, so keep a spot open for me."

"I've only got one massage booked today, so you're good any time after lunch."

"Why don't you and Luna get a jump on shopping for the trip if she's not busy today?" Lindy suggested.

Marley's eyes lit with excitement. "That's a great idea. Thanks."

CHAPTER TWO

Chancy Olsen was an easy person to read. In between tapping her fingers on the bar and continuing to flip her phone over to check on an update from Alex, Chancy wasn't surprised her nervous behavior had caught Janice's eagle eyes. Janice was her boss.

"What the hell is wrong with you today?" Janice grumbled. "You're as nervous as a feral cat. Please don't tell me you and Remy are already a distant memory. I warned you not to get involved with those straight society ladies. Even ones as nice as Lindy and Remy. They'll never be able to embrace any part of their queerness. Other people's opinions matter too much. Reputation is everything. It even trumps love."

"What? No. We're good. Better than good." Chancy scrunched her face. "Wait. Have you heard something?"

13

"Does this have anything to do with the reason you need every first Thursday of the month off? Did you get in over your head again? Please don't tell me that some crazy stalker is going to cause trouble in my bar?" Janice's eyes narrowed at Chancy before Selene, her wife, approached the bar.

Chancy breathed a sigh of relief that Selene once again would come to her rescue and save Chancy from having to tell another little white lie.

"This looks intense. Do I need to play referee again?" Selene winked at her wife.

"Why don't you ask the little cougar charmer?" Janice crossed her arms over her chest and glared at Chancy.

Selene turned her twinkling eyes to Chancy. "Are you in trouble? Hope it's good trouble."

"Don't encourage her," Janice chastised.

"Your energy seems a bit frenetic today. We appreciate you coming in to cover for your roommate. Did you have plans with Remy today? You could have said no. We would have figured it out." Selene settled onto a stool.

"Um, no. It's fine. I knew you were in a bind." Chancy decided to tell a partial truth without giving her bosses the whole story. "I'm sure Alex will fill me in on the meeting I had to miss."

"What meeting? Since when do you have meetings?" Janice asked.

"You know, I do have a life outside of the walls of this bar," Chancy answered with a degree of belligerence.

Selene patted Chancy's arm. "We know you do, hon. That's why I got concerned. Maybe we rely on you too much. You're always picking up additional shifts when we're short-staffed. Should we stop calling you so much?"

"No, no, I appreciate the concern, but I need the money, so it's all good." Chancy glanced at her phone as it danced on the bar. Pointing to the phone, she said, "Excuse me for a minute."

Chancy moved a short way down the bar and read the text from Alex.

Meeting is over. Lindy and Remy are on their way to Sisters.

WTF Alex. Can't you give me a clue? Is TWC shutting down?

Can't. Sworn to secrecy. Chill and exercise a little patience.

I got skipped when they handed out the patience gene.

LOL. TTYL.

"Fuck." Chancy shoved the phone into her back pocket. She wasn't sure how in the hell she was going to finish paying off her Christmas gift if they shut down the club and she didn't have her very lucrative Thursday night gig. Chancy hoped the experiment would catch on and grow, giving her more opportunities to make money.

She hadn't exactly been candid with Remy. Sure, she'd been entirely open and honest about her feelings for Remy, blurting her love like a volcano erupting hot, molten words of adoration and passion. What she hadn't been truthful about was her feelings of inadequacy. She wasn't blind to the whispers behind her back at the Women Strong fundraiser. Hell, Helena and Jules had come right out and said the words to her face. That hadn't been a big deal because Chancy could chalk that off to jealousy. But then, she'd been in the bathroom and overheard a group of women talking about the blue-haired bartender from Sisters and not understanding what magic the young woman had to attract three of Atlanta's finest. Of course, it wouldn't last. The women had noted that with such casualness, and Chancy had to agree their presumption wasn't too far-fetched. She wondered when Remy would bore of her dalliance on the dark side.

Everyone assumed Chancy was in it for the money. She wasn't about to become anyone's kept woman, not even Remy's, whom she loved with all her heart. Chancy needed to pay her own way and contribute equally to the relationship. She'd never have the kind of money Remy and her friends had, but she wanted to at least pay for some things. Chancy remembered when Lindy had first broached the idea of a gig. She had jumped at the chance without so much as a side glance at Remy to make sure she'd be okay with it. However, she hadn't completely ignored the deepening of that small worry line on Remy's forehead when Lindy had presented her vision to expand TWC.

†

After the Women Strong fundraiser, Chancy had escorted Remy home and led her to the bed, helping her change into lounging clothes. Remy had settled against Chancy's chest, falling asleep almost immediately. After a restful two-hour nap, Chancy nudged Remy awake, and they both relaxed on the couch as they waited for Lindy to arrive. Even in her exhausted state, Remy was the most beautiful woman Chancy had ever laid eyes on.

Chancy pinched her leg and dramatically cried out, "Ouch!"

Remy chuckled. "What in the world are you doing?"

"Yup, this is real, not a dream. When a person catches the eye of the most beautiful woman in Atlanta, you can't blame me for wondering if this is real. I'm thinking, *Matrix*, the sapphic version."

Before Remy had a chance to respond, Lindy bounded into the room after two quick knocks on the door. "Ready for our favorite Chinese takeout?"

"I am. I didn't have much to eat at the fundraiser, and I'm starved now," Remy responded.

Chancy jumped up and announced, "I'll get the plates, napkins, and utensils." On her way to the kitchen, she lovingly stroked Remy's cheek and leaned in for a short, sweet kiss. Remy smiled, and Chancy's heart skipped a beat. It was going to hurt when Remy tired of her. Chancy wasn't sure what she would do when that day came.

"Thanks, Chancy. No need for forks. We can use the chopsticks," Remy called out.

Lindy unpacked the bags and set the containers on the kitchen table. "I assume you want to eat here versus the dining room."

Remy lifted her hand in the air. "It doesn't really matter. If you prefer, we can eat here. Or you can set the bags on the coffee table and we can eat in the den. You know I'm not one for formal dinners."

Lindy furrowed her brow. "Would that be more comfortable for you?" Lindy was already putting the containers back into the bags and bringing them into the den.

"Yes, I suppose so. I should buy comfortable cushions for that kitchen set, but it covers the beautiful wood. I fell in love with the unique wood patterns in the Cocobolo." Remy settled against the couch pillow.

Chancy returned with three plates and a stack of paper napkins. "Can I fix your plate for you? A little of the orange chicken, spring rolls, crab wontons, and moo shoo pork, right?"

"I am the most spoiled woman in the world. Thank you, my adorable sprite. Small portions, please. I'd rather not be stuck on the couch because I can't move my massive body after eating all this food," Remy joked.

After Chancy made Remy's plate and settled with her own on the couch, she directed her attention to Lindy. "Okay, so I might be a sprite, but this sprite never learned patience like all the good little sprites in the forest. I'm dying to know what you wanted to talk to both of us about. I cannot imagine what I could contribute to the discussion."

Lindy tipped her head back and laughed. "Tact has never quite been a tool in my toolbox, so I'm going to just put this out there. I know you were not oblivious to the chatter tonight after you showed up on Remy's arm. And I'm sure the snide comments came from a place of envy. This has translated into a business opportunity where you will play a key role."

Chancy pointed to her chest. "Me? What do I have to offer?"

Lindy arched her brow. "You've charmed three of Atlanta's finest. Plus, you make the most unique drinks I've ever had. Ones that I assure you, I've never found anywhere else, and I've been all around the world to the best restaurants and bars money can buy. I'm not trying to compete with Sisters because our once-a-month club night will service a completely different clientele with offerings that Sisters does not have. My idea is to offer dancing, drinks, and then special services after the club shuts down at twice or maybe even three times the normal rate."

"Why increase the cost of those special services?" Remy asked.

"Because there will be a high demand and not enough supply. Chancy, this could also be a chance for you to make some additional money providing those special services. Alex told me you might be interested. However, although Luna, Alex, and Marley manage to maintain their relationships separate from their work at TWC, I did not wish to assume the same would hold true for you two. Think about it and perhaps talk it over. I would imagine the bartending part would be of interest without concern. I presume that a Thursday evening once a month would not conflict with your schedule at Sisters."

"How much money are we talking about here?" Chancy asked.

"I imagine that, along with tips, you'll make at least five hundred on just the bartending portion. Maybe more. The special services will bring in two to three thousand. I haven't quite worked out the percentage cut to provide to anyone who agrees to provide one session after hours."

Chancy whistled, then glanced at Remy, whose worry wrinkle had deepened. "That's a lot of money. I'd be crazy to say no to that."

"Like I said, no rush on an answer. Talk it over. I may have to recruit more workers if this goes over like I believe it will. You don't have to accept the second portion of the offer right away. You could see how the bartending goes and then decide."

Chancy grinned. "So, what kind of budget do I have for supplies? Some of my drinks require rare ingredients. Ooh, I could have specific drink specials, and they could change each month. That way, I could almost assure you we'll use up the expensive ingredients. They won't go to waste." Chancy's leg bounced in excitement.

"You can purchase whatever you need, and then we'll charge accordingly. The women who'll likely attend won't blink an eye at a drink priced higher than normal." Lindy grabbed a piece of orange chicken and popped it into her mouth, smiling as she chewed.

†

Chancy glumly walked to where Janice and Selene shot concerning looks her way. "Lindy and Remy are coming for lunch today."

"Well, that's good news, right? You love when they come for burgers. Why don't you look happy?" Selene asked while catching the eye of the other server. She mouthed a request that the server put a reserved sign on the booth that Lindy and Remy usually sat at.

"Um, I didn't want you guys getting all worried, so I didn't really tell you what I'm doing on those first Thursdays of the month, because honestly, it doesn't affect your business. I worried you might consider it a competition for your bar, but it's not, I swear. It doesn't matter anyway because they're probably going to tell me it isn't working out like they thought."

Janice waved her hand in the air. "Oh, we know all about TWC's Thursday night club where you serve your fancy drinks. And, before you get those nonexistent panties in a bunch, we know about the special services, too. Figured you were a part of that now. And given your propensity to attract stalkers who are not ready to let go, we worried you might get in over your head."

Chancy's mouth fell open in surprise. "H...how did you know?"

"Hey, we've got a few friends in high places. Plus, neither of us is stupid. We knew when Alex took the job at TWC. For the record, we think Lindy is a brilliant businesswoman. I can't say that I would be okay with Selene providing special services to anyone but me, but I hold no judgment. Is Remy really okay with you, uh..." Janice's words dangled in the air as Lindy and Remy pushed open the door and walked inside.

"Can we talk about that later? I really want to know who told you. But right now, I almost feel like I'm about to walk the plank. I'm going to have to find another way to pay for Remy's Christmas gift."

Remy waved, and her smile settled Chancy. Maybe it wasn't something to worry about. Both Lindy and Remy looked like the cat who caught the canary, which did not exactly track with bad news. But they were definitely up to something.

"Alex didn't spill the beans, did she?" Remy asked as she approached.

"No. Alex texted me to be patient, and you know how hard that is for me," Chancy grumbled.

"Can you take a short break after we have our burgers?" Lindy asked.

Chancy shifted to Selene and Janice for a response.

"Yeah, we'll fill in while you sit with Lindy and Remy," Janice answered.

"Thanks, boss." Chancy pointed to the reserved table. "Your booth is ready. Anything else besides burgers and sweet tea?"

"I'll probably want a slice of that delicious key lime pie if you have any," Lindy answered.

"Excellent idea. Me too," Remy added.

"Bacon?"

"Of course," Remy and Lindy both answered.

Chancy returned to the bar to give the order to the cook. She hoped they wouldn't take too long to eat their burgers. She would join them for dessert if she could force herself to wait that long to learn whatever it was that had prompted the special meeting. Chancy hadn't been able to attend because she'd already agreed to this last-minute shift at Sisters.

Selene nudged Chancy, then whispered, "It doesn't look like you'll be headed to the firing squad, so stop worrying."

"It *doesn't* look like bad news, does it?" Chancy's worry dissipated, but she was still eager to learn what the hell was going on.

CHAPTER THREE

"Are you sure you don't mind locking up tonight?" Marley asked Alex.

"No, not at all. I'm the only one with a late appointment, so it's all good. I may get some sauna time in, and a good workout beforehand," Alex replied.

"Let's go then, babe," Marley said and reached for Luna's hand. "I'm so excited about shopping for this trip."

"If you find some great deals, let me know. I wouldn't mind picking up a few new outfits," Alex told Luna.

"Text me your sizes and what you are looking for, and I'll keep my eyes open," Luna answered.

"Deal," Alex replied. "Y'all have a good time, and I'll see you tomorrow."

"Do you mind driving?" Marley asked.

Luna shook her head. "Not at all. I assumed I would drive anyhow." She grinned. "Did you have a good day?"

"Yes, not bad at all after the crazy start to the morning. I worked Lindy hard during her massage as payback." Marley laughed.

"She sure deserved it," Luna agreed. "Even though the news was terrific, it was mean for her to deliver it that way."

"I think she learned her lesson, and she truly regrets her poor choice of humor. You know Lindy will find a way to make it all up to us."

"She's been so good to us already, it's hard to be mad at her. Do you want to check out the mall? The girl at the store this morning said the Speedo shop may be our best bet for swimwear this time of year."

"I guess that's our first stop then," Marley said. "Do you want to shop for a bit and then hit the food court, or do you want something a bit healthier?"

"Let's see how the shopping goes," Luna answered. "If we work up an appetite, something more substantial may be in order."

Marley reached over to place her hand on Luna's thigh. "Is your carnivore kicking in?"

"That's a possibility," Luna replied. "A high dose of protein may be good."

†

Shopping in the mall during the holiday season had always seemed like a chore to Marley, but she found she enjoyed the activity with Luna. They both picked out several outfits and walked to the dressing rooms. Marley stepped into a form-fitting one-piece suit and looked at her image in the mirror when Luna knocked on her door. She opened the door, and her hormones skyrocketed. Luna had picked out a pair of black board shorts and a midriff top that fit her perfectly. "Damn, you look good enough to eat. That looks fantastic on you. Turn around so I can get the rear view, please. Oh, yeah, that's a keeper," Marley said.

"They have it in several colors, too," Luna replied. "That swimsuit fits you very nicely. Will you try the bikini on while I'm here?"

"The red or the black?" Marley asked.

"Both." Luna grinned.

Marley nodded and stripped off the one-piece suit. She was reaching for the red bikini when Luna laughed softly.

"When did you get so ripped? I don't remember you having such a nice six-pack?"

Marley smiled. "I have this drop-dead gorgeous personal trainer who works me hard. I've never felt or looked this good in my life."

"You should give her a raise. You look fantastic, and that suit shows off all your hard work." Luna crossed her arms as Marley turned around. "You look great. Would it be cheesy if we had a couple of matching outfits? Maybe not swimsuits, but shorts and shirts?"

"I don't think that's a bad idea at all. We don't have to wear the same color all the time, but the same style would be perfect. You look so much better in the bright colors than I do."

"I guess I'd better be picking out something besides black," Luna joked.

Marley smiled. "You look great in any color. I think we've got the swimwear nailed down. Let's look at shorts and tops next."

They both picked outfits that were similar in style in various colors.

"Do they have a baseball section in here?" Marley asked.

"I, uh, don't think so just yet. Why?" Luna asked.

"Because I'm going to need a bat to beat the women off of you. You look great in shorts and tank tops," Marley replied.

"They can look all they want, but I am one hundred percent yours," Luna said.

"That is such a perfect answer," Marley said. "Have you found anything for Alex?"

"I'm picking up some of the board shorts and midriffs in red and blue for her. I'm going to text her a few pics of these shorts to see what she thinks of them."

"I'll browse while you do that," Marley said. She walked over to a rack of lounge pants and T-shirts and selected a pair for her and Luna. Then she strolled over to the shoe department. There was a large bin of clearance items. Marley found leather flip-flops and no-show socks in both their sizes and found a pair of nice leather loafers for Luna.

"Alex said to tell you she likes your sense of style," Luna said when she joined Marley.

"Do you need any shoes? I found a nice pair of casual loafers for you," Marley said.

Luna shook her head. "I see you found flip-flops, too. I've got a couple of newer pairs of tennis shoes. Do you think we need a nice casual outfit or two for dinner out?"

26

"That probably wouldn't hurt. We can check out one of the department stores before leaving the mall. Have we done enough damage in here?" Marley asked.

"Probably so," Luna replied.

They had to pass by the food court to get to their next destination. Marley pointed to the pretzel shop. "I don't know about you, but I'd love a soft pretzel."

"I could eat at least one," Luna agreed.

The vendor had a special, so Marley got three with mustard for herself, beer cheese for Luna, and a drink to split while Luna took their bags and searched for a table. Marley found Luna and smiled. "I had forgotten how crazy malls can get around Christmas."

"I was lucky to get a table." Luna grinned as she reached for a pretzel.

"We won't be here long. We'll hit the department store and get out of this mayhem," Marley promised.

Finding two outfits was much more challenging than Marley had anticipated. They both ended up with light-weight linen slacks and pullover shirts. "Do you need anything else?" Marley asked.

"To flee this madhouse," Luna answered.

"Let's bolt then," Marley said. "If we find we need anything else, we can order online."

"Amen to that. We still have time," Luna replied.

"Dinner?" Marley asked.

"Steak or seafood," Luna suggested.

"Both." Marley grinned.

✝

The club was empty by the time they returned from their shopping trip. "Would you care to join me in the sauna?" Marley asked.

"That sounds lovely. I'll run these bags upstairs if you want to get the room heating?" Luna replied.

"I'll get it started and join you upstairs in a few minutes," Marley said as she locked the door behind them and reset the security system.

Luna carried the bags upstairs, slipped out of her clothes, then put on a robe. She grabbed a couple of fresh towels and emerged from the bathroom when Marley entered the flat. "All set downstairs?" she asked.

"Heating up as we speak," Marley replied. "I'm going to hang our new clothes while we wait."

"I'll help with that," Luna said and placed the towels on the breakfast table. "Did you get the cleaning and maintenance arranged this morning?"

"Yes, we're all good," Marley answered. She placed the linen pants on a hanger. "I can't wait to see you in these." She smiled at Luna.

"I'm sure we will have numerous opportunities to dress up while we're on the island," Luna said.

"Do you think we have enough?" Marley frowned.

"I think we'll manage with what we both have already," Luna said. "I think I will need to pick up some luggage, though."

"I'm set there."

"I was a bit more nomadic than you before we met. I traveled light, so I never accumulated luggage."

"You can buy some online or go back out to shop," Marley teased.

"Where's my phone?" Luna asked. "I don't care to go back into the fray again unless I have to, and it's only going to get worse."

"That's true," Marley said as she handed Luna her phone.

"What color is your set?" Luna asked.

"Blue with red trim," Marley answered.

"Is this a good deal?" Luna asked and turned her phone toward Marley.

"That's a great price," Marley said.

Luna pushed a button. "Done. It will be here on Thursday."

Marley put the bags with Alex's purchases on the couch. "Let me change, and we'll head downstairs. The sauna was still relatively warm, so it shouldn't take long to heat."

Luna had pulled her hair on top of her head with a clip when Marley returned. "How would you feel if I got a haircut?" she asked.

"Like a trim or what?" Marley asked.

"I was thinking of just below my shoulders," Luna replied. "I read an article about donating hair for cancer patients, and I need at least twelve inches."

"That would still leave you plenty for a ponytail," Marley said. "Do it if that's what you want to do. I think it's a very thoughtful thing."

"You wouldn't be upset?" Luna asked.

"I don't love you for your hair, sweetie. You're beautiful regardless of how long your hair is. Besides, it grows fast. It will be long again in no time."

"What if I go short and change colors?" Luna said.

"I'd adjust," Marley said. "I'm slowly getting used to Chancy's blue."

Luna chuckled. "I don't think my hair would even hold a color."

"You can do whatever you want as long as you leave me a handful to play with." Marley grinned.

Luna swung the door open for them. "That's good to know."

CHAPTER FOUR

As shifts at Sisters went, this was the most shit one she'd had since her broken arm slowed her to barely above a crawl while she attempted to make her fancy drinks. Already she had given the wrong food to two tables of her regular customers who never deviated on their order. Betty, a retired trucker, had been coming to Sisters almost every day, and Chancy knew her order—Grand Slam Sliders with blue cheese, bacon, mushroom, and arugula along with a side order of mozzarella sticks. But today, she'd given Betty and her wife, Alice, another couple's order. Then, after making the exchange, she forgot the limes for their beers on tap.

Chancy caught motion at Lindy and Remy's table and groaned. Shit, she'd forgotten Remy's honey mustard. *What kind of girlfriend am I if I can't even remember that today?* She hurried to retrieve the condiment for Remy.

31

Selene touched her arm before she delivered the forgotten item. "Hey, why don't you take a break? Clearly, you're not firing on all your pistons."

"I can't leave you and Janice with the lunch rush. It's still bananas in here right now. I'll be fine. Let me bus those two tables and deliver the correct order to tables four and five, and by then, I'm sure Lindy and Remy will be ready for their pie. I can join them for dessert. It should calm down by then."

"Okay, but one more wrong order delivered, and I'm afraid I'll have to insist." Selene winked.

"I know, I know. Thank the Goddess it was Betty. She's so good-natured." Chancy grabbed the honey mustard and headed to Lindy and Remy's table.

After she set down the two small containers, Remy grabbed her hand. "Hey, I know you're worried, but you have nothing to be concerned about. We would have told you already, but this place is crazy today, and we both wanted to have a bit more time to discuss everything. Although a fifteen-minute break is probably not going to be enough time. I can fill you in on more of the details tonight. You're coming over, right?"

"Of course. I will miss you too much. Besides, your bed is much nicer than mine." Chancy grinned.

Chancy had settled enough to finish serving during the rush because she certainly trusted Remy. And if Remy said everything was fine, Chancy believed her, despite that niggling sensation in the back of her mind that things were going too right for her and she was about to lose everything. Again. Gutter rats like Chancy did not deserve the good life with a gorgeous woman by her side. Carrying three slices of key lime pie, Chancy set the desserts on the table before sliding into the booth next to Remy. Under the table, she quickly squeezed Remy's thigh before slowly caressing the inside over the fabric of her linen pants. Remy shook her head in amusement.

"Okay, please spill now. My patience has now reached the end of the frazzled rope it's been attached to," Chancy declared.

Lindy had already taken a small bite of her pie and quickly chewed before responding. "I decided to close TWC for—"

"Fuck. I knew it," Chancy interrupted and, without taking a breath, continued, "but Club Night was going really well. At least, I thought it was. I know I disappointed some of the ladies when I told them I wasn't offering the special services, but I didn't want to jump into that without getting some pointers from Alex and talking it over with Remy." Chancy glanced at Remy. "If it makes a difference, I'll do it. Although, I'm not sure it's a good idea to offer those services to Helena. She asked, but that doesn't feel right to me." Chancy bowed her head to keep Remy and Lindy from seeing the tears that had built in her eyes. Frustration at not being good enough threatened her fragile state of mind. With great effort, she sucked in a breath and lifted her eyes to face Lindy.

Lindy shook her head, appearing partly amused and somewhat concerned. "Chancy, if you'd only let me finish. We're only closing TWC for deep cleaning and some minor maintenance. Since the club will be closed for two weeks, we plan to take everyone to St. Kitts for Christmas. Everyone has worked so hard to make TWC a success, including you, Chancy. It was way overdue for us to thank everyone properly."

Chancy's eyes blinked rapidly. "So, does that mean I'm not losing my new side job?"

"Of course not. As you said before, Club Night has been an enormous success. After the holidays, I plan to have Club Night twice a month. I might even consider every Thursday, as long as you're able to work that out with Sisters. And, yes, I know that you're a hot property. Even without the shortage of workers to provide special services after the Club Night shuts down, I have no doubt you would be in great demand. But, as I said before, the decision is yours and yours alone to make. With Remy's blessing, of course." Lindy dug into the pie again, taking a larger bite than before.

Remy narrowed her eyes. "You never told me that Helena approached you."

"Um, yeah. Helena apologized for her comments at the Women Strong fundraiser." Chancy shrugged. "It's not good to hang onto negative thoughts, so I told her it was okay. She totally surprised me when she asked if I was part of the special services staff. Even if I agreed to join the team, I would never provide those services to Helena. We have history, so it wouldn't be right. Um, I might not have enough money right now to afford to go to St. Kitts, but I appreciate you including me in the plans."

Lindy set her fork down. "None of the staff are paying for this. I thought that was implied in what I just shared."

Chancy shook her head. "I'm not your regular staff. I've only tended bar three times for you. Nine hours of work hardly warrants an expensive vacation to St. Kitts. I may not be all that worldly, but I know that will cost an arm and a leg. I don't have either to spare."

Lindy's jaw set. Chancy had never felt so intimidated by a mere glance in her direction. Even Janice's lectures paled in comparison as Lindy addressed her. "So, are you telling me you plan to quit TWC? I'm going to have to find another mixologist?"

"What? No. I was kind of counting on this job to pay some bills I have coming up."

Lindy folded her hands on top of the table. "Well, good, because if you don't allow me to be a good employer and sponsor this vacation for you, then that will only mean you aren't working for me anymore. That's the deal. The job won't be yours if you don't accept this small perk."

"That's blackmail," Chancy sputtered.

"You do know my husband is a judge. I doubt very much I'll spend any time in jail for that." Lindy chuckled, then picked up her fork again and took another large bite of pie.

Remy grabbed Chancy's hand. "Please, just accept Lindy's generosity. I don't want to go to St. Kitts without you. Besides, since I own the resort, Lindy only had to make arrangements for the private jet. It will be our first Christmas together, and I can't think of a better place to celebrate the holidays. Alex, Marley, and Luna have no problem with our plans. I believe they went shopping today for new clothes and bathing suits."

Chancy groaned. The hopeful look on Remy's face was Chancy's undoing. "I hate being poor. I'm not even sure I have clothes for this little excursion."

"I think an advance is in order. I have to make sure I don't lose the best mixologist in the state of Georgia. Hell, probably the whole United States. I'm going to pay you for the Club Nights I plan to schedule in January and February.

That should give you enough money to buy whatever clothes you need. Well, now that is all settled, any chance you can box up a whole pie for me to take home?"

✝

Fortunately, Sisters had a slow evening after the lunch rush. When Alex walked in, Chancy was able to chat with her while filling drink orders.

"Lindy is a scary woman," Chancy said.

Alex chuckled. "Don't tell me. I can almost hear the conversation. You were trying to let your stupid pride interfere with this incredible opportunity to spend quality time with your girl, soaking up the sun and having some other mixologist serve you. Sometimes, Chancy, good things happen to good people. You're well overdue."

"Wait. There is no way I'm letting some hack bartender make our drinks. Not going to happen. Did you know she threatened to fire me if I didn't accept this gift? I told her that was blackmail."

Alex threw her head back and laughed. "You did not."

"Oh, yes, I did. Lindy just laughed it off and reminded me that her husband was a powerful judge. That shut me right up. But honestly, it was the look on Remy's face that nailed it for me. I didn't want to disappoint her."

"I know a thing or two about pride, but never let that impede your relationship with Remy. Listen, Danna and I are about as opposite as two women can be. Ours is a similar circumstance. When I met Danna, I didn't have a pot to piss in, but we fit together like apple pie and ice cream. You'll find your way, and eventually, you'll feel worthy of her love. But you gotta do the work. And that means taking a hard look at yourself and where that stupid pride comes from. I'm good at two things—fixing stuff and pleasuring women. I take great pride in both. I'll admit I've found a lot more self-esteem after opening my business, but what I do matters."

"Sure, it matters. Sisters would be lost without your talents. You've saved them so much money. TWC, too. Having a place for women to go to is important. So many women's bars have closed in the last ten years. I honestly believe Sisters would have closed had you not come along to help them."

"Yup, that's the conclusion I came to. Plus, I make my services affordable for all those people in my community who can't afford a high-priced electrician, plumber, or another tradesperson," Alex acknowledged.

"Yeah, well, all I'm good at is making drinks. I'm not even sure I'd be very good at pleasing women. So, I wanted to ask if you would, uh, mentor me. If I join the special services team at TWC, I could make a shit ton of money. But I'm worried that Remy will think less of me. How did you and Danna work through that? Honestly, I don't know if I would be okay with Remy touching another woman. That's so hypocritical of me, huh?"

Alex smiled. "No, not really. It doesn't work for everyone, but Danna understands that. I am simply providing a needed service to these women. I don't let my emotions get in the way. I've always been able to separate sex from making love. I don't have sex with Danna. I make love with her. And, for the record, being a mixologist gives a lot of women great pleasure. Good food and drink go well together. People need to unwind, and you provide a most delicious way of serving them. A mixologist is a noble profession in my mind."

"Yeah, right," Chancy answered with derision.

"My papa used to tell me the story of the three different bricklayers. Want to hear it? I think it's appropriate to tell right now."

"Sure, why not?" Chancy answered.

"An architect observed three bricklayers one day. One was crouched, one was half-standing, and the third was standing tall with obvious pride. The third man, who stood tall, was working at two to three times the pace of the other two. The architect asked all three what they were doing? The first man answered, 'I'm a bricklayer, and this job allows me to feed my family.' The second man responded that he was a builder and was there to create a wall. The third man practically beamed his answer, stating, 'I am a cathedral builder creating a wondrous place where people will come from far and wide to worship. I do the work of the Lord.' The point of this parable is that every job has meaning. Find that meaning, and you will find your purpose. One that you can take great pride in."

"So, am I supposed to believe that my fancy drinks keep people sane in these crazy times?"

Alex shrugged. "Sure, that works. Giving people some joy and peace is a really good thing. Own it. Own your mad skills."

"Thanks, Alex. You're a good friend." Chancy glanced to the end of the bar and saw a small line forming. "Sorry, I guess the lull is gone. Gotta get back to work and provide those thirsty patrons some of that joy and peace."

"Can I get a beer after you finish serving them? I'm going to wait until St. Kitts, then I expect you to make me something extra special for all my sage advice."

"You got it." Chancy winked.

CHAPTER FIVE

"Man, time is flying by. Just think, in five more days, we will be basking on a beach, sipping umbrella drinks," Alex told Luna.

"Don't remind me," Luna said. "The beach and drinks sound great, but the flying part doesn't."

Alex cocked her head at Luna. "You've never flown?"

"Never, and I'm afraid of heights, too," Luna admitted.

"Are you serious? You've never flown anywhere?"

Luna shook her head. "Never. If I haven't been able to drive, I've taken the train, and even that was only once."

"Well, I'll be damned. You'll ride that Harley with your hair on fire, but you're afraid to fly? That just doesn't make sense, my brave friend." Alex shrugged her shoulders. "Does Marley know?"

"No. I haven't thought of a way to tell her yet."

"Just don't make the mistake of thinking alcohol will make it easier. You'll end up hurling, and that's no way to start a vacation," Alex teased.

Luna glared at her friend. "You think this is funny, don't you?"

Alex shrugged. "I guess it's normal for some people to have a fear of flying. I just never thought it would be you. I'm sorry. I didn't mean to offend you."

"I can't let this ruin Marley's vacation, but I get queasy every time I think of flying," Luna said.

"What? You're not considering not going, are you?" Alex cried out.

"I don't know. What can I do? Time is running out," Luna said.

"You do what we always do when we can't figure something out. Talk to Lindy," Alex recommended.

"I hate admitting to her I have a weakness," Luna said. "I don't know what else to do."

"Text her and see if she has time to talk with you," Alex suggested.

Luna nodded her head and pulled out her phone. She sent Lindy a text. Several minutes later, Lindy replied. *On my way.* "She's on her way."

"If anyone knows how to deal with your problem, it will be Lindy. Get a bottle of juice. You're looking a bit green around the gills. Step outside and get some fresh air. You can meet Lindy outside before she comes into the club."

"Good idea," Luna said and walked to the juice bar where she grabbed a bottle of apple juice. Marley had a massage scheduled, so maybe she could chat with Lindy without Marley knowing.

†

Luna walked outside, and the cool air was refreshing. She sat on a bench at the end of the building. Lindy pulled into the lot; she saw Luna and parked near her.

Luna jumped to her feet when she saw Lindy walking toward her. She felt ridiculous talking to Lindy about her problem. She gave Lindy a sheepish look as she walked over to her.

"Are you okay? You look pale," Lindy said.

"I have a problem I need to get your advice on," Luna said. "I'm embarrassed to admit this to you, but I need your help."

"Don't be embarrassed. Just tell me how I can help," Lindy said.

"I'm terrified to fly," Luna blurted out. "I've never flown, and I'm scared to death. Just thinking about it makes me queasy."

Lindy struggled to hold in her laughter, especially when she saw the look of terror in Luna's eyes.

"I don't want to ruin Marley's vacation, but I don't know if I can do it, Lindy."

"I understand your hesitancy, but millions of people fly every day, Luna." Lindy reached out to touch Luna's arm. "Do you love Marley?" Lindy asked.

"What? Of course, I do. She's my world," Luna declared.

"You know she won't go without you. Does she know you've never flown?"

42

"No, Alex is the only person I've told, and she told me to talk to you. I can't share this with Marley. You know she'll be determined not to go, and I can't have that on my conscience."

"Do you trust me?" Lindy asked.

"Yes, I do, boss."

"Then you must do something for me," Lindy said.

"Anything," Luna said.

"My daughter and her girlfriend are on a mission trip right now, and she's ordered a ring to propose to Maggie on Christmas. I need to fly to Memphis to pick it up from the jeweler in two days. As I see it, we have two options." Lindy looked at Luna, who was ghastly white. "You can fly by yourself and pick it up for me, or you can fly with me, and we can deal with your fear together. Maybe we can pick up something nice for Marley while we're there."

"I can't do it alone. There's just no way," Luna said, almost in tears.

"Then trust me to help you over this hurdle," Lindy said.

"Can I even get a seat this late?" Luna asked.

"You let me worry about that," Lindy said. "Just say yes, and you will learn there's nothing to flying."

"We'll have time to pick something out for Marley?" Luna asked.

"We'll have all day if we need it." Lindy smiled. "I'll have the best-looking bodyguard ever," she teased. "We could spend the night, but I don't want Marley to get suspicious."

"How will I explain that to her?" Luna asked.

Lindy smiled. "We'll tell her the truth. That I need your help for the day to pick up something for my daughter."

"What about my appointments?"

"Cancel them. It's not that big a deal this time of year. We're going to blow our diets over the holiday anyhow," Lindy teased.

"What do I wear?"

"Something that you're comfortable in, and bring a jacket. It gets cold in Memphis this time of year. Don't eat anything but some toast for breakfast. Once we arrive in Memphis, I'll treat you to breakfast before we shop."

"Thanks, Lindy. What if I get sick? Should I bring another set of clothes?"

"If you will feel more comfortable, then yes. I don't think you'll need to, though. I'll go back to the office, make our arrangements, and text you with the details. Go ahead and tell Marley I'm stealing you for the day."

"Just let me know how much I owe you for the ticket," Luna said.

"I'll make you earn it," Lindy said. "Be thinking about something you'd like to get for Marley, though."

"Yes, ma'am," Luna replied.

"Now, go get back to work and make some money," Lindy teased. "I'll text you the flight details. We can confirm the time and I'll come get you when I arrive for my massage tomorrow."

Luna finished the juice and walked Lindy to her car. "Thanks again. For everything."

"No problem. I'll enjoy spending the day with you," Lindy replied.

"I hope so." Luna smiled and walked to the front door.

†

"How'd it go?" Alex asked when she saw Luna return.

"You were right to have me talk to Lindy. She has a solution."

"Really? What is she doing?"

"I'm flying with her to Memphis to pick up a gift for her daughter. She's going to propose to her girlfriend for Christmas."

"Oh, wow. That's a great idea. It's a short flight, but you'll see how easy it is," Alex said. "Lindy's a genius."

Luna felt a bit more at ease, and when Marley's massage room door opened, she smiled. "I need to let her know I'll be gone for the day. Please don't tell her my secret, though."

"I won't mention it to anyone," Alex promised.

†

Marley stepped outside the door and stretched. *Man, she's beautiful,* Luna thought. "Hey, sweetie. Do you have a minute?"

"More than that for you." Marley smiled. "What's up?"

"Lindy asked me for a favor, and I couldn't say no. I'll be gone all day the day after tomorrow to help her pick up a Christmas gift her daughter ordered for her girlfriend."

"Okay," Marley said. "I'll try my best to survive a day without you. You'll be back that night, right?"

"Yes, ma'am, I will. I hope we never have to spend a night apart," Luna said. "Love you. I'd better get back to work. I've got some appointments to cancel."

"Join me for a salad for lunch later?" Marley asked.

"Just let me know when," Luna said and leaned down for a quick kiss.

†

Lindy felt herself smiling as she pulled away from the club. She hadn't expected to have that conversation with Luna, but she fully understood Luna's fear. She had flown so many times during her adulthood, but she remembered her first time flying when she went to Texas to visit family when she was ten. Luna was hardly ten, but the fear wasn't any less for her. Lindy would need to develop a plan to keep Luna's mind occupied during the flight. Thankfully, it was only a forty-five-minute hop. Lindy pushed a button on her console to call her travel agent to change her reservations. When the agent asked for Luna's information, Lindy told her she'd call her right back. "Crap, I forgot about the details." She pushed a button to call Luna. When Luna answered, Lindy asked her to text her a picture of her driver's license to book the flight. "I forgot all about needing your information. I'll text you later. Thanks!"

"Thank you, boss," Luna answered. She ran upstairs to take a picture of her ID and send it to Lindy.

†

Luna spent the rest of the afternoon calling to reschedule her appointments and then went up to the flat to stretch out on the bed. She intended to think about a gift for Marley, but the emotional turmoil of the morning had her

46

worn out, and the bed was too comfortable. Luna drifted off and didn't wake for two hours until Marley came up searching for her. Luna sat upright in the bed when she heard Marley call her name.

"Hey, there you are. Did I disturb your nap?" Marley asked as she sat on the bed.

"I hadn't intended to nap, but I guess I drifted off."

"Are you feeling okay?" Marley asked and felt Luna's forehead.

"Yes, I'm good," Luna replied. "I intended on planning something and fell asleep."

"What on earth were you thinking so hard about?" Marley asked.

"I've got this beautiful woman I'm totally in love with, but I can't figure out what to get her for Christmas," Luna explained.

Marley smiled. "That woman is so lucky to have your love. She doesn't need anything besides you."

"That's not the point. I need to get something, but I just haven't figured out a gift yet. Any ideas?"

"I'm sure she'd like anything that comes from your heart," Marley said.

"Like what?" Luna pressed.

"Something simple. A home-cooked meal and a night together. You're going to a romantic island soon. Maybe you can find something for her there. I'm sure whatever you do will be perfect."

Luna pulled her in for a kiss. "I do love you with every ounce of my energy."

"I know, and I love you even more."

"Impossible. I'm bigger than you," Luna teased.

"Speaking of home-cooked meals. What are we having for dinner?" Marley asked. "I forgot to take anything out to thaw."

"Next best option is a cheeseburger from Sisters," Luna said. "Are you game?"

Marley nodded. "We haven't been in a while. Maybe Chancy is working and can make us something delicious to drink."

Luna stood and grabbed her keys. "I'll drive and stick to tea. You can have whatever drinks you want. My treat."

"Maybe we can have a bubble bath when we get back," Marley said. "I need someone to wash my back." She grinned.

"Back or front, I've got you covered," Luna replied. "Let's roll."

†

Chancy looked up and smiled when she saw them walk in. "I haven't seen you two in here for a while. Am I missing a special occasion?"

"Hunger," Luna said.

"One of your delicious drinks, too," Marley added.

"I've been experimenting with something new," Chancy said. "You can test it for me."

"Just me. Luna is driving tonight," Marley replied.

"Do you know what you want to eat?"

"Cheeseburgers and onion rings," Luna said. "Sweet tea for me."

"Let me get your food orders in, and I'll be right back." Chancy walked into the kitchen. She carried a glass of tea when she returned and served it to Luna. "Are you okay at the bar, or do you want a booth?"

Marley looked around. "You don't seem too busy yet. We'll sit with you if that's okay."

"Perfectly fine with me. It's still early." Chancy pulled out a stainless drink glass and began mixing ingredients so quickly Luna and Marley lost track. Several different types of rum and juice with a generous shot of grenadine. Then she walked over to a blender and added ice before dumping the concoction in to blend. Chancy shut the machine off, plucked two cherries, an orange slice, and tucked it on the rim of the drinking glass. There was a small amount left, which she placed into a smaller cocktail glass. Chancy put the glasses in front of them. "A little taste won't hurt you." She winked at Luna.

Marley lifted the glass and smelled. "If it tastes half as good as it smells, I'm all set," she said. She lifted her glass and tapped it against Luna's. "Cheers."

"Damn, that is good," Luna said. "Not overpowering at all, which is surprising since we saw all the flavors of rum you added."

"That is tasty," Marley agreed.

"I'll take that as high praise since neither of you drinks that often," Chancy replied.

"I could see those becoming addictive," Marley said. "I bet several of them could knock you for a loop."

"Oh yeah," Luna replied after taking another sip. "The juice flavors camouflage the alcohol. It's definitely in there, though."

"I think I'll drop back on some of the alcohol," Chancy said.

"Beautiful color, too," Marley said.

"Hey there," Janice said as she brought two platters of food from the kitchen. "We haven't seen you two for a while."

"I'm allowing Marley to feed me cheeseburgers and try some alcohol on occasion," Luna teased.

"My, my. I've rarely seen you drink anything other than a beer once a blue moon," Janice teased. "I have to admit, though, there are many ladies who miss their favorite dance partner."

"Maybe I should let you out more often," Marley said with a wink.

"No way. I enjoy having a home life with you," Luna replied.

"I never thought I would hear those words come out of that mouth, but you look like you've been enjoying yourself," Janice said.

"Life couldn't be better," Luna admitted.

"Enjoy those burgers," Janice said. "Don't be such strangers in the future," she teased.

Luna bit into the burger. "As sinful as I remember," she added with a moan.

"You keep moaning like that, and I'll have to bring you more often." Marley grinned.

Chancy nodded. "That even got my attention." The door opened, and several couples came in. "Give me a nod if you need anything."

"Just a check when you have time," Marley said.

Chancy smiled and went to take drink orders.

†

"That was a real treat, but I am so stuffed," Marley said.

"Are you still up for a bath?" Luna inquired.

Marley grinned. "That will finish me off for the night."

"I noticed you were nodding on the way home."

"Even the size of that burger didn't lessen the alcohol in that drink. I'm so relaxed I thought I was going to slide out of your Jeep."

"I'll start the bath if you want to go ahead and peel off those clothes," Luna said with a chuckle. Luna started the bathwater and added some mango fragranced bubbles. "I hope this doesn't remind her of the drink," she said aloud with a grin.

Luna stepped into the room and saw Marley sitting on the edge of the bed. "Are you ready?" she asked as she pulled her shirt over her head.

"Yes, ma'am," Marley answered with a bit of a slur.

Luna undressed, stepped into the tub, and offered Marley her hand. She stretched out and positioned Marley with her back against her chest. "Just relax and let the bath do the work." Luna wrapped her arms around Marley's waist and closed her eyes. "This does feel great."

Several minutes later, Luna felt Marley relax, and she began snoring softly. She gently shook Marley. "It's time for us to dry off and hit the bed."

"You'll get no argument from me," Marley said as she took a towel from Luna.

When Luna climbed into the bed and wrapped Marley in her arms, it took only minutes for Marley to fall asleep. "I love you," she whispered and kissed Marley's forehead.

51

CHAPTER SIX

Chancy slid the key into the front door as quietly as humanly possible before quickly punching in the security code on the state-of-the-art panel Remy had installed several months ago. Remy had promptly called a locksmith and security company after her ex-husband had shown up unannounced and unwanted, using his key. The last thing Chancy needed was for sirens to come blaring down Remy's long driveway, unnecessarily waking Remy.

Neither Remy nor Chancy had attempted to define their relationship further after Chancy had asked what they were doing. It was poor timing, and Chancy knew that, but she had to know. Remy hadn't wanted to define their relationship further than declaring that she loved Chancy. That had to be enough for now. But it hurt that Remy hadn't officially asked Chancy to move in with her. Not that Chancy would have allowed her pride to accept an official proposal without having enough money to contribute her fair share. However, she would have liked Remy to at least extend the offer.

Instead, Remy had moved a portion of her clothes to the extra bedroom, clearing a corner of her closet and two drawers. As it turned out, only one drawer was necessary, as Chancy's meager belongings fit into the one drawer and half of the space allotted in the closet for her good clothes, including the tux she'd bought for the Women Strong fundraiser.

The tux was an expensive luxury, and Chancy knew she should have saved the money for a new bike—her previous mode of transportation before Remy came to the rescue after her accident. Chancy still used the leased car that Remy had arranged for the "business deal" they'd struck that had brought the two women together several months ago. Riding a bike to Remy's house after a long shift wasn't exactly doable, and Chancy had spent every night at Remy's since the Women Strong fundraiser. Driving the car was the logical choice, even though Remy still asked every night about whether Chancy was coming over as if it was the polite thing to do.

As Chancy crept up the staircase, the third step creaked, and she cringed. *That's it. Tomorrow I'm going to call Alex and ask her how to fix that step.* She took a moment to look at her lover asleep with her golden hair splayed across the pillow. It still took Chancy's breath away every single time she entered the bedroom, and she saw Remy peacefully sleeping. If she wasn't so exhausted, she'd spend hours just watching her chest rise and fall.

Before removing her clothes, Chancy went to the window to close the blinds. The full moon shed more light into the room, and Chancy feared it would eventually disturb Remy's sleep. Before Chancy had a chance to shut out the moonlight, Remy stirred, and her sultry blue eyes opened, blinking several times before she softly addressed Chancy.

"Oh, I'm so glad you're home. I get worried about you leaving the bar so late at night. It isn't like there aren't a bunch of crazies on the road after the bars close."

Chancy smiled. "True. But if I hadn't gotten crushed by one of those crazies, I wouldn't have had the perfect opportunity to woo you. The moon is especially bright tonight. I thought I'd close the blinds."

"The moon doesn't bother me, but if you can't sleep with the light of the full moon, go ahead and shut them."

"Won't bother me. After another double shift, I'm so exhausted I could probably fall asleep standing." Chancy removed her clothes and set them on the chair. Climbing into bed naked, she snuggled against Remy.

"Selene and Janice shouldn't have scheduled so many doubles to make up for the two weeks you'll be gone. It's not like you've ever taken any time off. Everyone needs a vacation to regroup and replenish their energies."

Chancy made small circles on Remy's arm. "I asked them to schedule me that way. It was easiest to have all of my shifts covered during the holidays. I'm picking up everyone else's shifts in exchange for them filling in for me over Christmas. I think I got the better deal. I can't believe Amber agreed to take so many shifts, but I guess her girlfriend is working a lot to help cover for her colleagues. She's low person on the totem pole and got all the crappy holiday shifts."

54

"Mmm, that feels nice, but you better get some sleep. You have another double tomorrow."

"Yeah, and I'm supposed to try to get in a quick shopping trip with Amber before I start my shift. I've never owned a swimming suit before."

"Didn't you ever go on holiday with your parents?" Remy asked.

"Nah, the closest thing that I had to vacation as a kid was church camp. They sent me to that sorry excuse for a camp with hand-me-down shorts and a T-shirt and told me I could swim in the lake without a fancy swimsuit. I've never even been anywhere but Georgia and Alabama where I grew up."

Remy shifted to her side to look Chancy in the eye. "So, you've never been on an airplane?"

"Nope. I'm going to try not to think about the physics of a four-hundred-ton machine lifting into the air and staying there for hours. It seems impossible, yet I know thousands of planes take off every day." Chancy shook her head. "Yup, not going to imagine that at all, or I'll freak the fuck out and not be able to go."

"I shouldn't be telling you this, but maybe it will help, and you can't share it with anyone else," Remy began.

"Ooh, gossip. I can keep a secret. A lot better than some people I know." Chancy chuckled.

Remy playfully nudged Chancy. "Just for that, I'm not going to tell you."

"I didn't mean you. I meant Helena. She was the one who blabbed about TWC and their special services."

"Yeah, I've been meaning to chat with you about Helena. I suppose I know you can keep a secret because you

were certainly tight-lipped about Helena's advances."
Remy's lip formed a straight line.

"They weren't advances. Helena was just asking if
I took part in the special services. I told her no, not yet, and
she asked me to let her know when I was offering those
services because she wanted to be first in line. I would never
agree to that additional work at the club without talking to
you first. I get the feeling you don't like that idea."

"Honestly, I haven't worked through my feelings
about that possibility yet. I know that Alex, Luna, and
Marley seem to keep their work at the club separate from
their relationships. I'm trying to wrap my head around how
that works."

"You and me both. I was going to talk more with
Alex about that. Get some sage advice from her. I could
really use the money."

"Having money isn't everything," Remy insisted.

"Says the woman who has more money than she
could spend in a lifetime," Chancy joked.

"Oh, I could definitely spend it all. I'd like to
spend a lot more on you, but you're such a prideful little
thing. Anyway, let's get back to that juicy piece of
information that should help you with your discomfort over
never flying before. Luna is deathly afraid of flying, and
Lindy is helping her out with her fear. Do we need to go on a
short flight to get you over your fear?"

"Luna? The total badass at TWC is afraid of
flying?" Chancy busted out in laughter.

"Hey, don't you dare say a word to her or anyone
else."

Chancy mimed zipping her lips. "I would never.
But, you know, maybe I should talk with her about my

trepidation and get her expert advice as a worldly woman," Chancy teased.

"You are so bad. I only told you so you wouldn't feel ashamed, knowing you're in good company."

"I know, and I really appreciate the kind gesture. As long as I'm sitting next to you and you hold my hand, I should be okay. But if that plane starts jiggling around too much, I'm climbing in your lap. Or, I'm taking you to the bathroom to distract me while we join the mile-high club."

"Who says I'm not already a member? Now go to sleep."

Chancy's eyes widened. But she did as told because eight in the morning would come far too fast for her liking.

†

"You look like shit," Amber remarked as she climbed into the Ford Edge.

"Working seven doubles in a row will do that to a person. I'm not as young and spritely as I used to be." Chancy put the vehicle in drive and eased onto the road.

"Ha, you're not even thirty yet. I'd say you're plenty young enough to handle it. Something else must be stressing you out. I know you. It's not like you've never survived on less than five hours of sleep at night. Is your woman keeping you up all night, too?"

"None of your business," Chancy quipped.

Amber held up her hands. "By the way. You haven't spent a single night at our place since the fundraiser. I suppose that means you'll be moving. Jen and I wanted to talk to you about that since our lease is up soon. I've kind of committed to Briana. She wants me to look for another place in a better neighborhood. Since she makes pretty good money as an imaging tech, she suggested moving in together. Jen doesn't really care one way or another. She had an offer to move in with her study buddy. I think they're actually an item now, which totally shocked me. You know how Jen is. I thought she was asexual."

"She's on the spectrum, you ass. She's able to form loving relationships, you know." Chancy knew she sounded way too irritated, but bringing to the surface her insecurities about Remy not asking her to move in brought about her foul mood.

"Whoa. Something is wrong. Tell your best bud what ails you."

"It's nothing. I don't really have an answer for you regarding our living situation. Remy and I haven't talked about it."

"Do I detect trouble in paradise?"

"Blunt as always. No, not exactly. Everything is fine. I understand that Remy's had a lot going on with her divorce, cancer, and surgery. Having a double mastectomy is a big fucking deal. She's still coming to terms with losing her breasts and not feeling attractive. Of course, she's a fucking goddess to me, but getting her to believe that has been challenging." Finding an open parking spot near Atlantic Station was a miracle that Chancy wasn't about to second-guess. "At least the parking goddess has recognized I don't have much time before my shift at Sisters starts. We should make a plan. I need a swimsuit, shorts, tank tops, and maybe one nice summer outfit."

"The Gap is a good bet for many of those items. A swimsuit this time of year could be tough to find." Amber waggled her eyebrows. "You could always get some lingerie from Victoria's Secret and use that as your swimsuit."

"Yeah, and advertise how much I am white trash. Funny."

Amber used her thumbs to type something into her phone. "Ha. I'm a genius. Bet you didn't know that Victoria's Secret actually sells swimsuits."

"I doubt very much that any of the swimwear in that store would be remotely close to something I'd choose to wear. Does the Gap have swimsuits? I want something closer to workout clothes. You know, boi short bottoms and like a sports bra top."

Amber continued typing. "Got it," she exclaimed. "We'll find exactly what you're looking for at Athleta."

Chancy undid her seatbelt and climbed out of the car. "All right, let's go. Time's a wasting. I need to get in and get out in less than two hours."

After running through the stores with the kind of style Chancy was comfortable with, she'd spent well over six hundred dollars in new clothes for the trip. Her wardrobe was small, but it would have to do because Chancy had never invested this much in clothes except for the tux she bought for the fundraiser. If Chancy were honest with herself, it made her a little sick with worry that she'd spent that much for the trip. The Christmas gift she had planned for Remy was going to cost thousands, money she didn't really have, but hoped to amass with Club Nights happening more frequently, and the likely prospect of making even more if she offered those special services.

As soon as Remy had confessed that her favorite thing as a child was her horse, the idea took root. Chancy had already started working on having the small horse stable built—

possibly while they were in St. Kitts, but things were not coming together as she hoped. Instead, she might have to consider approaching Lindy for help with a loan and Alex to help build the stables. After all, Alex's business was specifically for people who couldn't afford the high building prices often advertised by others. At least she had a picture of the horse she bought that was still being boarded until she arranged for someone to build the stable on Remy's property. Chancy planned to put the picture in a box and explain her gift on Christmas. She hoped Remy would appreciate the gesture for what it was, her way of showing her love with the most personal gift she could think of. Of course, she could have gotten her jewelry, but somehow, she believed that was less personal. And it was way too soon to buy her a ring.

CHAPTER SEVEN

Luna was between clients when she checked her phone and saw the text from Lindy. *We're all set to fly at nine, and we'll be back by seven tomorrow night.*

"Damn, tomorrow is the big day."

"What was that?" her next client asked as she entered the room.

"Nothing. Just mumbling to myself," Luna replied with a smile. She had one more client after lunch, and then she planned a heavy workout so she'd be able to sleep tonight. Luna snapped back to attention and barked at her client.

"Do those stretches all the way. I can't have you pulling something this close to Christmas," she teased.

"Yes, Luna," the woman replied and began stretching the way Luna had instructed her.

61

When the hour session was up, Luna praised her client. "Great job today. Walk for another five minutes to cool down. Are you hitting the shower or the sauna?"

"I was thinking of the sauna."

"I'd still recommend walking for a bit," Luna said.

"No problem, Luna." The woman smiled at her. "Do you have any openings for extra services this week?"

"Sorry, I'm all booked until we come back after the New Year," Luna replied.

"I may die." The woman groaned.

"Check with one of the others," Luna suggested.

"I will, but there's not another you."

"Thanks, Mrs. Wilkerson." Luna smiled.

"Have fun on vacation. You all deserve to have a great time."

"We plan to do just that," Luna assured her. She began wiping down the equipment, and when finished, sat down on a bench and scrolled through her phone. She pumped her fist in the air when she found an email confirming one of the unique gifts for Marley in St. Kitts. She and Marley had reviewed the website and booked several tours and activities they wanted to enjoy while on the island. Luna was looking forward to the ATV excursion and snorkeling trips. One of the presents she had purchased for Marley was an underwater camera. It would be an early gift once they reached the resort so that Marley could use it on their trips. She had also selected several new CDs for Marley's massage area. Luna had been devious and snooped on Marley's phone to see what music she had been researching. In addition, Luna hoped to find several other small gifts on the island. She would have them wrapped and under the Christmas tree Lindy had ordered to be decorated in their common area.

"There you are," Lindy said as she stepped into the workout room. "I'll pick you up at seven in the morning. How are you feeling?"

"Nervous as hell," Luna said. "I plan on a hard workout this afternoon and a long soak in the bath to help me sleep tonight."

"That's a great idea. Can you break to eat some sushi?"

"I can always break for sushi," Luna said.

"Good. I brought enough for a small army." Lindy chuckled.

"Alex will be here in a bit. She can probably clean up any leftovers," Luna teased. "I'll text her to skip lunch."

"Or come in and join us if she can," Lindy replied.

"I'll see what she's up to and meet you in the juice bar?"

"Please. Marley is already setting out the food," Lindy answered.

"I'll be right there," Luna told her and grabbed her phone. She sent a quick text to Alex.

I'll be there in five. Don't eat it all.

I think you're safe. Lindy bought, and she typically orders one of everything. Drive safe.

On my way.

†

Luna walked into the juice bar and smiled at the table filled with sushi. "Alex will be here in about five minutes."

"What do you want to drink, sweetie?" Marley asked.

"Water, please. I need to go wash my hands."

"Lindy, what are you drinking?"

Lindy grinned. "I think I'll stick with water, too. I know you'll make me drink plenty after my massage, so I'll get a head start."

"Smart move," Luna said as she left the room.

Alex arrived while Luna was washing her hands. "Now that's a sushi spread. Let me wash up, and I'll be right back."

"We'll try to save you some," Marley said. "Water?"

"Yes, please."

†

They couldn't finish the sushi even with Alex's appetite. "I guess I know what we're having for dinner," Marley said to Luna.

"That's fine with me," Luna replied. "I'll take the leftovers upstairs after everyone finishes."

"Stick a fork in me," Lindy said. "I can't eat another bite."

"That sure was good," Alex said. "Thank you."

"My pleasure. I always enjoy watching you and Luna devour sushi." Lindy chuckled.

"I'm so happy Luna got me started on sushi, but it's become an addiction," Alex said. "Danna has even begun to enjoy it."

"I can't wait to try some of the local food down on the island," Luna said. "Especially the jerk chicken. The pictures on the travel site look delicious."

Alex swallowed a drink of water. "There's so much to do there. I don't see how we will be able to see half of what there is to see."

"We'll just have to give it our best. Maybe we'll make this an annual trip," Lindy said. "I haven't been snorkeling in years. I'm looking forward to that."

"Me too," Marley said. "I picked up a couple of those disposable underwater cameras to use."

Lindy was about to say something when Luna caught her attention and shook her head with a panicked look.

"That's a great idea. I think I'll get a few, too," Lindy quickly answered.

"My afternoon appointment canceled on me, so I plan on a hard workout and then some time in the bath. Would you ladies like to join me after your massage?" Luna asked.

"That sounds great," Lindy said. "Are you free afterward?"

Marley nodded. "You are my last appointment for the day."

"Alex, can you join us?" Lindy asked.

Alex shook her head. "No can do, boss. I'm booked up this afternoon and into the evening."

"No rest for the wicked," Lindy teased. "Maybe next time."

"Yes, ma'am." She looked up to see her first appointment had arrived. "I'll see you later."

"Enjoy," Luna replied.

"You, too. Don't strain any of those pretty muscles of yours working out," Alex teased.

†

Luna stored the leftovers in their refrigerator and hit the gym. After stretching, she began a slow jog on the treadmill and worked into a run. Sweat soaked her T-shirt within minutes, and after a four-mile run, Luna stepped off and wiped down the machine. Her schedule called for an upper body workout, so she began hitting the machines going through her training circuit with a heavy load of weights. It was a hard workout, but that was what Luna had planned. The exhaustion in her muscles as she worked the different groups felt great. Luna wiped down the machines with arms trembling from exertion and then finished her routine with deep stretching.

"We're on our way to the bath," Marley said when she stuck her head into the gym.

"I'll be there in just a minute," Luna answered.

†

"I never knew someone could look so delicious coated in a sheen of sweat," Lindy said when Luna walked into the bath. "You are a lucky woman."

"Yes, I am. I have to agree with you. Luna glows after a workout like that. I wouldn't walk for days, but she does them with little to no soreness."

"Here we go. Wait for it," Lindy teased as they watched Luna pull the shirt and sports bra off in one easy motion. "Ah." Lindy sighed at the sight of Luna's firm muscles. "Jaydub never looked even half that good in his prime."

Luna slid her shorts off and then stepped out of her shoes. She turned to look at them. "Did you enjoy the show, or should I begin again?"

"You are such a tease. Rinse off and get your gorgeous self in here," Lindy said.

Luna rinsed off and walked to the bath. "Damn, this feels great," she said as her body slipped beneath the steamy water.

"Yes, it does," Marley agreed. "Did you have a great workout?"

Luna smiled. "Yeah, I did. It was nice to go that hard." She looked at Lindy. "How was your massage?"

"Heavenly as usual. Marley has such magical hands," Lindy replied.

"I have to agree with you there. Marley can make every ounce of tension disappear in minutes," Luna said.

They made idle chat until Lindy looked at the clock. "I'd better get moving. I've got a date with a gorgeous young woman tomorrow. I'll see you at seven."

"Yes, ma'am. I'll be ready," Luna answered.

"Remember. Toast only in the morning." She smiled. "I can't wait for you to experience Brother Junipers for breakfast. The best omelets you'll ever eat, eggs, pancakes, virtually any breakfast item you can imagine, so be hungry."

"You're making me hungry already." Luna smiled.

"Goodnight, ladies," Lindy said.

"Are you ready to head upstairs to shower and hit the sushi?" Marley asked.

"If you are," Luna replied.

"I know you've worked up an appetite, and I'm hungry, too," Marley said as she stood and offered her hand to Luna.

Luna took her hand and stood, then pulled Marley into her body for a kiss. "Dessert later?"

Marley took a step away from Luna, turned back toward her, and smiled. "That could be arranged."

†

"That was just as good as earlier," Marley said.

"Yes, it was," Luna agreed. "Just enough to feed us one more time, too. I couldn't survive the thought of disposing of leftover sushi," she teased.

"I hear that. Are you excited about your day out with Lindy tomorrow?"

"Yeah. I'm sure it will be a day filled with excitement," Luna said. "Will you miss me?"

"Terribly," Marley answered. "I've gotten used to having you only a few rooms away from me. I think it's great that you're helping Lindy out, though. She's done so much for us."

Luna smiled. "She's changed our lives for the better. I still look back on the night you walked into Sisters to discuss the plan with me as one of the best nights of my life."

"Are you ready to go make some more memories?" Marley asked as she reached for Luna's hand.

†

Marley's hands untied the belt to Luna's robe and then slipped the garment from her body. Her fingertips glided over the smooth muscles down Luna's arms until she reached her hands. Marley lifted them to her mouth and kissed each one. "You are so beautiful. I could look at you for hours, but right now, I want your hands all over me."

Luna smiled and removed Marley's robe before leading her to the bed. She positioned Marley on her back and laid beside her as her right hand began gently caressing Marley's face. Marley shivered at the intense look of passion in Luna's eyes as her fingertips glided down to tease her nipples. Marley wet her lips in anticipation of a kiss as Luna bent her head down.

†

Luna felt Marley shiver under her touch. She had never felt so deeply in love with anyone before Marley. Every inch of her body was beautiful, and Luna wanted Marley to feel her passion. Her mouth closed over Marley's for a slow, tender kiss as Luna's hand cupped a breast, softly stroking her erect nipple between her thumb and forefinger. Marley's hands encircled Luna's waist, urging her closer as their tongues danced seductively. Luna moved her body on top of Marley without breaking the deep kiss they enjoyed. Her hips instinctively began undulating against Marley as Marley's hands caressed her ass. Luna ended the kiss and whispered to Marley. "I love when you play with my ass, but I've got to taste you." Luna's mouth blazed a fiery trail down Marley's neck to cover her left breast as her hand slipped between their bodies to tease her lower lips with the moisture flooding from Marley. "You must like this too."

†

"I love everything you make me feel," Marley purred. She spread her legs wider to give Luna better access. Marley buried her hands in Luna's damp hair as it cascaded onto her body, causing ripples of pleasure and goosebumps as the cool, wet hair drew across her skin. As Luna moved lower, Marley lifted her feet and rested her thighs on Luna's broad shoulders, inviting her to feast until they were both sated.

†

Luna wasted no time after receiving Marley's invitation, and the tip of her tongue traced Marley's outer lips. "You taste so good," Luna replied in a sultry voice, then her tongue dipped deeper inside, curling to lap at the forming droplets of moisture. Her left hand spread Marley's entrance open as two fingers entered her slowly, and Luna's tongue teased her clit to attention.

"Oh, hell yes," Marley cried. "That feels so good, Luna." She used her hands to bring Luna's mouth fully onto her. Marley felt her world begin to spin as Luna's warm mouth sucked on her throbbing clit. Luna's fingers curled upward, caressing Marley's G-Spot and Marley's orgasm ripped through her.

†

Luna felt Marley's muscles contract around her fingers as her body released, and wetness coated her chin.

Her fingers continued to move slowly as she drank in every ounce of Marley's pleasure. Luna carefully removed her fingers and moved beside Marley when she fell silent.

"I hope that felt as good for you as it did me," she whispered against Marley's cheek.

"That felt fantastic. My world was spinning as you were making love to me. I love you so much."

"I know, and I love you, too," Luna replied and pulled Marley against her body. "Goodnight, my love."

"But," Marley began speaking.

"I'm content. As long as you're in my arms, nothing else matters."

CHAPTER EIGHT

Chancy sniffed the air and smiled. Remy was making bacon. She stretched her body, then hopped off the bed and grabbed a pair of shorts and a T-shirt from her designated drawer. Chancy had quietly stuffed the packages from her shopping trip with Amber into the corner of the walk-in closet before climbing into bed late last night. She wanted to model her new outfits for Remy to see if she liked what Amber helped her pick out, but that could wait until after brunch.

Chancy suspected that Remy had let her sleep in. She'd voiced her concern about Chancy working so many double shifts in a row. She liked how Remy cared about her well-being. None of her other lovers had given any consideration to Chancy burning the candle at both ends. They'd expected Chancy to be at their beck and call, even after she'd broken her arm and struggled to maintain her work schedule. Remy was everything that Chancy could ever hope for. She wasn't afraid to admit that Remy had the power to destroy her fragile heart if things didn't work out between the two of them.

Hurrying down the stairs, Chancy grinned when she saw Remy swaying to the music quietly playing through her Bluetooth speaker. Remy was so damn sexy in her skimpy robe. Chancy wanted to drag her back up the stairs and make love to her. Food could wait. Maybe she'd have time to scarf down some breakfast before her shift. However, her stomach expressed its discontent with her by growling loudly and announcing her arrival.

"You're up. I was going to let you sleep just a little longer. Brunch is almost ready."

"I see that. Actually, I smelled the bacon, and now the coffee is calling my name. Although, you look so damn irresistible right now, my libido is fighting with my stomach. What to do? What to do? Drag you back upstairs or eat the delicious meal you've prepared. Have I told you how much I love the little things you do for me? I haven't been such a great partner lately, have I?"

Remy turned toward Chancy, holding a spatula in her hand. "What do you mean? You're a wonderful partner."

"I used to be the one that brought you breakfast and lunch," Chancy answered.

"I'm amazed you haven't collapsed with all the extra shifts you've taken. I'll be so glad when we head to St. Kitts so you get to relax and enjoy yourself like a normal person. I'm going to find a way to entice you to take more time off. All work and no play..."

"Please tell me you aren't calling me dull already?"

Remy laughed. "No, never, but you do have an oversized work ethic for someone of your generation."

"Ouch. Are you saying Millennials are slackers? I thought Boomers were the highly critical generation, not Gen Xers." Chancy grinned.

"Sit. You don't have a lot of time before you have to leave, and I want to send you off with a full stomach."

Chancy glanced at the clock and waggled her eyebrows. "I have plenty of time. Maybe even enough time to make you purr this morning." Chancy reached around to turn off the burner and then pulled Remy into a tight embrace. She kissed her neck, right at the place she knew drove Remy wild.

"Mmm, that feels nice. What a little charmer you are."

Chancy's stomach growled again. "Damn stomach. Why are you always complaining to me at the most inopportune moments?"

"Did you have dinner last night?" Remy asked.

Chancy sheepishly shook her head. "No, I didn't get a chance. It was so crazy at Sisters, I barely had time to pee."

Remy gave Chancy a relatively chaste kiss and led her to the table. "We'll have plenty of time to reconnect when we get to St. Kitts. How was your shopping trip yesterday with Amber? Will you bless me with a fashion show to show me what you bought?"

Chancy nodded enthusiastically. "I'd love to. I spent way more than I wanted, but hopefully, you'll like what I got, and I won't embarrass you."

Remy scrunched her face. "Why in the world would you ever think you'd embarrass me? You are a beautiful, charming woman who is apparently a hot new commodity at TWC. I'll likely have to beat off the women when we get to St. Kitts."

"Nah. I only have eyes for you..." Chancy crooned. "Are you sure we don't have time for a quickie?"

Remy laughed again before dishing up a large portion of eggs, bacon, French toast, and potatoes onto Chancy's plate. "As tempting as that offer is, I'd rather us relax and have a nice breakfast together. One that isn't rushed. And then you can model your new clothes for me?"

"Will you return the favor? Have you decided what you're taking?"

Remy frowned. "I haven't worn a bathing suit since my surgery. I don't know if I should shop for a suit with a built-in bra or just go with the flow and simply accept my new flat chest. It's been several months, and I still haven't decided what to do. Some days I want to explore reconstructive surgery, while other days, I'm ready to hit the tattoo parlor. Thoughts?"

"You know, I think you're stunning exactly as you are. Whatever you decide is right for you is the perfect answer. I'll find you sexy no matter what you choose. I pinch myself every single day, thinking I'm dreaming. Like being here with you can't be real for a gutter rat like me."

Remy filled both cups with coffee, setting them and the creamer on the table. "I wish you would stop referring to yourself as a gutter rat. That is not how I see you or any of your friends."

"I guess we both have some work to do on our images. Hey, don't tell me you're only having coffee. You better load that plate of yours up as high as mine. This is way too much food. I should find time to work out with Luna now that I'm driving versus biking to work." Chancy grabbed at her stomach, checking to see if she could pinch an inch.

Remy laughed. "I doubt you have anything to worry about. Biking or not, you get plenty of exercise at Sisters. I haven't noticed a change in that washboard stomach of yours. Although, I can attest to Luna's magic in developing the perfect training schedule for each client she works with." She added a smaller portion of food onto her plate. Pointing to Chancy's plate. "Eat up. Cold eggs are horrible."

†

Looking into the floor-to-ceiling mirror in Remy's master bedroom, Chancy tugged at the top of her new swimsuit and repositioned her breasts. She wondered if she should have gotten the next size up. She hated when her sports bra rode up under her breasts, not unlike when underwear gathered in her crack. Boi shorts didn't do that as much as regular bikini underwear. She'd switched several years ago after having to pluck the offending piece of cloth from her ass crack every five minutes.

Remy had sprawled on the bed, watching Chancy change into her new suit. "Very nice. I like it. It's perfectly suited to your body and style. It's not a skimpy bikini, but it still shows off your figure. Will you show me what else you bought?"

"Yeah. I wanted to get your opinion on the one nice outfit I got. If you don't like it, or it isn't fancy enough, I can try to find something else."

76

"I'm sure it will be perfect. You worry too much. You'd look good in a paper bag," Remy declared.

"I always feel so...ugh, I don't really know how to explain this. When you dress up, you look so glamorous. Except for the tux, I always feel like I don't have the right wardrobe to stand beside you." Chancy removed the suit and pulled the white linen pants and patterned tunic from the bag.

"That's nonsense. Your style is unique and wonderful, and Lindy is not the only one that thinks we look great together."

Without bothering to put on a bra or underwear, Chancy donned her nice outfit and twirled for Remy. Amber had told her the pants showed off her ass nicely, so she hoped Remy would notice. "Well? What do you think?"

"Wow! I didn't think you could rock anything more than that tux, but this outfit shows off all your assets."

"Amber told me my ass looks especially nice in these pants."

"She's right. It really is too bad you have to go to work soon. I'd love to help you out of those clothes, but I'm afraid that will lead to bedroom calisthenics that will undoubtedly make you late for work."

"Oh, now you tempt me with so little time left. I'm hoping tonight is slower, and I'll be able to duck out early. I really feel the need to reconnect with you."

Remy sighed. "Me too. I'll grab a good book and wait up for you. How does that sound?"

"Heavenly. I only have to keep up this pace for less than a week and then fun in the sun. I'm so excited about my first true vacation. I can't think of a better group of women to hang with for this milestone in my life."

"Although it saddens me to know this is your first vacation, I'm glad I'm the one that gets to spend it with you."

"I couldn't agree more. I am slowly but surely replacing my early life experiences with memories I'll cherish well into my golden years. Years that I hope to spend with you."

†

Chancy bounced into Sisters ten minutes before the official start of her shift. Janice and Selene sat at the bar with a stack of sheets in front of them. Janice frowned as she looked at the papers.

"Hey, what's going on?" Chancy asked.

Selene shuffled the papers together into a small stack. "Nothing. We were just going over the schedule and our recent expenditures."

"Janice has that worry wrinkle on her forehead. Come on. Tell me the truth. Am I leaving you high and dry?"

"Don't worry. We'll figure it out. Sandy just quit. She found a higher-paying job. I wish we could offer more in salary, but we took quite a hit during the pandemic. Finding quality staff is proving quite challenging. To be honest, Sandy is no substantial loss. All the time she called out was becoming a problem, anyway. We need people committed to working, not simply flirting with attractive patrons. I think Sandy was only working here to get a new girlfriend," Janice grumbled.

"I was kind of wondering why you kept her on. Want me to ask around to see if anyone at TWC is looking to pick up additional shifts? A few young women who work at the juice bar might want a second job. I'm not sure if they're queer or not, but they're certainly queer-friendly. Of course, they would have to be to work at TWC."

"If they have a work ethic like yours, please do send them our way," Selene answered.

"What about the finances? Are you guys still doing okay?" Chancy asked.

"We're getting there. The budget called for a new refrigerator, but that isn't happening now. So, I called Alex to see what she might be able to do to cobble together a fix until we recover a bit more after the losses earlier this year. Lately, it seems like everyone wants to get out of the house, so hopefully, we won't have to wait too much longer before replacing that clunker." Janice shoved the papers into a folder and stood.

Chancy glanced up to see Alex stroll through the door. "Hey, speak of the devil."

"I thought I was the angel of maintenance, come to save your asses again," Alex quipped.

Janice walked to Alex, greeting her. "Thanks for coming so quickly. Could you also look at our heating unit? We've had unseasonable cold weather lately, and I'm worried it might go out with the strain."

"That old fridge isn't going to last much longer. I hope you have a plan to replace it. The last time I worked on it was two months ago. I remember telling you the fix wouldn't last much longer than a few months."

"It was in our budget, but then the pandemic..." Janice shrugged.

"Okay. I'll try to construct a miracle for you, but you're going to need a longer-term solution," Alex stated. "I can give you two more months, max."

"We'll take it," Selene said.

Chancy leaned in to whisper in Selene's ear. "I wish I had some money to loan you, but I had to get an advance from Lindy to buy some new clothes. I know this probably isn't the best time to ask about this, but Lindy might open Club Night every Thursday. After returning from St. Kitts, I could give you the money I earn from Club Night. Of course, that means you have to give me Thursday nights off." Chancy grinned.

"Of course, you can have Thursday nights off, as long as you don't quit on us. But we can't take money from you, not even a loan. I know you're planning that big Christmas gift for Remy, which is a brilliant idea. You'll need a lot of money for that, even if you do plan on asking Alex to help."

"I would never quit on you. Not for all the money in the world." Tears formed in Chancy's eyes. "You two literally saved my life when you offered me a job. I won't forget what you did for me. I owe you everything."

"I know you make a lot more money at TWC, so I wouldn't blame you, you know."

Janice narrowed her eyes. "What are you two whispering about?"

"My undying loyalty to both of you." Chancy grinned.

Janice waved her hand in the air. "Yeah, yeah. Pain in the ass, but at least you mix a good drink."

With Selene reminding Chancy about her plan to build a stable for the horse she bought Remy, Chancy decided she should ask Alex about that sooner rather than later. Alex's business was hopping lately, and she wanted to get on her schedule before she booked up. "Hey, Alex, after you fix the dinosaur, can I talk to you about something?"

"Sounds serious." Alex focused on Chancy.

"Not exactly, but I do need your help with Remy's Christmas gift. It might require a lot of your free time, but I'll pay you, of course."

"Intriguing. What's Remy's gift?"

"A horse. And she'll need a home. That's where you come in. I need you to build a stable for maybe two to three horses. I trust you won't overcharge me."

Alex stroked her chin. "Well, that'll be a challenge. I've never built stables before."

Chancy's face fell. "Oh. So, you can't do it?"

"Nope, not saying that. I'll ask my father for some help. Even if I have to scour the internet for tips and tricks, we'll build you the most luxurious stable a pampered horse could hope for. How hard can it be?"

"Um, not that this isn't a riveting conversation to follow, but can you look at the fridge and heating system now? We'll be opening for lunch soon," Janice reminded.

"Sure, sure. Sorry. Let me get my toolbox from the truck. It shouldn't take too long to fix the fridge. Not sure about the heating system yet. I'll have to look and see what's happening."

"Thanks, Alex. You're a lifesaver. I know you're doing this as a favor to us. You probably had to rearrange another job to squeeze us in." Janice offered Alex a rare smile.

Alex waved her hand. "You and the blue-haired sprite will always be a priority. Chancy is not the only one who has benefited from your generosity. We've both got your number, you old softy."

"I am neither old nor a softy," Janice grumbled.

Chancy and Alex both burst out in uncontrollable laughter.

CHAPTER NINE

Luna paced until she saw a car arrive in the parking lot a few minutes before seven. She rushed over to kiss Marley and double-check she had her wallet. "I'll see you tonight."

Marley smiled at her excited lover. "Have fun, and I'll wait for dinner with you."

"That sounds great." Luna grinned and picked up her cell phone. "See ya."

Luna rushed out to the car and climbed into the back seat with Lindy.

"No bag of spare clothes?" Lindy said with a quirked eyebrow.

"I've decided I'm going to be a big girl today," Luna answered with a grin.

"You're going to be just fine. I've already printed our boarding passes, so we just have to get through security, and we're good to proceed to the gate."

Luna nodded. "I had some toast and a glass of juice."

"Excellent. Once we get to the gate, we can pull up the menu and start dreaming about breakfast when we get to Memphis."

"Did you rent a car?" Luna asked.

"No way." Lindy smiled. "We are going in style today. I rented a driver who will be waiting for us when we arrive and will take us anywhere we want to go."

"What time is your appointment at the jeweler?" Luna asked.

"It's at eleven, so we'll have plenty of time for a leisurely breakfast at Brothers. It's only a few blocks from the store, so we're all set. Afterward, we can do some shopping in Memphis if you want, or go downtown to see some sights and have a late lunch."

"That sounds good," Luna replied with a smile. "I'm feeling both excited and nervous about our adventure."

"Just trust me when I say you are going to do just fine," Lindy replied.

Lindy paid the driver, and they entered the airport. Lindy pulled out Luna's boarding pass to Memphis. "You will need this and your driver's license to go through security," she instructed. She grinned at Luna. "I wouldn't be surprised if you got flagged for a pat-down, especially if women are working the security post. Don't take it personally. They are doing their jobs and enjoying it in the meantime." Lindy couldn't hold back her chuckle.

"Should I feel violated?" Luna pouted.

"Worshipped is more like it," Lindy replied. "You have a great body, and you should be proud of it."

"I know. I'm just teasing you. I just hope Miss Security is cute," Luna tossed back.

"We'll know in just a minute," Lindy said as she nodded to the short line ahead of them. "Not Marley, but still cute."

Luna took a deep breath as she handed her boarding pass and ID to the screener.

"First time flying?" she asked.

"Yeah, how can you tell?" Luna asked.

"Just a guess. Besides, your feet haven't stopped moving since you got to my booth. Relax and have fun in Memphis."

Luna smiled at the woman. "Thanks. I'll try my best. No strip search?" she asked.

"Only if you want one," the woman answered with a wink as she gave Luna her pass and ID back.

"I think I'll pass this time. Maybe next trip," Luna answered.

"That's the spirit. I hope to see you again soon. I'd gladly volunteer for the search."

Luna chuckled. "Thanks, I'll keep that in mind."

"I'll be disappointed if you don't get in my line," the woman continued to tease.

"Got it," Luna said. She walked through the metal detector and retrieved her shoes before meeting Lindy, still wearing a smile.

"See, I told you they would gladly search you." Lindy laughed softly. "Let's go. We still have a ride to our gate."

†

"Damn, this all looks delicious," Luna said as they scrolled through the menu for Brother Junipers.

Lindy shook her head. "If you leave there hungry, it's your fault. It's known for the best breakfast in the state. I think I've had almost everything on the menu, and I've never been disappointed."

Luna's stomach growled. "I'll be more than ready to eat by the time we get there."

"Which shouldn't be long now," Lindy said as the counter person opened the door to the walkway. "We're in first class, so they will call us to board first."

"First class?" Luna said. "Isn't that super expensive?"

"It's a bit more than flying coach, but it has more room and a few other perks. You would feel like a sardine in one of those cramped seats."

"Thanks, Lindy," Luna said.

"I learned a long time ago to go for creature comforts whenever possible."

The lady invited all first-class passengers to board, and Lindy nodded to Luna. "Let's roll."

†

Luna's legs felt like Jell-O as they walked down the jetway to board the flight. She was happy to see a handrail but was determined not to use it. *I've got this,* she had to keep reminding herself.

"Do you want the window or aisle seat?" Lindy asked.

"Do you have any preference?" Luna asked.

"Not really. I've seen the geography on this flight many times if you'd like the window. It's pretty impressive from the air. Your choice."

Luna nodded and accepted the window seat as other passengers began boarding.

"May I offer you ladies something to drink?" a flight attendant asked.

"I'd love a cup of coffee," Lindy replied. She looked at Luna.

"Water or juice, or both," Luna replied.

"First flight?" the woman asked kindly.

Luna nodded. "Do I have a note on my forehead or something?" she asked.

The woman smiled at Luna. "After a while, you can sense who is a first-time flyer. Relax, we will take good care of you."

"That's what I keep hearing," Luna answered nervously.

Lindy sipped on her coffee as they waited for take-off. "We will probably be stuck in a line of traffic for a few minutes while we wait for permission to take off."

"So once we start moving, we won't go straight up?" Luna asked.

"Nope," Lindy said. "It'll be a slow roll as we move up in line. Take off is quick once we get the go-ahead, and we'll be up in the air in seconds, probably before you even realize it's happened. Your ears may pop, so put this in your mouth before we take off," Lindy said and handed her a piece of gum.

Luna's leg was bouncing, and Lindy reached over to place a comforting hand on her knee. "I promise it will be fine. Tell me about what you have planned for Marley. I assume from the look I got from you yesterday that you have a camera in mind."

"Yes, I bought her a camera that she can use underwater and on land," Luna said.

"Do you have a picture?" Lindy asked as the boarding doors closed.

"Yes," Luna said as she pulled her phone out and began scrolling. She hadn't realized the jet was moving until the brakes squealed at the end of a runway. "Whoa, I didn't realize we were moving."

"Now the wait begins. Oh, that's nice," Lindy said as she studied the photograph. "Marley is going to love that. I can't wait to go snorkeling. I've seen most of the island already, but underwater is like a whole other world."

Lindy kept Luna distracted until the engine revved. "We will start rolling fast, and then the pilot will pull the front of the jet upward, and we'll be in the air. I'd recommend you look out the window as soon as we take off. There's no better view of Atlanta than from the sky." Lindy reached over and covered Luna's hand with her own, and Luna turned her palm to grip Lindy's hand. "Here we go," Lindy said.

Luna heard the engines roar to life as the heavy jet began to creep forward and pick up speed. She squeezed Lindy's hand gently and concentrated on breathing slowly as the plane left the runway.

"Now would be a good time to peek out the window," Lindy said.

Luna released her hand. "We're in the air?"

"Yes, we are. Leaving Atlanta quickly, so get a look."

Luna leaned toward the window and was amazed by the view of Atlanta that was fading so fast. The golden dome of the capital glittered in the early morning sun. "That's beautiful," Luna whispered. She continued staring out the window as they began flying over farmland and rivers. "It looks like a huge patchwork quilt," Luna said. "All the different colors of fields and forest."

"It's even prettier in the winter with the ground covered by snow," Lindy replied. "It doesn't happen that often here, but when it does, it's wondrous."

"I'm flying," Luna said.

"Yes, you are," Lindy replied. "See, nothing to it. If it gets a little bumpy as we go up and come down, it's turbulence in the air. Nothing to be worried about, but it can make your heart flip the first time you experience it. Landing can be a bit bumpy at times, depending on the status of the runway, but it's usually not bad." Lindy smiled at Luna. "Wait until you see the view after dark."

"Thank you for giving me this opportunity to overcome my fear," Luna replied. "It's nothing compared to what I had imagined."

"It will be even smoother on our flight to the islands. A smaller, faster, private jet with more opportunity to get up and move about," Lindy told her.

"A private jet?" Luna asked.

Lindy nodded. "Remy provided the resort accommodations, and I agreed to the transportation."

"That's amazing and generous of both of you," Luna replied.

"We want you to know how much we appreciate you all. Now tell me more of what you have planned for Marley."

"I've booked a private, candle-lit dinner on the beach for Christmas Eve for us. I want to propose that she consider marrying me in the future."

"I've no doubt she'll say yes," Lindy said. "She adores you. Have you found a ring you like yet?"

"No, but I hope to find something today. Because Marley works with her hands, I don't think she'd want something with a tall setting. I want something she can comfortably work with and not have to remove for massages."

"Something like a channel setting?" Lindy asked. "The diamonds or whatever stones you select inside a band," she explained. "Let me see if I can find something to show you." Lindy pulled out her phone and started searching the internet.

"Wait, we have Wi-Fi up here?" Luna asked.

"Yes, of course. You're in first-class, baby," Lindy teased.

"Can we do a quick selfie I can send to Marley?"

"Of course," Lindy replied.

Luna took her phone, leaned into Lindy, and snapped several shots. "I like this one," she said and turned the phone toward Lindy.

"That's perfect for sending," Lindy replied.

Luna typed in *I'm flying* and hit send.

†

Marley set up her room for her first appointment when her phone pinged. She picked it up and smiled when she saw the photo of Lindy and Luna. *Looking great. Are you having fun yet?*

So far, so good, Luna answered. *Love you.*
Love you too.

†

"This is what I was talking about," Lindy said. She handed her phone to Luna. "Low profile so she can still wear it and it will be beautiful on her hand."

"Did you think they will have these at the jewelers?"

"I would think so, but I can email them to find out," Lindy said. "What size?"

"A seven and a half," Luna answered.

Lindy began creating an email while Luna gazed out the window. They received another choice of drinks, and then Luna could feel they were starting to descend. "We can't be there already, can we?"

Lindy looked at her watch and nodded her head. "We'll be on the ground again in just a few minutes."

"That went by quick," Luna said. "Is that a pyramid?" she asked as she gazed out of the window as they approached Memphis.

"Yes, initially it was built to be a sports and entertainment complex, but Bass Pro Shops has bought it out."

"Bass Pro as in major outdoor suppliers?" Luna asked.

"The same. The other large arena is FedEx Arena, where the Grizzlies play. The Red Birds baseball team also has a complex downtown, but I can't remember the name. They are a farm team for the Cardinals. St. Jude's Children's

91

Hospital takes up several city blocks, and there are numerous other famous places to visit."

"Such as?" Luna asked.

"Graceland for Elvis Presley fans. Sun Records, the Pink Palace, BB King's, and Beale Street. The list could go on endlessly."

"Wow. I've never been to Memphis," Luna said. "It sounds like a cool place."

"We may have to road trip here in May when they have Memphis in May. BBQ cooking contests every weekend, loads of music, entertainment, arts, and crafts. A bit of something for everyone," Lindy replied.

"That does sound like fun," Luna said. She felt a bump, and her eyes got big.

"That's just the landing gear lowering. You want to hear that sound," Lindy teased.

"Is that the Mississippi River?" Luna asked.

"Yes, Memphis is a huge port city. It was an important location during the Civil War for the Confederate forces. It remains a key commerce port to this day. Hundreds of barges flow past the city every day."

The jet landed with two heavy bumps. Lindy looked at Luna. "Welcome to Memphis. You have survived your first flight," Lindy informed her. "Now it will take five minutes to taxi to the terminal from here. I swear you land in Mississippi or Arkansas and taxi into Memphis. Both states are within a half hour's drive or less from the airport."

They disembarked from the jet and headed for transportation. A beautiful young woman in a form-fitting suit held a sign with Freemont on it. Lindy smiled. "There's our ride for the day."

"Nice ride." Luna grinned.

"Are you Mrs. Freemont?" the young woman asked as they approached.

"Yes, I'm Lindy Freemont, and my associate, Luna."

"I'm Celeste, and I'm at your service today," she replied. "Any baggage?"

"No, we're just here for a day trip," Lindy replied.

"Follow me then. I'm parked right outside."

Luna offered Lindy her arm, and Lindy looped her hand around Luna's elbow. "To Memphis," Luna said with a chuckle.

"Where to first?" Celeste asked.

"Breakfast at Brother Junipers," Lindy replied. "Will you join us?"

"I'm sorry, Mrs. Freemont, but that's not allowed. I will wait in the lot until you've finished your meal."

"After that, we're off to an appointment at Gattas," Lindy said.

"Very nice choice," Celeste said. "Best in town."

"That's why we're here to pick up a gift for my daughter," Lindy said.

"Is this your daughter?" Celeste asked as she held the door for them.

"No, but I would claim her if I could," Lindy answered. "She's a very dear friend."

"I see. Well, let's get you fine ladies some breakfast," Celeste said and closed the door. She climbed in behind the wheel. "There's a small refrigerator with a variety of drinks if you are thirsty," Celeste told them.

"I think we're good for now," Lindy answered.

†

"Welcome to Brother Junipers," a woman greeted them as they entered the restaurant.

"Reservation for Freemont," Lindy said.

"We've got you all set," the woman said and led them to a table. "Enjoy your experience."

"Thanks," Lindy replied.

"Good morning. My name is Wanda, and I'll be taking care of you this morning. What can I start you off with to drink?"

"Coffee for me, please," Lindy answered.

"Apple juice and water for me, please," Luna replied.

"I'll be right back with your drinks," Wanda told them.

"Have you decided?" Lindy asked.

"I think I'm going with the eggs Benedict and a Belgium waffle."

Lindy nodded. "Great choices. I think I'm going with the cinnamon roll pancakes with a side of eggs and bacon."

Wanda delivered the drinks and took their orders.

Lindy's phone chimed to notify her that a new email had arrived. She took out her phone and checked the email. "Oh, my. One of these will do nicely." She looked up at Luna and smiled. "Take a look."

Luna took Lindy's phone and scrolled through several channel-set diamond band pictures. "These are gorgeous."

"Have you considered what type of metal? White gold, platinum, or traditional gold."

"Traditional gold, I think, but they are all beautiful." Luna scrolled back and forth between a couple of the pictures. "What do you think of this one?"

Lindy looked at the photo of a band with three emerald-cut diamonds embedded in a heavy band of gold. "That's gorgeous. I think it would be perfect for Marley."

"I'll wait to decide until I see them all in person," Luna replied.

"Photos can be deceiving."

"Yes, they can," Lindy agreed.

Wanda arrived and set a large serving tray on a stand. Luna's eyes grew wide at the amount of food on the tray. "It's a good thing we're hungry," Luna said.

"Maybe Celeste can drive us around for a nap later," Lindy teased.

"No napping today. We've got a city to explore," Luna replied.

"Yes, we do," Lindy agreed.

†

Luna sighed when she swallowed the last bite of waffle. "I made it," she said. "For a second, I didn't think I would be able to finish."

"You did good, but I want you to take one more bite. You have to try these pancakes." Lindy took Luna's fork and offered her a bite.

Luna's eyes lit up as the sweetness assaulted her taste buds. "Wow, those are sweet, but oh so good. Marley would love those."

"We will have to bring her here then." Lindy smiled.

"Yes, we will," Luna agreed.

"Have you given thought to when you will have a wedding and where?" Lindy asked.

"She has to say yes, first," Luna said.

"Do you honestly think she'll turn you down?"

"No, I sure hope not, but it may be too soon for Marley. She's been burned by a lover before."

"Not you, though."

"No, not me. I think Marley has realized my womanizing days are over, and she provides everything I need." Luna smiled, thinking about Marley.

"I think you make the perfect couple. May I make a suggestion?" Lindy said.

"Certainly, I'm open to ideas."

"Remy has a beautiful garden with a gazebo that would make the perfect venue for a wedding. I'm sure she would be honored if you asked to use it for your celebration."

"That's a fantastic idea. Neither of us attends church, and an outside service would be great." Luna smiled. "Yeah, that's great. I'll ask Marley about it if she says yes before approaching Remy. Thanks, Lindy."

Wanda returned to see if they needed anything else and delivered the check. "How about a cup of this wonderful coffee to go?" Lindy said and handed her a credit card.

"I'll be right back. Would you like anything to go?" Wanda asked Luna.

"No, ma'am. I am all set. That was a terrific breakfast," Luna replied.

"I'm happy you both enjoyed your meals," Wanda replied.

Lindy signed the bill and smiled at Luna. "Let's go shopping."

†

"All set, ladies?" Celeste asked.
"Stuffed to the gills," Luna replied.
"Next stop Gattas, please," Lindy requested.
"Yes, ma'am," Celeste answered.

†

"Good morning, Mrs. Freemont," the manager, Gerard, said when they entered the store.
"Good morning, Gerard. Let me introduce my friend, Luna, who is looking at the channel-set bands."
Gerard smiled and shook Luna's hand. "It's a pleasure to meet you, miss," he said. "I believe we will have whatever you are looking for, but if not, we can make something you desire."
A young man stepped over to them. "This is William, my assistant. He will be assisting you while I take care of Mrs. Freemont's order," he explained.
"I'm Luna," she said as she offered him her hand.
William returned her smile and handshake. "It's my pleasure to serve you. Come with me, please."
Luna followed him to a counter, where he pulled out a tray of channel set bands. "A size seven and a half, I believe."
"That's correct," Luna said. "I saw a gold band with three emerald-cut diamonds that caught my eye."

William smiled. "That is a beautiful piece." He searched for it and took it out for Luna's inspection.

"If I may ask, is there a special occasion?" William asked.

"I want to propose to my girlfriend on Christmas. She's a massage therapist, so I wanted something she would be comfortable with that she didn't have to take off between clients."

"The channel set is a perfect choice for that." William smiled. "Congratulations."

"She hasn't said yes, yet," Luna said.

"I hardly doubt she could say no to you or this ring," William said. "Do you want to compare it to a few others?"

"Yes, I would. I'd like to see the difference between white gold and platinum," Luna answered.

"I don't have the exact cut in white gold, but I do have platinum." William pulled out another band to hand to Luna.

"That's a beautiful piece as well," Luna said. "What other cuts of stone do you have?"

"Rounds and I think an oval," William said as he inspected the tray. "All of our stones are the highest grades possible."

"The stones look smaller than the emerald cut. What was the carat weight on the first ring?"

"With the three stones, it is slightly larger than one total carat. There is a princess cut band that's closer to two carats, with a total of five stones."

"May I see that one?" Luna asked.

"Of course," William answered.

Luna inspected the band closely. She liked that the total weight was more significant, but the cut's squareness wasn't as attractive to her.

Lindy walked over with a gift-wrapped package in hand. "Have you found something you like?"

"I'm still leaning toward the emerald cut. He also has a princess cut that is nice, too. What do you think?" Luna pointed the two rings out to Lindy.

Lindy picked up the princess cut. "The stones are larger, but I think the emerald cut is more Marley."

Gerard had opened a small safe behind the counter. "Would something with more diamonds be more appealing?"

He handed Luna a band with four stones.

Lindy watched as Luna's eyes lit with excitement. "I think that's the one."

"I agree," Luna replied.

"Gift wrapped?" William asked.

"Yes, please."

"Let me polish it nicely for you, and I'll be right back. Gerard will get you written up." William took the ring from her.

"I guess I should have asked how much," Luna whispered to Lindy.

"The price doesn't matter. It's your special ring for Marley," Lindy said.

"I only brought three thousand in cash with me. I could put the balance on a card," Luna replied.

"Three thousand will be plenty," Lindy replied. "I've already instructed Gerard to make sure you get the best he has for my two favorite women. Any difference he will put on my card, and it will be my wedding present to you."

Luna hung her head. "I can't let you do that, Lindy. I appreciate the offer, though." Her eyes glistened with tears. "I have more money in savings. I would take a short-term loan, though. I can get the rest to you tomorrow."

"That's fine. Please give me your cash and look at the bands while William gets your ring ready."

Luna pulled the cash from her pocket and handed it to Lindy.

†

When Luna was out of earshot, Lindy looked at Gerard. "Write the ticket for thirty-five hundred and put the two thousand on my card," she instructed.

Gerard smiled. "As you wish, Mrs. Freemont." He had her sign a ticket for the credit card charge and then gave her the additional receipt for the amount she requested. "Thank you for your continued business."

"Thank you for reducing the price on that ring. I'm certain it was worth much more," Lindy said.

"Not near as valuable as your continued business," Gerard said with a wink. "You bought two beautiful pieces today, and I'm sure you will return."

"I always do," Lindy replied, and tucked her receipt into her purse.

"Here we go," William said. He looked around for Luna.

Luna saw him return and walked over.

William handed her a gift bag. "Your certificate of appraisal is in the envelope. Again congratulations. I know she'll say yes."

"Thanks for all your help," Luna said.

100

"My pleasure. Have a great holiday season."

"You, too," Luna replied. "Are we ready?"

"Have a great day, gentlemen," Lindy said with a wave. "Memphis, here we come."

Lindy handed Luna the receipt as they reached the car. Luna looked at it and frowned. "That seems a bit low," she said.

Lindy smiled. "He gave us a great deal. Trust me, Gerard has made plenty of money off of me over the years."

Luna pulled Lindy into a bear hug. "Thank you so much. I'll get your money to you tomorrow."

"No worries. I know where you work," Lindy teased.

"Yes, ma'am, you do."

Celeste pulled up to the curb, and Lindy and Luna climbed inside. "Where to next, ladies?"

"Downtown. We'll figure it out when we get there. Do you have a safe in the car?"

"In the trunk. Do you want me to secure your packages now before we head downtown? Far fewer prying eyes here," Celeste said.

"Yes, please," Lindy said and handed Celeste the two gift bags.

†

They walked around downtown and visited numerous gift shops for souvenirs. "How was your stomach on the flight?" Lindy asked.

"It was okay. I worked myself up over nothing," Luna said.

"Fear of the unknown isn't nothing," Lindy corrected her. "Do you think you could eat something spicy for lunch?"

"What did you have in mind?" Luna asked.

"Memphis is known for its great BBQ, but it also has some of the best fried chicken I've eaten at a hole-in-the-wall place called Gus's Fried chicken, but it's a tad spicy."

"I think I can handle it. The BBQ place at the airport smelled pretty tasty. Maybe we could get some to take home to Marley for dinner?"

Lindy smiled. "Neely's. I like that idea. Let's go eat some yard bird."

†

Celeste welcomed them back. "Did you have a nice stroll?"

"We did, but we worked up an appetite," Lindy said. "Is there any chance of getting into Gus's?"

Celeste looked at her watch. "I think it's late enough for the lunch rush to be over."

"I must insist you eat with us this time. We won't tell if you won't," Lindy said.

Celeste nodded. "I can't resist Gus's."

"Sitting outside smelling that would have been cruel," Lindy said.

†

Luna completely understood Lindy's comment about the aroma of fried chicken filling the air. As soon as she stepped from the car, the delicious smell hit her like a brick. Her stomach growled in response. "Damn, if it tastes half as good as it smells, we're in luck."

"It tastes even better," Lindy replied with a smile.

"I'm going to have to work out for hours to burn off all these calories today," Luna teased.

Lindy chuckled. "I'm sure Marley will be glad to help with that."

Luna's eyes scanned the plates and the happy faces of the customers as they made their way to a table. She picked up the menu and put it right back down. "I don't even have to look. I know what I'm having."

"You looked up the menu already, didn't you?" Lindy asked.

"Yes, ma'am, I did," Luna said. She looked up at their server. "I'll have a three-piece all white, with beans and slaw. Sweet tea to drink, please."

"I'll take the same, but only two pieces," Lindy said.

"Same here with the two-piece," Celeste added.

"Y'all made that way too easy," the woman said. "My name is Sally. I'll put your orders in and be right back with drinks."

Lindy handed her the menus. "Thanks, Sally."

†

Luna's eyes grew wide when Sally placed a platter of chicken in front of her, containing two large breasts and a wing. "Maybe I should have ordered the two-piece," she said to Lindy.

"I have every confidence in the world that you can tackle that," Lindy replied.

103

"I'm danged sure going to give it a try." Luna smiled and bit into the chicken. Her eyes lit up when the spices reached her taste buds. "This is tasty."

"Not too spicy?" Lindy asked.

"No, ma'am, it's perfect," Luna said.

"There's some hot sauce if you need to add more of a kick," Celeste teased and offered her the bottle.

"Not needed," Luna replied as she took a drink of tea.

†

"Is there any place else you would like to see, or do you want to head to the airport?" Celeste asked when they were back in the car.

Lindy shook her head. "The airport, I think. We're taking some Neely's home for dinner tonight, so I'd like to give them plenty of time to prepare it for our flight."

"Make sure they give you some extra sauce, and you've got to try some of their ribs. The sandwiches are great, but the ribs are out of this world," Celeste advised.

"That's good to know. Thank you for being such a knowledgeable guide today," Lindy said.

"It's been my pleasure," Celeste replied and handed them the two gift bags from the trunk safe. "We sure don't need to forget these."

"I'll tuck them in my purse so they can go through the scanner," Lindy replied.

Luna grabbed the bags from the souvenir shops and combined them to make carrying them more manageable. Once they cleared security, they went straight to Neely's to place their order. They reached the gate with twenty minutes to spare. "I'm going to hit the restroom. Do you need a drink or anything?"

"Thanks, Luna, but I'm good. I'll use the facilities when you return. We'll be boarding soon, so I'll wait to get a drink onboard," Lindy replied.

Luna nodded and began walking toward the restroom. *We're bringing dinner home, so don't cook*, she texted Marley.

Sounds great. Did you have a great day?

Memphis is awesome. See you soon. Love you.

Love you too.

Luna returned and took the seat beside Lindy. "I texted Marley that we were bringing dinner so that she wouldn't cook."

"Great idea. I'll be right back," Lindy replied.

Luna took out her phone and scrolled to the picture of the ring she bought for Marley. "I hope this will be enough to convince you to say yes."

†

Once they were seated for the flight home, Lindy turned to Luna. "Did you enjoy your trip to Memphis?"

"This has been one of my best days ever. The company was great, the food fantastic, and the experience of flying was nothing like I dreaded."

"You'll be fine to fly next week, then?" Lindy asked.

"Yes, ma'am, I believe so."

"The flight will be longer, but I think you have the basics of take-off and landing. Being over the ocean offers more of a chance for turbulence, but I think you did great."

105

"You don't know how much this means to me," Luna said.

"I had a blast with you today. Maybe we should get out more often," Lindy replied. "Do you like wine?"

"I can give it a try," Luna said.

Lindy ordered two white wines and bottled water when the attendant came around.

Luna took a sip of the wine and tried not to make a face, but her expression gave her away.

Lindy chuckled. "That's okay. I'll drink yours, and you can stick to water. She raised her glass. Thanks for a great day."

Luna twisted the top off the water and tapped her bottle against Lindy's wine glass. "Thank you for a day I'll never forget."

†

When the driver pulled in front of the club, Luna stepped out and picked up her bags. Lindy handed her the gift bag and the food.

Luna cocked her head. "Aren't you coming in for dinner? I'll drive you home later."

"No, that dinner is for the two of you. I'm going home, have another glass of wine and a nice bath, and hit the sheets. Thanks again for such a great day."

Luna nodded. "See you tomorrow?"

"Without a doubt," Lindy replied. "Have a great night."

†

Marley met Luna at the front door and took the bag of food. "Where's Lindy?"

"She decided to skip out on dinner. I hope you're hungry," Luna said. "Do you want to eat upstairs?"

"That will work." She locked the door behind them and set the alarm. "No one here but us." She grinned.

Luna followed her upstairs, and while Marley set the food out, Luna tucked her gift bag in a drawer.

"How was your trip?" Marley asked.

"It was a fun day," Luna replied. She walked into the kitchen carrying a Beale Street T-shirt. "I bought this and a few other things for you."

"Thank you, sweetie," Marley said.

"I thought you'd get a kick out of this in your Jeep," Luna said, and handed her a box with an Elvis bobblehead.

"He's so cute," Marley said as she took him out of the box. "He will be a perfect dash mate."

"Wow, we got a lot of food, didn't we?" Luna said as she looked at the containers on the table.

"Do you want me to heat the beans and corn?" Marley asked.

"I'll pour our drinks if you warm them just a bit. The smell of this place was intoxicating inside the airport."

"This is the most delicious airport food I've seen." Marley smiled.

"We've got enough left for two more meals," Marley said when they finished. "One if we invite Alex to join us."

"Will she be out tomorrow? Do you know?" Luna asked.

"I think she's got an early appointment at five. Do you want to invite her to dinner or a late lunch?"

"She'll probably have dinner plans with Danna, but you can see if she wants to join us for lunch. Lindy, too, if she'll still be here."

Marley sent Alex a text. "Nope, she says she'll have to pass tomorrow, but thank you."

"Lindy then? She has got to try some of these ribs," Luna said.

"We can ask her when she gets here in the morning. It's getting kind of late for her," Marley replied.

"That's true. We did have a long, eventful day, too," Luna said. "I bet we walked a few miles in Memphis."

"Let's put the leftovers away and relax tonight," Marley suggested.

"That's perfectly fine with me," Luna agreed.

CHAPTER TEN

"I still think you're nuts for working a double again. We leave tomorrow, you know? As in O Dark Hundred," Alex teased.

Chancy shook her head. She loved Alex like a big sister. Alex was always so protective of her, but Chancy had taken care of herself way before her parents kicked her out of their house at fourteen. She was sure that Remy had called Lindy, who probably asked Alex to stop by. Chancy narrowed her eyes at Alex. "I thought you'd be packing tonight. So why are *you* here?"

"I couldn't find the part for the refrigerator and had to order from fucking overseas. It just got here today. That fridge will not survive even two weeks, so I promised Janice I would swing by and install the new part. I didn't want to jerry-rig the thing together again. The part was spendy but worth it if they want the thing to last another

109

year. Don't tell Janice, but I paid for half of it, and I'm not going to charge her for labor."

"Sly. You big softy. But that is not going to work. Janice isn't stupid. Neither is Selene, but it's Janice's ire I'd worry about." Chancy absently ran the bar rag over the spotless bar.

"I'm going to present her with a combined bill for the heater and refrigerator. She doesn't know how long I work on things. And you will not say a word. We all have to do our part to keep Sisters open." Alex hitched up her heavy tool belt. "I better get to it because I have last-minute packing I need to take care of tonight. You should try to get off a little early. I'm sure Janice and Selene will let you. Those bags under your eyes are probably going to exceed the weight limit on Lindy's fancy private jet if you don't get a few hours of sleep."

"Honestly, I'm way too excited for sleep. And nervous. I've never been on an airplane."

"Neither had I before Danna went with me to visit my parents. I think I know you well enough to state without hesitation that you're going to love it. Still, you don't want to get sick before we leave. With you running yourself ragged, you're more susceptible to illness. I'd hate for you to get the new variant going around."

"That's sweet of you to be concerned, but it's already getting busy. These past few weeks have been total tit busters. I guess everyone is so tired of staying home, they've decided to hell with it. Two vaccines and a booster, and I'm good to go. Thank goodness the people in our community have the good sense to follow the science. I'd never set foot in a straight bar. Most of those ass wipes are listening to the conspiracy theorists and dropping like flies."

Alex shook her head, and as she walked away, she grumbled, "Well, at least I tried. Such a stubborn little shit."

"I heard that," Chancy called out.

"Wasn't trying to hide my thoughts," Alex retorted.

†

"I'm so sorry you had to stay until closing. While I won't complain about how busy it's been lately, I know your flight leaves early tomorrow. Hopefully, you can sleep on the plane." Janice finished putting the last chair on the table.

Chancy grabbed the mop and pail from the utility closet. "It's fine. I'm too wound up to sleep, anyway."

"Gimme that." Janice grabbed the mop. "Selene and I will finish up. Go home and at least try to relax. Cuddle with your woman. Three hours sleep is better than none."

"You know, I can still back out of this. Are you sure you have everything covered?" Chancy asked.

"You are not backing out. You deserve this vacation more than anyone I know. We'll be fine. You showed Haley how to make those fancy holiday drinks you added to the menu. They've been going like hotcakes. Since TWC is closed, we're thrilled to have Haley work during the holidays. She's attractive enough to get good tips, too. It's a good thing her girlfriend, Pepper, isn't the jealous type."

Chancy snorted. "Hardly. Besides, Pepper would have absolutely nothing to say about it anyway, considering half her salary at TWC is from her additional work upstairs."

"Wow! Really? By the way, why aren't Pepper and Haley going to St. Kitts?" Janice asked.

"Pepper's family is coming to Atlanta for the holidays. She hasn't seen them in years. She plans to introduce them to Haley. I don't know if she's going to propose or not. Haley is pretty nervous about meeting them. It thrilled her to have somewhere to go for the two weeks."

"We're certainly happy about that. She's a quick learner. Getting this temporary job works out well for everyone. So don't worry. We have everything covered. Now git home to your woman. That's an order," Janice declared.

Chancy stuck out her tongue. "You're not the boss of me." She danced away from Janice.

"I most certainly am."

"Not for the next two weeks," Chancy continued to tease. "Maybe I'll decide to become a beach bum and stay in St. Kitts."

"Yeah, right. And leave that beautiful woman you're currently shacking up with."

Chancy frowned. "I'm not shacking up with her. I love her. She's the one."

Janice held up her hands. "Whoa, sorry. I didn't mean anything by that. Has she finally asked you to move in with her?"

"No, but..."

"I'm sure she will. Remy isn't like your other affairs. I can see that clearly."

"No, she isn't." Yet even as Chancy said the words, that tiny niggle of doubt remained in the back of her mind. She wasn't ordinarily pessimistic or insecure, but she needed to know that this relationship would endure because Chancy wanted to marry Remy more than she wanted anything else in the world. This wasn't because Chancy was young and brash, letting her feelings overrun all sense of logic. On the contrary, she knew without a doubt that Remy was the woman she wanted to grow old with.

†

Chancy smiled when she saw the two bags neatly stacked together by the front door. She'd had to borrow one of Remy's suitcases because she didn't own a proper one. Why would she? She hadn't ever gone anywhere. In her epic accident, Chancy had scuffed the backpack she used while biking to and from work. Besides, the old thing wouldn't hold everything she planned to bring to St. Kitts.

Carefully making her way up the stairs, Chancy debated about crawling into bed with Remy. She was still keyed up and afraid her tossing and turning would wake her lover. In the end, she needed the warmth of that glorious body she'd come to know so intimately. Removing her clothes, she gingerly pushed aside the covers and settled next to Remy, draping her arm over Remy's stomach. Remy made a cute sound of pleasure but didn't fully wake. Chancy kissed her shoulder, then brought her lips against Remy's neck, sniffing her perfume as if it were ambrosia from the gods.

"Mmm. I'm glad you're here," Remy mumbled in her adorable, sleepy voice. "I had hoped Janice and Selene would send you home a bit earlier. You stayed until closing, didn't you? I set the alarm for 5:30. That should give us enough time for a quick shower. We can grab breakfast on the way. Actually, if I know Lindy, she'll have a spread already prepared for when we arrive at the airport."

"I'm sorry. I didn't mean to wake you. Your shoulder was just too tempting."

113

Remy turned to face Chancy, touching her face, then bringing their lips together. "You can wake me anytime you want. You know how sensitive my neck is to your kissing assault."

"Well, in that case..." Chancy began kissing Remy's neck as she pushed the straps of Remy's negligee to get better access to her shoulders and the top of her chest, but Remy was having none of that.

Remy quickly sat up and pulled the nightgown over her head, removing it entirely and leaving her skimpy lace underwear as the only article of clothing. "That's much better," Remy said as she settled back against the mattress.

Chancy grazed Remy's clit over her panties and found that she was already wet. "So, were you having fun before I came home because your panties are already soaking wet? Admit it. You weren't really asleep."

Remy laughed. "This is just what you do to me all the time. One brief touch, and I'm a goner."

Chancy continued her pleasure assault on Remy's body, kissing and licking her way down to Remy's dripping wet lace underwear. She spent a few extra minutes lavishing Remy's chest as if her breasts were still there. It had taken some time, but with determination, Chancy hoped she had made Remy feel beautiful about her new body. Complicating matters was the time it took for Remy to regain any sensation in her breasts, but slowly, the sensation had returned. Remy had started to feel less self-conscious, and Chancy could tell she enjoyed when Chancy touched or kissed the area around her scars.

As Chancy's warm breath came in contact with the delicate fabric, Remy moaned in delight. Playfully grabbing Remy's panties with her teeth, Chancy tugged until they revealed the prize she was after. Remy helped push them down and opened her legs, giving Chancy greater access to her drenched center.

Lightly dragging the tips of her fingers over Remy's folds, Chancy followed with her tongue. Then, using the end of her tongue, her laser focus allowed her to flick Remy's sensitive clit, causing Remy to buck her hips to maintain contact. But Chancy was not about to let Remy control the pace as she lifted her head and grinned.

"Someone is impatient tonight," Chancy drawled in her exaggerated southern accent.

"Go inside, please," Remy begged.

"In due time." Chancy returned to her previous position, and after ratcheting up Remy's arousal to the point where Chancy was sure she would explode any minute, she plunged two fingers inside while simultaneously stroking Remy's G-spot and sucking on her clit for good measure.

A long, low moan was Remy's response. "Yes," Remy cried out as her juices flooded Chancy's mouth.

Chancy crawled up Remy's body, caressing her face before kissing her tenderly. "I love you, and I can't even describe how wonderful it feels when you come undone like that."

"I love you, too. You make me feel so incredible, like nothing I've ever experienced before. Would you consider moving in with me after returning from St. Kitts? And I'm not asking just because you've given me one of the best orgasms of my life. I've been meaning to talk with you about this. I just didn't know where you were at with it. I know how much pride you have regarding your independence. So, if you don't..."

Chancy placed a finger over Remy's lips. "I'd love to. But we will need to talk a little about how I can contribute to the household. I'm not some gold-digger bent on living off my sugar mama." Chancy winked to add some levity to her comment. Yet, she meant it. She didn't want to depend on anyone but herself. She might have to seriously consider providing those special services to keep her pride intact. Chancy couldn't even begin to fathom how much the mortgage on Remy's place was. She worried about being able to pay half.

Remy reached over and stroked Chancy's cheek. "Hey, I can almost see the wheels turning in your cute little head. We can talk about all of that later. Right now, I'd like to help you relax enough to get maybe a couple of hours of sleep before the alarm rudely wakes us."

"I'm good with zero sleep if you are? Sleep is definitely overrated."

"Says the woman twenty years younger. Speak for yourself. I need my beauty sleep. Besides, I've been watching those bags under your eyes, and if you're not careful, you're going to prematurely age. People will stop thinking you're my daughter."

"No one ever mistakes me for your daughter. That's ridiculous. Mostly, they all wonder how in the world I attracted such a hot woman."

"Enough talk. If you don't let me touch you in the next ten seconds, I'm going to explode from sexual frustration."

"We can't have that, can we?" Chancy answered.

†

The sleek jet was a lot bigger than Chancy thought it would be. As the sun reflected on the shiny silver plane, Chancy took a deep breath. *Piece of cake, slice of pie, I can do this.* Grabbing both handles of the luggage, she rolled the bags to the bottom of the stairs. As she struggled with both cases, Alex's head popped out of the entrance to the plane, and she rushed to grab Remy's bag, which was the larger of the two.

"Thanks, bud. I could have carried them both, but the staircase is kind of narrow, and it's awkward to drag both pieces. Appreciate the assistance."

"No worries. Everyone else is already on board and settled. Lindy said we'll have breakfast as soon as we reach our cruising altitude. She hired someone to serve us. You should see all the food she bought." Alex climbed the stairs carrying the large bag in front, and duck-walking as she made her way into the plane.

Chancy turned to Remy. "Do you want me to take your other carry-on bag?"

"No, I got it. This has all the stuff I might need while we're in the air. I'll just put this under the seat."

"Okay. I'll follow Alex and store my bag with yours." Chancy followed Alex, similarly holding her smaller bag in front of her as she waddled up the stairs and into the plane. "Breakfast sounds good right now. I'm starved. Remy thought Lindy would make those arrangements. We kind of got a late start this morning. If we'd stopped for breakfast, y'all would have been waiting for us even longer."

"You look remarkably chipper this morning. How is that possible? Didn't you get home at like 2:30 or 3:00 last night?"

"Uh huh. And then I was a little wired from work, so..." Chancy waggled her brows.

"No wonder you two are late. Geez, it's not like you two will lack any opportunities while on a romantic island getaway." Alex made her way to the back of the plane and found an open storage spot, stuffing Remy's bag into the dedicated compartment.

Chancy nodded at Marley, Luna, Danna, and Lindy as she passed them to reach the storage area for luggage. "Hello, ladies. Sorry to hold you guys up." She set her smaller bag next to Remy's and waited while Alex secured the luggage partition. A woman she didn't recognize stood at the back of the plane and greeted Chancy, who nodded her own greeting.

"No, you're not," Lindy teased.

Remy blushed as she set her carry-on down on the seat, waiting for Chancy to join her. "Aisle or window?" she asked when Chancy made her way to the plane's center, where Remy stood.

Chancy's nerves finally kicked in as she shuffled her feet. "Um, it doesn't matter to me."

"Why don't you take the window seat? I'm sure the view will be stunning."

"It will," Lindy chimed in.

"Okay." Chancy slid into the large leather seat. Wiggling her butt before grabbing the seatbelt and securing it across her lap. She began nervously tapping her thigh before Remy took her hand, squeezing it, and providing Chancy with a reassuring touch to settle her.

Remy leaned in to whisper to Chancy. "I'm right here."

"If Luna can do this, so can I," Chancy declared.

"Once we're in the air, you won't even know you're on an airplane unless we come across turbulence," Remy soothed.

Chancy assumed the tall woman was the person Lindy had hired to serve them breakfast and perform flight attendant duties. She ambled down the aisle, glancing at each woman as she passed.

"Everyone ready? I see you already have your seatbelts on. I'll tell the pilot we're ready to go, unless anyone needs to use the lavatory before we take off."

Chancy couldn't see anyone else but heard the muffled sounds indicating everyone was ready. She wasn't sure she was prepared for this, but Chancy didn't need to use the washroom unless you counted puking in a little silver hole, which she was determined not to do. Chancy wasn't going to use one of those barf bags, either. She would swallow whatever bile threatened to rise in her throat. She'd faced a lot worse while living on the streets, she kept telling herself.

"Breathe," Remy advised. "I can see you getting worked up already. I promise it will be fine."

"Okay, I'm holding you to that." Chancy returned the earlier hand squeeze.

"Hello everyone, my name is Dawn Reynolds, and I'll be your pilot today. Hopefully, you've all met my beautiful wife, Candice, who will take care of you while we're in the air." The sultry voice came over the speaker above Chancy's head. "We'll be taxiing to the runway in a few minutes. Relax, and I'll have you in St. Kitts by noon at the latest. The weather looks good, only one storm that might cause a little turbulence two hours into our journey, but other than that, smooth flying. Don't forget to look out your windows. The view will be spectacular as we reach the island. I'll let you know when we approach. Just sit back and enjoy the flight."

After a few moments, the plane began to move, and Chancy didn't think it was so bad. She was acting like a big baby for nothing. "It sort of feels like I'm in a car. This isn't so bad."

"Lift off is a little different. Right now, we're going slow and getting in line for take off," Remy explained.

"Oh." Chancy gulped loudly.

The silence in the cabin was slightly unnerving. As the plane moved again, only much quicker, Chancy realized they were about to take flight. Her stomach did a tiny flip flop as the aircraft ascended into the air. She glanced out of the window and saw how everything reduced in size as they got farther from the ground. She was flying, and it was glorious.

"This is so awesome." Chancy's smile widened as she took in the sights. She was glad they were flying in broad daylight. The patchwork of green, gold, and other colors on the ground was so unusual. It looked like one of those quilts sold at the farmers markets. Chancy could see blue rectangles dotting the more upscale neighborhoods with built-in outdoor pools. She imagined seeing that same cerulean blue color when they reached the island. Alex had shown her pictures of St. Kitts. She couldn't believe she was on her way to such a beautiful paradise with the most exquisite woman in the world. This was a trip Chancy knew she would never forget.

CHAPTER ELEVEN

The morning of their flight, Luna raced to load their bags into the taxi's trunk and then back inside to grab her backpack and reset the security system. She peeked in her bag to make sure the ring was inside. Luna punched in the code with a smile of comfort and closed the door. She tapped her pocket to ensure her wallet was there and jogged back to the car.

"All set?" Marley asked from the back seat.

"Yes, ma'am. Do you have your ID?" Luna asked.

"Checked and double-checked." Marley smiled. "Let's go to the private jet entrance," she told the driver.

"Yes, ma'am," he answered.

"This is much better than flying commercially and not having to go through security and all the other lines. We just climb a few steps, and with passports in hand, we're going to another world," Luna said as they pulled onto the tarmac.

"You are such a pro at flying," Marley teased.

"Ha! If you only knew." Luna reached for her hand as the driver removed the bags.

†

"Good morning, ladies," Lindy said from the top of the stairs. "You can leave the bags if you don't want to carry them up these steps."

"Not a problem," Luna said. "I've got these." Luna quickly carried their larger bags and helped the attendant store them.

Alex had arrived with Danna and helped Marley with the smaller bags. "Hand yours up, and we'll get them stored," Luna told Alex.

"Y'all get settled in, and once Remy and Chancy arrive, we'll get going. We'll have breakfast in the air," Lindy said.

"Do you want the window or aisle?" Luna asked Marley.

"You can have the window," Marley replied.

"You can both have a window seat," the attendant replied. She pulled a lever on the seat in front of them and swiveled it around to face them. "A table will pop up between you once we are in flight."

Marley shook her head. "Too far apart," she said as she took Luna's hand. "I'll get the window coming back."

"Can we join you then?" Alex asked.

"Absolutely." Marley smiled.

"You can have the window," Danna said. "I know how much you love looking out."

"Thanks. I'll wait to take my seat until Remy and Chancy are onboard," Alex answered. "Chancy is probably dragging from working so late."

"Did she close the bar last night?" Marley asked.

"Yes, even though Haley is filling in for her, Chancy feels a bit guilty taking two weeks off from Sisters," Alex said. "I'm sure Janice and Selene were fine with her being off. Especially since she's worked so many doubles."

Luna smiled. "She's going to need a few days to catch up on sleep."

"Not Chancy. I've never seen someone with the energy she has," Alex replied. "By the time we leave, she'll have seen and done everything on the island twice."

"There's nothing wrong with youthful energy," Lindy said. "From the size of those bags, she could probably use some of your muscle."

"You need help?" Luna asked.

"Nope, I've got this," Alex replied.

†

"Last call for a lavatory stop," Candice said. "If we're all set, just sit back and relax."

Luna took Marley's hand and lifted it to her mouth. She kissed it. "Love you."

"I love you, too." Marley smiled.

"That was so sweet." Alex grinned.

"I've been taking lessons from you." Luna winked.

"Yeah, right, I should be the one taking lessons." Alex laughed.

"You are perfect just as you are," Danna told her.

"Now, that was sweet," Marley answered.

†

"Here we go," Alex said as the jet started to move. She glanced over to look at Chancy. She was staring out the window and gripping Remy's hand. Chancy turned her head, and Alex nodded and smiled at her. Then she looked across to Luna, who looked perfectly at ease, excited even. "I sure hope St. Kitts is ready for us."

†

Luna felt the nose of the jet elevate quickly and felt the landing gear tuck back into the belly of the plane. She looked at Lindy, who shot her a wink. Marley's hand in hers was all the comfort Luna needed. She watched Atlanta disappear from her small view and turned back to Marley. "Here we go."

†

"We're all set." Dawn's voice came over the speaker.

"Watch your knees, ladies," Candice said and flipped a switch. Two large tables rose and unfolded from a compartment in the floor. Candice began setting baskets of croissants and bagels on the table and plates and silverware.

"Is there anything I can do to help?" Marley asked.

"Just sit back and relax. I'll have everything served in a minute," Candice said. "Thanks for the offer."

124

Candice served steaming bowls of scrambled eggs, bacon, and hashbrowns. "Would anyone like their bread toasted?"

"I wouldn't mind a toasted bagel," Lindy replied.

"Anyone else?" Candice asked.

"Yes, please," Marley, Luna, and Alex replied.

Pitchers of juices were placed on the table while Candice toasted the bread.

The door from the cockpit opened, and a striking young woman stepped into the galley. "Do you need my help?"

"You can make sure I don't burn the bagels." Candice smiled.

Dawn saw a panicked look on Chancy's face. "Don't worry. I've got it set on autopilot while I check on my passengers. It's safe." She smiled.

Chancy relaxed in her seat.

"Autopilot flies smoother than I can," Dawn admitted. "Here you go, love." Dawn handed Candice a basket of toasted bagels. "I'm grabbing a cup of coffee, but let me know if you need help."

"All set, sweetie," Candice replied.

"How long have y'all been married?" Remy asked.

"Three years in a couple of weeks," Candice said. "We're going to spend a couple of days on St. Kitts before Christmas to relax before we come back to bring you home."

"Will you join us for dinner tomorrow night then?" Remy asked.

"That would be great, but let me check with Dawn," Candice answered.

"Of course," Remy replied. "We're staying at the Villas."

"You've got to be kidding? We have a room there," Candice replied.

"Maybe y'all can join us for some fun in the sun," Alex said. "Snorkeling, ATVs, windsurfing."

"That does sound like fun. We've flown customers into Bradshaw International many times, but we've never stayed over." Candice smiled.

"Now is a perfect time," Remy said. "Can you stay through Christmas?"

"Unfortunately, no, we're flying a family to Maine on Christmas Eve," Candice said.

"Maybe you can join us for New Year's Eve, then?" Remy suggested.

Candice nodded. "I'll have to check with our schedules. I think Dawn has tried to keep that week clear." She smiled. "Enjoy your breakfast, and I'll be back to check on you in a few minutes."

"Thanks," Remy replied.

†

"That was a great breakfast," Luna said.

"Yes, it was. Not Brothers, but still good." Lindy grinned.

"You went to Brother Junipers without me?" Remy cried out.

"Yes, Luna and I went last week," Lindy said.

"It was so good, too," Luna added. She rubbed her stomach.

"That's just cruel, Luna," Remy teased.

126

"We had Gus's Fried Chicken and Neely's BBQ that we brought home for dinner." Luna continued to twist the knife.

Remy cocked an eyebrow at Lindy. "Do I need to look for a new best friend?"

"Heavens no," Lindy answered. "You'll always be my number one. I do admit, Luna was a heck of a replacement, though." Lindy broke out laughing at the feigned look of shock on Remy's face.

"Good food, I take it?" Chancy asked.

"Some you and I will experience for ourselves soon." Remy smiled at her young lover.

"Lindy suggested a Memphis in May trip," Luna said.

"Oh, that could be fun," Remy said. "We haven't done that in at least ten years."

"With this crew, it would be much more fun," Lindy said.

"I'm in," Danna said. "Good music, good food, and great friends. What's not to like about that?"

"Amen, sister." Remy held up her juice glass. "If we can decide on a weekend, I'll set us up in a resort."

"Is there any place you don't have a resort?" Danna asked.

Remy smiled. "Vegas, but I'm working on that."

†

Luna glanced out the window to find they were over water. She could see the coast of Florida in the distance. Islands looked like tiny dots in the deep blue waters of the

Atlantic. Cruise ships from Miami and Ft. Lauderdale cut a trail south.

"I'm glad we're not on one of those," Luna said to Alex.

"What's that, baby?" Marley asked.

"A cruise ship," Luna answered.

"I did that once," Marley answered. "By day three on the water, I was bored stiff. You didn't have enough time in the ports to see hardly anything."

"You have two weeks to do all the exploring you want on St. Kitts," Luna said.

"Just don't plan on anything for tomorrow," Lindy said.

"What have you got planned for us?" Alex asked.

"We are going to catch lobsters for our chef to cook for our dinner," Lindy informed them.

"What? We have a chef?" Marley exclaimed.

"We can't be spending our time shopping and cooking. Remember, this is a fun trip," Remy said.

"We've got a boat to take us out in the morning to go fishing for lobsters on the coral reefs. The chef will grill them with steaks for dinner," Lindy said.

"Catching them ourselves?" Alex asked.

"While snorkeling," Lindy said. "They also have traps we can select from if we don't catch our own."

"With our bare hands?" Luna asked.

"No, with some special tongs," Lindy said.

Marley smiled. "That sounds like great fun."

"I hope so. I've wanted to do it for years. Jaydub would prefer to buy them off the docks," Lindy said.

Luna squeezed Marley's hand. "We will be great lobster catchers tomorrow," Luna promised Lindy.

"Do you have other activities planned?" Danna asked.

"Nothing set in stone, but several recommendations. If you don't want to ride ATVs or go zip lining, there are many other things to do," Lindy said. "We can go as a group or break up into smaller groups, if that's what you prefer."

"We always have fun together," Alex said.

"I know some people enjoy shopping, but that's not my cup of tea," Lindy said. "If y'all want a shopping day or two, I can go snorkeling."

"I'm with you on that," Luna said. "I can't wait to get in the water." Luna looked at Marley. "I know you enjoy shopping. Would you mind if I stay behind and snorkel?"

Marley smiled. "Not at all. I can't guarantee you won't get a tacky island-print shirt under the Christmas tree."

"For you, I'd wear it with pride," Luna said.

"I love you too much to make you do that, but I don't need to have you attached to my hip. Do what makes you happy," Marley replied.

"You make me happy," Luna answered. "I appreciate that you won't drag me through every store in town, though."

†

Lindy stood to hit the lavatory. She didn't want anyone to see the tears welling in her eyes. It was so evident that Marley and Luna were in love, and it made her heart yearn to feel that again. She had lost that feeling for Jaydub years ago. Being around three loving couples was refreshing, but it also made her realize what was missing in her life.

"Maybe one day you'll feel that fire again," she said, as she wiped the tears from her eyes and washed her face.

†

"Ladies, if you'll look out your windows, we are crossing over to the Bahamas. Let the island adventure begin," Dawn's voice announced.

"I don't think I've ever seen sand so white," Luna said.

"Or water such a brilliant blue-green," Alex added. "How much longer?" she asked Candice.

"We should be on the ground in St. Kitts in another hour or so. Dawn said we missed the rough weather, so it's smooth flying the rest of the way."

"That's a blessing," Chancy said.

"If you two don't have plans in the morning, we are going to catch lobsters for dinner tomorrow night," Lindy told Candice. "We'll leave around ten."

"That sounds like fun," Candice replied. "Dawn is a fish in water, so I'm sure she'd love that."

"Great, we'll add two more to the boat," Lindy said.

†

"Whoa, look at that," Luna called out. "It looks like there are two lines in the ocean. One green and one blue."

Candice smiled. "That's the convergence where the Atlantic and the Caribbean join. The Caribbean is green or, in some places, a blue-green."

"Beautiful," Marley said. "I can't wait to get into that and take some pictures."

Luna shot a look at Lindy, who was smiling at her. Luna would give Marley a Christmas present early to take full advantage of her gift. She may have to go shopping after all.

"What do we have planned for tonight?" Luna asked.

"Settling into our rooms. I distinctly remember someone commenting about the Jerked Chicken they saw in the photo gallery, so we thought we'd start with that for dinner tonight," Lindy answered.

"After a few rounds of umbrella drinks," Remy added.

"Do I at least get to make those?" Chancy asked.

"There's no better bartender," Remy said and kissed her.

"Yes!" Chancy did a fist pump. "That's not like work for me."

Luna settled back into her seat, staring out the window until she felt Dawn lower the landing gear. "You've got to be kidding me? This place is gorgeous."

A lush forest of deep green loomed ahead of them, low clouds shrouding the top of the mountains. "What, wait? White, tan, and black sandy beaches? All in one place."

"This is a volcanic island," Remy replied. "That accounts for the black sand. The tans are due to the shells that wash up from the ocean, ground to bits by the water. The white is the pure sand on the Atlantic or southeast side of the island."

"We are going to have so much fun," Chancy replied.

"Yes, we are," Alex agreed.

"I hate to break up the fun, but you ladies will need to return to your seats and put your seat belts on in preparation to land," Candice said. When everyone was secure, she returned the tables to their storage and took her seat.

"I've gotten permission to circle and come in from the south to give you all a better view," Dawn said from the cockpit, and banked the jet.

"You can't see the ground through the rain forest," Marley said.

"No, you can't, but you can see the fields of banana and coconut trees," Luna pointed out through the window.

Candice smiled at the young women's excitement at seeing the island.

†

Dawn expertly guided the jet to a smooth stop outside of the terminal. When the engines fell silent, Candice unbuckled her belt and walked to the door to lower the steps to the tarmac.

Dawn joined them from the cockpit.

"That landing was so smooth. I didn't know we were on the ground until we came to a stop," Luna praised.

"I try my best not to jar your teeth from your mouth." Dawn smiled. "I've had my fair share of rides where we bounced onto the runway. I didn't appreciate that as a passenger, and I try my best to land as smoothly as possible."

132

"Wonderful flight, ladies," Lindy said. She gave them each a business card. "Give me a call if you decide to join us tomorrow."

"No call needed. Where do we need to meet you?" Dawn asked.

"In the lobby at 9:30." Lindy smiled.

A large black van arrived on the tarmac. "I do believe your ride is here. We'll see to transferring your bags while you go through customs with your passports. It's an easy process in the private terminal. I'll have the driver meet you at the front door," Dawn informed them.

"Thank you both for a lovely flight. Please join us tonight for a cocktail if you'd like," Remy offered. "Just give us a call so that we can give you access to the private floor."

"I make some mean cocktails," Chancy promised.

Dawn smiled at Chancy. "Let me get this baby tucked away for service, and we'll get checked in to the resort. What time are cocktails?"

Lindy looked at her watch. "Will five give you enough time to get everything settled?"

"That should be great," Dawn replied.

"I'll be waiting for your call then," Lindy said.

"What are y'all waiting for?" Remy teased. "Let's get moving." She led them into customs, and they were all good to go within fifteen minutes.

"I can't believe I'm going to say this, but I'm hungry," Marley said.

Lindy smiled. "Excellent. Our chef will have crabmeat salad sandwiches waiting for us. We can eat while the porters deliver the bags, then get settled in."

†

Remy led them into the resort. "Welcome back. I hope your flight was good, Ms. Remy." The ebony-skinned man greeted them at the desk.

"The best flight ever, Marcus," Remy replied. "Our flight crew, the Reynolds, will arrive this afternoon. Please make sure they get upgraded to a suite."

"As you wish. I'll have your bags delivered promptly."

"Thank you, Marcus. You're looking well. Is Ms. Beth taking good care of you?"

"Very much so, Ms. Remy. I've gained five pounds since we married," he said, patting his stomach.

"It looks perfect on you. Thank you for making our preparations."

He nodded. "Your chef arrived earlier and should have lunch ready when you arrive."

"I hear she comes highly recommended," Remy said.

"Only the best for you, boss." Marcus grinned.

"Why do I feel like I'm missing something from that exchange?" Lindy asked as they rode the elevator.

"Our chef is Marcus' eldest daughter, Emelia, from his first marriage. She was recruited by the best in New York but will not leave her father since her mother's death a few years ago," Remy explained.

Remy led them into the extensive suite of rooms, and then directly into the kitchen. A young woman was busy at the counter. When she looked up, a brilliant smile lit up her face. The whiteness of her teeth made her smile glow against her flawless dark skin.

"Ms. Remy," she said as she rushed across the room. "It's been so long." She wrapped Remy in a gentle hug. "How are you doing? You look radiant."

"I'm well, Emelia. You look fantastic, too. Is life treating you well?" Remy asked.

"Yes, except for Father harassing me about not going to New York." Emelia grinned. "Sometimes, I think he's trying to get rid of me."

"You know he only wants what is best for you," Remy said. "These are my friends." Remy introduced everyone.

"Just let me know whatever you desire to eat while you're here, and I'll make it happen," Emelia said. "I hope you're hungry. The crab salad sandwiches are ready to toast."

"I think it's safe to put them in. Can I offer any help?" Remy asked.

"You can sort out drinks for everyone," Emelia said. She opened a double oven and placed a tray of sandwiches beneath the broiler for several seconds to put a slight crunch to the sweet rolls.

"Grab a seat, friends. Chancy, you can help me with drinks," Remy said.

"Sodas, sweet tea, water, and juices are in the fridge," Emelia said.

†

"Dear Lord, this is the best sandwich I've ever eaten," Lindy said.

"Thank you. Eat up," Emelia replied. "I have jerk chicken on the menu tonight, with fresh island vegetables and a salad. Is that still good?"

"That's perfect, Emelia." Remy smiled. "We're going to fish for lobsters tomorrow to go with the steaks. I know you have them marinating. Will it be a problem to add two more to the guest list?"

"Not at all, Ms. Remy. I've got a new lobster recipe I want to try out for you."

"That sounds interesting. Have you been creating some new dishes?" Remy asked.

"Yes. I'm putting your high-priced education to good use." Emelia chuckled. She saw the look of surprise on Lindy's face. "She didn't tell you she put me through two years of culinary school in New York, did she?" Emelia said. "She wanted me trained by the best."

"Money well spent, if these sandwiches are any indication," Lindy said.

Emelia's face beamed with pride. "Thank you. Are there any dietary restrictions I need to be aware of for any of you?"

"Only that we appreciate good food and lots of it," Danna replied. "Somehow, I don't think that will be a problem."

"Not at all," Emelia promised.

†

The porters knocked on the door and Remy answered. "You can leave them in the foyer. We've been so busy with Emelia we haven't even selected rooms yet." She handed each of them a bill and closed the door behind them.

136

CHAPTER TWELVE

Chancy had been to a few high-priced hotel rooms during her brief affairs with Helena and Jules, but she had seen nothing like the suites Remy had arranged for their small group. After lunch, each pair and Lindy had gone to their respective rooms to check out their new digs for the next two weeks.

After bouncing on the bed to check out the mattress and grinning at Remy, who had already changed into her swimwear ensemble, Chancy was itching to do the same and break out her brand-new swimsuit. She didn't have an elegant cover-up like Remy, but a tank top and shorts were okay with her.

The water and sand had looked incredibly enticing from her vantage point in the air as the plane had descended. Atlanta was humid in the summer, but nothing like St. Kitts. Chancy thought a dip in the pool would cool her down.

Although the rooms were comfortably air-conditioned, Chancy had ventured out onto the balcony, and since she was used to much colder temperatures in the winter, the ocean breeze wasn't quite enough to reduce the somewhat oppressive humidity. She felt the beads of sweat form on her face and absently brought her T-shirt up to wipe her face. In times like these, not wearing make-up was a blessing.

"Mm, I love the view," Remy called out to Chancy as she opened the sliding glass door to the large balcony.

Chancy bounced on the tip of her toes. "I know. It's so awesome. I've never been to such a beautiful place before."

Remy chuckled. "I meant you."

"Can we take a walk on the beach and maybe have a quick dip in the pool?" Chancy asked.

"That sounds wonderful. Let me pull together a beach bag. With our fair skin, we better cover every inch of our bodies."

"I'd be more than happy to rub lotion on your back and any other inch of your delectable body. In fact, right now, I have some warring emotions going on inside my head. One part of me can't wait to hit the beach, but the other segment of my brain is shouting at me to break in that wonderful bed." Chancy ran her hand seductively down Remy's arm.

Remy chuckled. "We have plenty of time for that. But I will take you up on your offer to cover my body in sunscreen."

Chancy grabbed Remy's hand. "Let's go then."

"Should we knock on the doors to the other suites and see if anyone wants to join us?" Remy asked.

"Sure. I'll do that while you pull together the beach bag," Chancy answered, then frowned. "Do you think they'll want me to make them cocktails before we hit the beach?"

"I know that you're excited to make drinks for everyone and it's not really work for you, but I want you to relax while you're here. Even though the drinks at the bar probably won't come close to your mastery, I think we'll all survive if we order something like a simple mojito. That should tide us over until tonight."

"There is nothing simple about making a proper mojito. I'll watch the bartender and make sure they muddle the mint correctly and only add fresh lime, not some piss-poor imitation."

Remy laughed again. "I doubt very much they will use a premixed substitute for fresh limes. This isn't a two-star hotel."

"True. Okay, but if the drink is not up to my standards, I'm taking over," Chancy insisted.

"Fair enough."

†

Everyone in the group had opted to join Chancy and Remy on the beach. The others offered to find chairs for everyone as Chancy and Remy leisurely made their way through the hotel. Chancy looked around as they walked through the lobby, taking in the beautiful view, and subsequently failed to notice the woman on a collision path with her. As they bumped into one another, both mumbled their apologies. Chancy looked into the startled green eyes of an attractive woman who would definitely have sparked her interest before Remy. The woman's long, wavy, reddish-brown hair fell delicately across her shoulders. She had an air of no-nonsense about her, coupled with a hint of melancholy. Chancy wondered briefly about her story as she headed straight for the outdoor bar, sat alone and ordered a drink. Unfortunately, she couldn't hear what the woman ordered, which drove her crazy. After quickly sizing someone up, Chancy prided herself on knowing precisely what drink a person would order. This woman did not seem like the fruity, tropical drink kind of person. Chancy craned her neck, attempting to determine what drink the bartender was making for the woman.

"Hey, should I be worried?" Remy playfully asked. "You seem ultra-focused on that beautiful woman over there."

"What? No. I can't figure out what kind of drink she ordered. She looks a little lost, kind of like Lindy lately."

"Lindy? What do you mean?"

Chancy shrugged. "I'm a bartender. Part of my job is to pick up on subtleties. Lindy has seemed a little off lately. I get the lonely vibe from her. I know Lindy suggested this vacation, but I don't think she realized how hard it would be to hang with three couples in love."

Remy frowned. "Damn. What kind of best friend am I? I've been so self-absorbed lately and so happy. I suppose I have noticed her looking a little out of sorts lately. Jaydub is gone so much, the loneliness must get to her. I know if you were away as much as Jaydub, I would feel lonely."

"I think she was crying earlier. She did a good job of covering up. In fact, it's so subtle I'm not surprised no one else has noticed. Jaydub not being around a lot has to be hard on her." Chancy took Remy's hand and walked closer to the bar.

"Jaydub's as big a jerk as my ex. I wish Lindy would leave him. I don't think she loves him anymore. But it isn't my business to tell her that."

"Why not? You're her best friend. She didn't have a problem encouraging you to have a tongue-wagging racy affair with a young sprite. Which, for the record, I am one hundred percent grateful for," Chancy added.

"I think I have to wait for her to open that door with me. Then, I think I will let my opinion be known."

Chancy smacked her head. "Mint Julep, that makes sense. Classy cocktail."

"What are you talking about?"

"Oh, I kind of play this little game at work. It keeps me from getting bored on slow nights. I try to figure out what kind of drink a person will order before telling me what they want. I was curious about the woman's drink preferences. I would have guessed Cosmo or a zingy gimlet."

The woman turned to smile at Chancy and Remy. "Well, those were my second and third choices."

"Shit. You heard me. I'm sorry," Chancy mumbled.

The woman's eyes traveled to Remy and Chancy's clasped hands before waving her hand in the air. "Don't worry about it. My favorite pastime is figuring out a person's occupation and preferred investment type. Most people tend to be more conservative with their investments than what I generally propose. It helps to have a read on my clients or prospective clients before I make my pitch. That way, I can slightly alter my advice to their level of comfort." The woman opened the bag she'd set on the bar and pulled out a card, handing it to Remy.

Scrunching her face in confusion, Remy accepted the card. "Thank you, Remy Beckham."

Chancy didn't mind that the woman was giving her card to Remy. She suspected the woman was as good at her job as Chancy. She'd sized up who had the money and handed the card to that person. It wasn't exactly hard to decipher based on the clothes they'd worn to the beach. Remy reeked of money and grace. Chancy did not.

"Angel DuBois. My contact information is on the card if you ever need my services. I run an all-woman financial planning services company. I prefer giving women their fair share of opportunities in the business world. It is my small way to even the playing field. Although, I don't discriminate in who I take on as clients. Men still have the lion's share of money in our world." Her lovely tinkle of laughter filled the air.

Chancy had a crazy thought that this woman might be a good match for Lindy, but she couldn't overstep her bounds and suggest that Angel join them for dinner. That invite would have to come from Remy. That wouldn't stop Chancy from making that suggestion later when Remy and Chancy were alone.

†

Alex and Luna played in the surf while Lindy, Marley, and Danna stretched out in lounging chairs. Someone had dragged two empty chairs with rolled-up towels to the right of Lindy.

143

Lindy shielded her eyes from the sun and said, "Took you long enough to get here."

Remy chuckled. "Chancy is like a heat-seeking missile for attractive women. We met a woman who owns a financial planning company. Chancy was trying hard to figure out what kind of drink she would order. She gave me her card. I might check her company out. She only hires women."

Lindy raised her eyebrow. "Interesting. Was she here by herself?"

"Pretty sure she was," Chancy piped in.

"How do you know that?" Lindy asked.

"Well, you kind of get a feel for it after a while. Being a bartender is certainly about making awesome cocktails, but the real job is the ability to read people quickly. She reminds me of you, Lindy. She had this air of self-confidence about her. I'd bet everything I own, which I admit isn't much, that she's very good at what she does."

Marley turned her head. "Maybe we should invite her to join us for dinner. I could certainly use some advice on investments. Before I started at TWC, I didn't have two pennies to rub together and was living paycheck to paycheck, but now I actually have to think about retirement investments."

Remy smiled and settled on the chair next to Lindy. "Not a bad idea."

Chancy thought to herself, *Not a bad idea at all*.

"And what drink did she order?" Lindy asked.

"Mint Julep," Chancy answered. "Classy drink. It fit." Chancy adjusted the lounger so she could sit up and look at the view of the ocean. She wanted to play in the water with Alex and Luna, but she also wanted to see where the conversation would end.

Lindy nodded her head in appreciation. "That sounds divine right about now." Lindy scanned the beach until her eyes tracked the young man taking cocktail orders. The minute she lifted her hand in the air, the man hurried to where they had settled on the beach.

"Good afternoon, ladies. What can I get you to drink? Mojito, pina colada, something else?"

"Well, I, for one, have a hankering for a Mint Julep right about now," Lindy answered. "Anyone else?"

Danna lifted her finger in the air. "Make that two."

"Three," Marley and Remy answered together.

"I guess that makes four, but I'm going to be the odd woman out and have a simple mojito with spicy rum, please. But if you don't use fresh lime and mint, just give me a bottle of water."

"Drink snob," Marley teased.

"Damn right I am," Chancy retorted.

"Don't worry, miss, we only use fresh ingredients for all our drinks," the man answered.

"Would you mind if I followed you back to the bar? I want to see how the bartender makes their drinks." Chancy turned to Lindy. "I can extend an invitation to Angel while I'm there."

"Lindy, are you okay with that?" Remy asked.

"Sure, why not? The more, the merrier. Besides, she could prove to be a valuable connection."

Chancy mentally pumped her fist in the air and followed the young man to the bar.

†

"Well, hello again," Angel greeted. "Where's your, uh, colleague?"

Chancy broke out in a fit of laughter. "Yeah, right. In what universe would Remy be my colleague? Lover," Chancy corrected.

"Sorry, I did not mean to offend."

"No worries. I know we're an unlikely pair, but Remy is an extraordinary woman who has blessed me with her love, and I'm completely besotted with her."

"I could tell. You two look good together." Angel smiled.

"Listen, um, we're here with some friends and have a chef planning a meal for us tonight in our suites. We wanted to invite you to join us if you're free," Chancy said.

"Oh, I don't want to intrude."

"You're not intruding. It's just a bunch of women. I might not be the kind of person you'd typically hang out with, but several of the other ladies seem to be in your social circle. Besides, I think you might have a chance for some new business, and I doubt you'd ever turn that down."

"Don't sell yourself short. You seem like a perfectly charming young woman who would be great fun to socialize with. Okay, then, if you insist."

"I do, but just for clarity, I'm taken."

Angel threw her head back and laughed. "Oh, I know. I would not dream of getting in the middle of you and Remy. I don't think I caught your name."

"You didn't because I didn't give it to you." Chancy stuck out her hand. "Chancy. It's nice to meet you."

"What time is dinner?"

"Why don't you come by around six? We'll have cocktails before dinner. Let me know if you have any special requests. I know my way around a bar."

The woman raised her eyebrow. "I'm sure you do."

"No, really, I'm a bartender back home, and I'm pretty sure you've never had as good a cocktail as I make."

"I like your confidence. But, if you're as good as you claim to be, you're not a bartender. You're a mixologist."

Chancy shrugged. "Potayto, potahto, fancy names for what I do don't mean a lot to me."

"That's refreshing. I spend far too much time with pretentious people. Somehow, I believe your group is not that way, even with women who probably have enough money to buy this resort."

"Yup, you're spot on with that assessment. Lindy, Remy, and Danna, who are the rich ones, are some of the most down-to-earth people you'll ever meet, so bring your A-game and don't act like a snob."

"Oh, Chancy, you are a delight. It is too bad you're taken. I'll try my best." Angel smiled.

"We're staying in the Presidential suites."

Angel whistled. "Wow, that is impressive. I've never even seen the Presidential suites, and I've been coming to this resort for years."

Chancy grinned. "It's pretty awesome. Definitely not what I'm used to. Although I've been in a few nice hotel rooms before, it's nothing like this. Um, sorry, do you mind? I wanted to make sure the bartender is making the drinks correctly." Chancy turned her attention to the bartender, who frowned after hearing her state her intentions.

Angel leaned in and whispered to Chancy, "Now who is being the snob? I think you just offended the bartender. My Mint Julep was very good, so I don't think you need to worry."

"Oh, hey, man, I'm sorry. I didn't mean to be rude. I'm a bartender in the states and kind of picky about my drinks, but that was completely uncalled for. I've just been to some places where they use this disgusting sugary mix, and to most people, that's fine, but I really like fresh ingredients in my mojito."

"This hotel only serves top-shelf alcohol, and we never use mixes." The bartender muddled the mint and then the lime.

"So I've been told." Chancy watched as he made the drink precisely like she would have. She nodded her head in acknowledgment of his skills.

He pushed the finished drink in her direction. "Please, miss, have a taste and let me know if the drink meets your satisfaction."

After taking a small sip, Chancy smiled. "Good. Thanks."

"My pleasure."

"I guess I'll get out of your hair now." Chancy turned to the server and asked. "Do you need help to carry the other drinks?"

"No, miss."

"Okay, I'll see you later. Sorry again. Thanks for the awesome drink." Chancy lifted her glass in the air and took a sip. She wondered if she should have brought money to tip the bartender. Chancy felt terrible now. Not only had she offended the man, but she didn't even bring any money to tip him.

†

When Chancy approached her beach lounger, she leaned in close to Remy. "I didn't bring any money to tip the bartender, and I was kind of an ass to him."

"Don't worry about that. We'll add a generous tip for both the server and the bartender. Did you invite Angel?"

"Sure did. I like her."

Remy quirked her eyebrow. "You do?"

"Yeah, I think she and Lindy will really get on."

"Are you trying to play matchmaker?" Remy chuckled.

"Would it be so bad to even consider? I mean, they're both attractive women who are here by themselves. A little vacation fling wouldn't be the worst thing to happen to Lindy, would it?"

"I suppose not. But I'm staying clear of Lindy's love life unless she asks for my opinion," Remy answered. "You shouldn't be so obvious, either. I don't want Lindy to feel bad or for this to somehow blow up in all our faces."

"It won't. I have a good feeling about Angel."

"What are you two lovebirds whispering about over there?" Lindy asked.

"Remy was just asking me if I found Angel to invite her for dinner," Chancy answered. "And, I was making sure we were going to tip the bartender. I was shitty to him and acted like one of those pompous rich people, which I am the furthest thing from. I'm kind of embarrassed about what I did. I'm not going to hassle any more bartenders at this hotel. They know what they're doing. Of course, I'm still a better bartender, but he was pretty good. This drink is delicious."

"I'm sure you weren't that bad," Lindy noted.

"No, I was, I really was. Here come your drinks. Angel said her Mint Julep was scrumptious, so I'm sure you'll be pleased. Tonight, I'll make you something that will knock your socks off."

"I'll hold you to that." Lindy accepted her cocktail and pointed to the table for the young man to set the other drinks.

Remy plucked the paper from the young man, and Chancy noted the very generous tip she added to the bill. "Can you make sure the bartender receives half this tip, please?"

"Yes, miss."

"That ought to make up for my boorish behavior," Chancy whispered. "Thanks."

CHAPTER THIRTEEN

After several hours of playing in the surf and relaxing in the sun, Luna announced to the group. "I think we're going to head to the room and get showered for drinks and dinner."

"Maybe we can even get a quick nap in," Marley said.

"Is that what you call it these days?" Lindy teased.

"No, that would be a quickie, but seriously, that sun and those drinks have drained me," Marley said.

"I'm just playing with you," Lindy said. "It probably wouldn't hurt any of us to get a shower in."

"Especially me, since I've got to get to work on some out-of-this-world cocktails," Chancy said.

"I'll be your welcoming committee," Remy volunteered.

151

"That would be lovely, gorgeous," Chancy said and kissed Remy's cheek.

Luna looked around. "Do we need to take these chairs and towels in?"

"The beach staff will take care of those," Remy replied.

"That just doesn't feel right," Luna said.

Marley grabbed her hand. "That's what the beach staff are paid for, sweetie. Don't take their jobs away."

"Especially this crew." Remy nodded toward youngsters racing toward them. "Marcus pays them a dollar per chair and fifty cents a towel when they are out of school on breaks."

Luna took her hand off the chair and draped the towel around her shoulders.

"That's how many of them earn Christmas money," Remy continued.

"We may have to request more towels tomorrow," Alex said. "I can remember what it was like trying to scrape up the money to buy my mama and papa a gift."

"Is tipping allowed?" Marley asked.

"No, Marcus says that leads them to beg, and he will not tolerate that behavior on his property," Remy replied.

"That's probably a wise decision," Danna said.

"He wants them to grow into men with dignity and respect. As soon as they are old enough, he puts them to work at the resort," Remy added. "Several, including a prominent physician, began their careers here."

"I don't imagine you had anything to do with that," Lindy said, eyeing Remy suspiciously.

Remy shrugged. "Maybe a student loan or two. All repaid with high-quality health care for some of our neediest communities."

"You are such an angel," Lindy replied.

"Nonsense, I just believe in investing in the communities whenever possible." Remy smiled. "Let's head inside now, so they can do their jobs."

Luna smiled at the young boys of ten to twelve years old. Some of them were barely larger than the chairs they hefted onto their shoulders and proudly carried off the beach while the younger boys scrambled for towels. She turned and caught Marley smiling at her. "What?"

"Nothing, just admiring the view," Marley answered.

"It amazes me the little things we take for granted that mean so much to others," Luna said. "Were you serious about a nap?"

"Yes, but you don't have to nap with me if you'd rather do something else," Marley suggested.

"Something else would take me away from you, and I don't want to be anywhere but with you right now," Luna replied. "Let's go shower and check out that bed."

†

Remy showered and dressed before leaving the empty suite in search of Chancy. She found her lover sitting at the kitchen counter, slicing fruits while talking with Emelia. "Here you are," Remy said as she circled Chancy's waist with her arms and kissed her neck. "Are you two getting acquainted?"

"Emelia has been educating me on the island culture. She's also shared with me how much your presence has meant to so many lives," Chancy said. "You truly are an angel."

"Oh, stop it now before you make me blush," Remy said.

"That looks good on you," Emelia said.

"What's that?" Remy inquired.

"That beautiful smile you wear whenever you are close to this charmer," Emelia said, pointing a knife at Chancy.

"She has been a breath of fresh air in my stale life, Emelia. I am blessed to have met her."

"If anyone has received a blessing, I think it's me," Chancy said. "I was just a poor young woman with a broken arm, a crashed bicycle, and a life so confusing I didn't know which way was up any longer."

"You've both been good to and for each other, then." Emelia smiled.

"Most definitely," Remy said. "I could buy her any bar she wanted and set her up to manage it, but she'd rather earn it herself."

"There is nothing wrong with that. Hard work always pays off in the end." Emelia resumed chopping ingredients for the salad.

"Are you about ready to start mixing drinks, my love?" Remy asked.

"What's your pleasure? Wait, let me guess, a glass of dry white wine or maybe a Cosmo," Chancy teased.

"Hmm, wine would be light, but that wouldn't allow me to watch you work. A Cosmo sounds perfect. Oh, wait for a second before you start. I think that is Dawn and Candice, texting."

"Right on time, too. I'll ride down and bring them back with me," Chancy said. "Text them that I'm on my way."

"Yes, ma'am." Remy chuckled. "Do I need to get anything for you while you're gone?"

"A bucket of crushed ice," Chancy called from the door.

Remy turned and smiled at Emelia.

"She adores you," Emelia said. "I hope you don't break her heart. So young and yet not so innocent. Chancy needs someone like you in her life."

"How long did you two talk?" Remy asked as she picked up the ice bucket.

"Long enough to hear how special she is and how lucky you both are to have each other," Emelia replied.

"I hope she doesn't break my heart when I'm old and ugly," Remy said.

"That will never happen. Wild horses couldn't pull Chancy away from you. She doesn't see your looks or your money, she sees your heart, and that's what she loves."

"Maybe I should have sent you to medical school to become a psychiatrist instead of culinary school," Remy teased.

"Then I wouldn't be doing what I truly loved." Emelia grinned.

Chancy returned with Dawn and Candice in tow.

"Welcome," Remy said and introduced them to Emelia.

"Pleased to meet you, and thanks for the room upgrade. That was unexpected but very much appreciated," Dawn told Remy.

"My pleasure," Remy said. "Have a seat. Chancy is preparing to wow us with some of her delicious cocktails."

"I've been looking forward to that," Candice replied with a wink to Chancy.

"Let me start working some magic then," Chancy said, and picked up the bucket of ice. She walked outside to the wet bar on the patio.

"Should we join her outside?" Remy asked.

"It's a beautiful evening," Dawn replied.

Remy looked back at Emelia. "Do you need anything?"

"No, ma'am. I am all set to start cooking in about half an hour, if that's still good with you," Emelia answered.

"That sounds perfect. I can't wait to try your jerk chicken." Remy smiled.

Emelia nodded. "I'll send the others out as they arrive."

"Lindy's here," Lindy announced as she walked into the room. "I don't think the others are far behind."

"Come with us then. Chancy is dying to start mixing." Remy chuckled. "I know she's been experimenting with some new drinks."

Moments after everyone arrived and began sampling Chancy's new drinks, Remy's phone pinged with a text. "I'll be right back. Our final guest is waiting downstairs."

"Do you want me to go?" Lindy asked.

Chancy sent a quick nod to Remy. "That would be great. She's waiting outside elevator 2."

"I got this," Lindy said.

†

Lindy rode the elevator down to the lobby. She looked up when the doors opened to a beautiful smile and the most amazing emerald-green eyes she had ever seen. Lindy felt a low gasp leave her body and hoped the woman didn't hear it as Angel stepped forward. "Angel?" she asked with a hopeful tone.

"Yes," the gorgeous woman replied and offered her hand.

"Lindy Freemont," Lindy answered without stammering. She felt her heart hammering in her chest. "It's a pleasure to meet you. I hope you're thirsty. Chancy is already serving."

"I'm feeling parched from the sun," Angel replied. "Chancy's mixology talents are very enticing."

The sultry tone of the woman's voice had a visceral effect on Lindy, who couldn't wipe the smile off her face as the woman stepped inside. Lindy slid her key into the slot for the suite.

"Chancy has been experimenting with a few new cocktails to try out on us, so it should prove interesting," Lindy said. "I'm delighted you could join us, and I hope you'll consider staying for dinner."

Angel smiled. "After a few of her cocktails, I may not have a choice."

Lindy opened the door to the suites.

"Everyone is out on the patio," Emelia replied. "I'm getting ready to start cooking."

"Do you need help with anything?" Lindy asked.

157

"Just keep everyone out of my kitchen." Emelia laughed softly. "That means the grill outside, too."

"I'll try my best." She gestured to Angel. "Angel will be joining us for dinner."

Emelia's smile beamed. "The more, the merrier."

"Let's go get you something refreshing," Lindy said. She placed her hand softly on Angel's shoulder to guide her toward the door to the patio.

Chancy looked up from the bar. "Hey, hey, now we are complete. Take a seat, and I'll bring out two more drinks. Lindy, will you make the introductions?"

Lindy noted that the two empty seats were next to each other as she offered Angel a chair and began introducing the group. She smiled at Angel. "There will be a test later tonight to see how many names you remember," she teased.

Angel waved a hand toward Lindy. "Piece of cake. I am very good with names," she promised.

"Here you go, ladies," Chancy said as she placed tall drinks in front of them with cherries and an orange slice on the rim. "Enjoy."

Angel smiled at Lindy. "I know what the handsome mixologist does for a living. What about the rest of you? I'm in investments, as maybe Remy has informed you. An all-woman firm in Atlanta."

"She didn't mention the Atlanta part," Marley replied.

"I think I may have missed that detail." Remy shrugged.

Angel shook her head. "My card also has an 800 number. You wouldn't have picked up on the phone number, but it's likely in this heat and my rush to get a cool drink, I may have omitted that information."

"We are all from Atlanta," Lindy said. "I own a few businesses in the area."

"I'm mostly in resorts and entertainment," Remy said. "This is one of my flagship resorts."

"It's beautiful," Angel replied. She took a sip of her drink. "Oh my, that's good."

Marley was seated next to Remy. "I'm a massage therapist."

"Do you do private work? I'd love a card if you do," Angel requested.

"No, I stay booked working for Lindy," Marley replied.

"I'm a personal trainer," Luna replied. "Also, well booked working for Lindy."

"It seems I need to get to know Lindy better," Angel teased.

Alex was next. "I'm a general contractor with my own business. I also do work for Lindy and other women-owned businesses."

Danna ran her hand down Alex's arm. "I have several of those businesses, and Alex is my wife."

"Noted." Angel smiled.

Dawn looked at Candice. "I am Dawn, a private jet owner and pilot with my wife, Candice, as my flight attendant and assistant."

"I would love to have your information," Angel replied. "Flying commercially, even first-class, is such a risk these days." Angel looked around the table. "You are such a diverse group. It's lovely to see you traveling together."

"This is our first of, hopefully, many vacations together," Lindy replied. "We've all worked hard and accomplished so much in the last year that we decided to celebrate together."

Angel's smile filled her face. "That's a beautiful idea. I'm sure you don't want to spend your leisure time discussing business, but thank you for giving me a glimpse into your worlds."

Lindy asked, "How long will you be staying at the resort?"

"I'll be here until the New Year, then it's back to work for me," Angel said.

"Are you traveling alone?" Luna boldly asked, despite Marley pinching her thigh.

"Yes, I am. I'm single and just here to relax and enjoy the peacefulness of the island."

"So, you wouldn't be interested in joining us on some excursions?" Marley asked.

"Now, I didn't say that," Angel replied. "I'm all in for exciting adventures, but it's never fun doing them alone."

"You'd never feel alone with this group," Chancy called out from the bar.

"What do you think? Game for some adventure?" Lindy asked.

No one missed Lindy's veiled attempt at innuendo. The pinch from Marley had turned into a squeeze. She could barely keep from giggling.

Dawn, who had known Lindy the least amount of time, reached for her drink to cover her growing smile.

"We are going lobster fishing tomorrow for our dinner if you'd care to join us," Lindy offered.

"That sounds divine," Angel said, returning Lindy's smile.

Chancy pumped her fist in the air, and Remy was thankful Lindy and Angel had their backs to the bar.

Emelia pushed a food cart onto the patio and rolled it toward the heated flattop grill. Luna stood and began to walk toward her. Emelia shook her head. "Oh no, you don't, missy. Sit back down. The grill and kitchen are my domain and strictly off-limits."

Luna's shocked facial expression was priceless and quickly turned into a smile. "Yes, chef," she replied and returned to her seat. "I guess I just got schooled."

Marley laughed. "Yes, you did, sweetie. No different from how you would react to your gym, though."

"I guess you're right." Luna grinned back at her.

Chancy served another round of drinks while Emelia cooked.

"You've got the air smelling wonderful, Emelia," Remy called out to her.

"It won't be long now," Emelia promised.

Remy and the others watched Lindy closely and smiled at how easily she and Angel fell into conversation. Remy couldn't remember the last time she'd seen Lindy smiling like that. It was way past due for Lindy to have some fun.

"Lobster fishing tomorrow, and then what, ladies?" Remy asked. "We have so many options."

"What do you recommend?" Marley asked.

"One of two things. Either jet ski out to the reefs for more snorkeling or ATVs around the island. We could zip line or take a tour of the rain forest," Remy answered. "Or we could split into groups and do both."

161

"I vote to stick together as much as we can. We have so much fun together," Lindy said.

Marley looked at Dawn and Candice. "You two have to leave the soonest. You choose what we do on your last day on the island."

"You have to leave so soon?" Angel asked.

"Yes, we've got reservations to fly a family to Maine on Christmas Eve, but we will be back the day after Christmas through New Year's Day, if that's okay," Dawn said.

"I've already booked the suite for you," Remy told them.

"Jet skiing and snorkeling then," Dawn replied. "I figure the rain forest may take more than a day."

"That's an excellent choice," Remy replied. "You can uncross your fingers now, Lindy."

Marley leaned over and bumped shoulders with Lindy. "Who knew you were such a water baby, boss?"

"No, boss, for the next two weeks, remember?" Lindy reminded her.

"Yes, ma'am." Marley grinned.

"To me, there's no greater joy in the islands than underwater," Lindy said.

Angel laughed softly. "I couldn't agree more. It's even more beautiful than the island itself, and you never know what you will see or find. The last time I was here, I found a Spanish gold coin."

"That must have been an incredible experience." Lindy smiled.

"It was. It kept me underwater for the rest of my visit." Angel laughed. The group seemed mesmerized by the interaction between Lindy and Angel, allowing them to dominate the conversation around the table.

Emelia finished cooking and began rolling the food toward the door. "Hey, barkeep, you want to arrange drinks for these ladies?" she asked Chancy.

"You got it, chef," Chancy called back. "What will it be, ladies? I know there are wines, beer, tea, soda, milk, and juice in the fridge. Or if you want something else, I will do my best."

"I think I spotted a Pinot Gris that would match well with the jerk chicken spices," Remy said.

"That would be my suggestion too," Emelia replied. "I'll pull it out of the chiller," she said, then disappeared inside.

"All right, who all wants wine?" Chancy asked and took a headcount.

"I think I'll stick to tea," both Alex and Luna replied.

"It gives me a headache," Luna said.

"Y'all make it too easy on me." Chancy grinned. "Get set for dinner, and I'll pick up here and come pour the wine when everyone is seated."

"Do you need help?" Luna asked.

"Do you need to be schooled again?" Chancy laughed.

Luna threw up her hands. "Let's go wash our hands, baby," she said and offered her hand to Marley.

"You can use my washroom," Lindy told Angel. "It's the first door to the left."

"Thanks," Angel said and followed the crowd inside.

Only Lindy stayed outside. "Are you playing matchmaker?" she asked Chancy.

"Who, me?" Chancy gave her the most innocent face she could muster.

"Yes, you," Lindy replied.

"Is it working?" Chancy asked.

"She seems very nice and is fun to talk to, so who knows?" Lindy said.

"What will be, will be," Chancy replied. "So let it be."

"You are so incorrigible, but I love you anyway."

"Love you, too, Lindy, now go wash up."

Chancy stored her supplies and wiped down the bar before slipping into their suite. She kissed Remy sweetly. "What do you think about Lindy and Angel?"

"They seem to be hitting it off. I don't think I've seen Lindy smile like this in ages," Remy reported.

"We can only hope it will continue," Chancy said. "Let's go. I'm starving. Emelia's cooking was killing me with that delicious aroma."

CHAPTER FOURTEEN

Of course, Angel knew who Lindy, Chancy, and Remy were before she handed Remy her card. She'd seen them at the Women Strong fundraiser. Tongues had wagged at the fund-raiser as she hung back in the corner, simply observing the crowd. Remy and Chancy were a hot topic of conversation, but Lindy was the one who caught her attention. She was exactly Angel's type. Angel needed to learn more about this enticing woman.

Angel had attempted to balance her client list by attending the fundraiser and making connections with investors who possessed considerable assets. Unfortunately, she'd had more trouble than she thought she would, breaking into polite Atlanta society. Most men preferred male-dominated firms to manage their money, and the few women who were independent of their husbands weren't exactly eager to associate with an out-and-proud lesbian. She preferred having a large contingent of working-class women as clients. Besides feeling proud that she could help them dig their way out of near poverty, they were much easier to manage because they did not question every single piece of advice she provided. Men were the worst, but the society women came in a close second.

Angel sighed. It was a Catch 22. She needed more wealthy clients, but those clients would end up taking what little free time she had because they were so high maintenance. Somehow, she thought Remy, Lindy, and Danna would be different. After the initial getting-to-know-her stage, which was always present when taking on a new client, most new investors gave over their trust. She had no doubt that if Remy, Lindy, or Danna used her firm, there would be a lot of questions at first. After all, they were savvy businesswomen. Angel would expect nothing less of them.

Jules was one of the few who had trusted in her services. Of course, they'd had a brief affair, so Angel suspected Jules did not care one bit what others thought of her. In fact, if the rumors were true, she had a string of young lovers, both men and women, and the handsome blue-haired mixologist was one of them.

Angel was astute enough to pick up on Chancy's subtle attempts to bring her and Lindy together. This was a stunning development for Angel. Almost equal to what she could easily have interpreted as a double entendre from Lindy after asking if she was game for an adventure. Following the fundraiser, she'd googled Lindy Fremont and found out she had married a prominent judge. Angel was no home-wrecker, but Lindy was almost too irresistible. If she'd known about Jules' marital status, she never would have taken up the short dalliance with her. Fortunately, Jules had moved on to another lover soon after the affair started, saving Angel from an uncomfortable conversation and the loss of her business.

Angel plastered on a smile and walked back into the main suite, where Emelia had set out the various dishes. The delectable aroma of jerk spice filled the air, and Angel's mouth was already watering. The presentation was equally impressive. Angel could admit that she'd become a food snob since her business had taken off. Excellent food and drink were her aphrodisiacs and a surefire way to begin a delightful evening with a woman. This certainly wasn't a date or a business meeting, but it was nice to be around so many fascinating women.

"I believe I've died and gone to heaven. What more could a woman want, good food, drink, and company," Angel announced before taking the open seat next to Lindy.

Lindy smiled back at Angel. "Indeed."

"Shall I serve all of you, or would you prefer to do this family-style?" Emelia asked.

"Definitely family-style," Remy answered as she took the plate of jerk chicken from Emelia. Selecting several pieces, she passed the dish to Chancy. Emelia had already handed Luna one of the sides to pass around.

"So, lobster fishing tomorrow. Will we also be spearfishing?" Angel joked.

"Oooh, can we?" Chancy piped up before adding chicken to her plate.

"Yeah, I'd love to give that a try," Alex added.

"Maybe we should wager a little bet," Luna suggested and then passed her plate to Marley, who scooped a generous proportion onto her plate.

Lindy and Remy laughed together. "That's what we get for inviting all these competitive women to St. Kitts," Lindy said. "I don't believe I'll be hurrying to the front of the line for that challenge. We should leave that to the young, athletic members of our group."

"You can count me out, then. I'm neither young nor athletic," Angel noted.

Lindy's eyes roamed across Angel's body, and that mere look caused shivers up and down Angel's spine. She felt like Lindy's eyes had caressed her skin.

"Nonsense. You absolutely look as though you can hold your own," Lindy purred. "But while the hunters are showing off by sending spears into unsuspecting fish for dinner, we can gather all the lobsters that will crawl into the traps all on their own. And we'll be able to enjoy the underwater treasures as they swim by. Finding multiple varieties of tropical fish is my kind of competition."

After everyone's plates were heaping with food, Remy picked up her glass of wine. "To good friends and outstanding food."

"Isn't that a little premature?" Emelia asked.

"Not at all. If there is one thing I am absolutely sure about, it's that the meal you prepared will put any five-star restaurant to shame. And that, my dear friends, is a bet I'd be more than willing to make with any of you sitting at this table." Remy grinned.

The group lifted their glasses in the air and sipped.

"Thank you for inviting me. I feel so blessed right now to be included," Angel stated. And she meant every word. Perhaps this group of women would become close friends. She'd spent so much time lately on her business. Building its reputation left little room for enjoying the simple pleasures of life. She wondered how often she'd missed out. Perhaps it was time to put as much effort into her personal relationships as she had done with her work connections.

✝

Lindy leaned back in her chair and groaned. "That was so scrumptious, but I definitely ate too much. I think a long walk on the beach is in order. I know we're all on vacation, but all of Luna's hard work will go by the wayside if I don't at least move my body a little."

"Well, if you and Remy wouldn't have made fun of our spearfishing challenge, you would have been able to work off that dinner tomorrow," Luna teased. "I can guarantee the amount of effort we'll engage in will sculpt your body similarly to when I put you through the paces in the gym. Care to amend your plans for tomorrow? We can give you slackers a handicap, like in golf. You get two fish to start."

Lindy smiled and flipped her hand in the air. "I think I will stick to a moonlit walk on the beach. Does anyone care to join me?"

"I'd love to," Angel offered. "Anyone else for a more reasonable form of exercise?"

Danna shook her head. "I might try out the gym early tomorrow."

"I think I'll let my food settle. Perhaps we'll see you a little later. A walk sounds nice, but in a little while," Remy added.

"We can wait for you," Lindy suggested.

"No. You two go ahead. We'll catch up later. Perhaps have an after-dinner drink before we all head to bed," Remy said.

"All right." Lindy stood and held out her hand to Angel. "Shall we?"

Angel smiled, taking Lindy's hand and then linking their arms together as they left the suites for the beach.

†

The almost full moon shimmered above the ocean, shedding a path of light on the water. The leaves on the palm trees swayed gently with the tropical breeze. A few errant clouds moved lazily across the sky but didn't dare block the moon.

"May I be honest with you?" Angel blurted.

Lindy turned to face Angel. "Honesty is always the best policy."

"I knew who you, Chancy, and Remy were before we officially met."

Lindy's eyebrow quirked in the sexiest expression Angel had ever seen on a woman. "Do tell."

"I attended the Women Strong fundraiser. A few of my clients were previous winners. You are a hard woman to forget. And, well, I heard a small amount of chatter about Chancy and Remy. None that I took part in because I tend to stay on the periphery, especially with the socialite crowd."

"Do I detect a note of derision? The way you say *socialite* suggests you aren't enamored with Atlanta society. I hope we've altered your perspective because many of us are part of that socialite crowd, whether or not we like it."

"No, no, I meant no offense. I have nothing against the fine ladies and gentlemen of the upper crust society in Atlanta, but I don't believe they share the same view. I tried to develop a specific clientele early in my career, believing it would be less work to have fewer clients with massive wealth to invest." Angel looked away, choosing to stare at the ocean as she continued to explain. "Unfortunately, I was wrong on so many levels. First, being an out lesbian is not what most desire for an investment manager, especially the men. But it was also true for many of the women I approached. Second, I've found most wealthy clients expect far more effort than the middle-class women who have entrusted me with their hard-earned dollars. And, of course, I would be lying if I didn't admit to being enamored by you."

"Nice catch. I'm surprised I didn't notice you at the fundraiser. I most certainly would have taken note. You're an extremely attractive woman. One who would be hard to miss." Lindy shot Angel a seductive look.

"Can I be so blunt to ask about your husband? He wasn't with you at the fundraiser, and he isn't here in this wonderfully romantic place. Unfortunately, you being married messes up my plans to seduce you." Angel winked.

Lindy sucked in a big breath. "Jaydub and I have an understanding. He doesn't get too involved in my friendships or my club, and I pretend not to notice his ongoing affairs with young women."

"Do you also take young lovers that he pretends not to notice? It seems to be a common occurrence in your social circle. Although I don't believe Jules's husband ignores her dalliances."

"Jules? How do you know Jules? I'd stay clear of her if I were you."

171

"Too late. I'm reluctant to admit this, but we had a brief affair. It was over before I knew Jules was married. That saved me the trouble of an awkward conversation to end the relationship. Although I'd hardly call a few romps in the bedroom a relationship. To be fair, Jules is one of my better accounts to manage. She leaves me alone to do what I do best—make gobs of money for her. And you didn't answer my question."

"What does it matter? You seem to be allergic to affairs with married women." Lindy's tone sounded irritated, which was the last thing Angel wanted. But Angel was not a game player, and setting her cards face-up on the table had always worked for her.

"I suppose I'm curious. It will not affect how I view you. I have no judgment. It's just not my thing to take up with married women. The mistress always gets the shaft in the end. I care too much about my self-worth to be anyone's dirty little secret. I'd love nothing more than to take you back to your suite or mine and make love with you all night, but you're married. Even if from my small vantage point, it doesn't seem like you could add happily to that fact. And...in for a penny, in for a pound...you seem a little lost and lonely." Angel held up her hand. "I can only recognize this because I often feel alone, and that is something I hope to change in the future. What I valued before, I no longer value as much. What good is having all this money if I have no one to share my life with?"

"I'm not sure why I'm going to admit this to you, but I started my club to offer lonely women a chance at the intimacy they aren't getting in their marriage. Taking part in the special services that my club offers has made life more bearable for me."

"Are you telling me your club is a high-class brothel?" Angel burst out in laughter. "Well, shoot, if I'd known that, I would have coughed up the fee to join. Of course, I'm assuming that only women offer those services to other women."

Lindy smiled. "Your assumptions would be correct. It would seem that not all of Atlanta's finest are opposed to a little sapphic loving. The club is a very lucrative venture. Behind closed doors, it would amaze you how much these women let their hair down. I wish they would be less concerned about their reputations. I'm sorry to hear that so many treated you with disrespect. I could certainly open a few doors for you. I may be interested in checking out your services."

"That's very kind of you, but not why I shared what I did. I prefer to be completely open and honest with someone I'm interested in. Game-playing is simply not part of my portfolio."

"Ah, but you're no longer interested, since I am still married," Lindy responded.

"I didn't exactly say that. It's a hurdle. A big one, but if I'm honest with myself, you're simply too hard to resist." Angel turned Lindy to face her and cupped her face, bringing their lips together. The kiss began with a slow exploration of Lindy's lips. Before long, Angel sought entrance into Lindy's mouth. Swirling inside with her tongue, the kiss deepened until Angel couldn't tell who moaned first.

After the two women broke apart, Lindy whispered, "Well, that was unexpected. Nice, but you certainly caught me off guard."

"I caught myself off guard, and I'm breaking every rule I've established for starting a relationship," Angel admitted.

"Rules are meant to be broken, or at the very least bent to the point of breaking. Let's just say you're bending a rule, not breaking it. I won't ask you to be my mistress if you simply accept that we're two grown women destined to explore something that, in reality, is hurting no one."

"Speak for yourself. I think hurt is entirely possible. My heart is a bit more fragile than I might let on. Since I've decided I no longer want my business to be my entire existence, perhaps I have more work to do on what is and is not acceptable in my private life. My new motto is carpe diem."

"Wonderful. This vacation is suddenly looking up. Let's agree to enjoy these two weeks and then see where we go from there. How does that sound?"

"Dangerous but exciting," Angel answered.

"Hey, there you guys are," Chancy called. She held Remy's hand as they walked closer to the location where Angel had just kissed Lindy. "We aren't interrupting anything, are we?" Chancy's grin widened with mischief.

"Nope. Join us. We were going to walk down to that large rock off in the distance. It's such a beautiful evening, isn't it? Are the rest of the gang still in the suites?" Lindy asked.

"Yeah, they were chattering away. I think I even saw Luna grab another bite of chicken. I swear that woman has hollow legs," Chancy responded. "I told them we'd be back in a little bit, and then I can prepare a special after-dinner drink for everyone."

"Sounds like a plan. If the drink is anywhere near as perfect as the cocktail you made earlier, I don't know if I'll survive these two weeks without turning into a raging alcoholic. But, Goddess, that siesta cocktail went down way too easily." Angel slipped her arm inside Lindy's and began to walk toward the rock.

"Wait until you taste my dessert drinks. I'm prepared to make a Grasshopper, a Golden Cadillac, or Brandy Alexander." Chancy nearly skipped along the beach as she explained her plans for the evening cocktail.

"What? No Pink Squirrels or Golden Dreams?" Angel teased.

Chancy grinned. "I like this woman. I can make anything your little heart desires. Do you think the bartender will let me raid his well-stocked bar for some of the liqueurs I didn't bring up to the suite?"

"I was just kidding. I'd love a Grasshopper. I haven't had one of those drinks in years," Angel answered.

"And I'll have the Golden Cadillac. Galliano is one of my favorite Italian liqueurs," Lindy added.

"Come on, let's hurry to that rock and get back to the suite. My mouth is watering. Now I don't know which drink to pick. Too many rocking choices." Remy kissed Chancy's cheek, who beamed under her attention.

The women hurried down the beach. Angel worried about what she was getting herself into, but Lindy proved too enticing to resist. Underneath her confidence, there was something fragile and vulnerable about Lindy, and Angel wanted to touch that part of her she suspected few ever reached. Most would probably give up before finding that special kernel. But Angel was not like most women. She would discover what made Lindy tick and perhaps end up helping Lindy to find a better path in her life. Maybe she'd also find a more suitable direction for her own lonely existence.

CHAPTER FIFTEEN

Marley was the first to finish her drink. She had chosen a Brandy Alexander that went down much too quickly. "I hate to be a party-pooper, but tomorrow morning will come all too soon for my choosing."

"It has been a long, eventful day. We were all up early, and tomorrow will be a full day out on the water," Lindy said. "I'll walk these ladies to the elevator and see you for breakfast in the morning at eight."

"Goodnight, ladies," Marley said and accepted the hand Luna was offering.

"I'll clean up here and meet you inside in a few," Chancy said.

"Nonsense. I'll sit right here and wait for you," Remy replied.

"Fine," Chancy said. "You can help me bring the glasses to the sink, then."

Alex laughed. "We'll see you in the morning."

"Goodnight, ladies," Danna added.

Lindy looked at Dawn, Candice, and Angel. "Ready?"

"Lindy, why don't you ride down to the lobby with them and get two additional keys made? That way, they can join us without hesitation," Remy suggested.

"That's a great idea," Lindy said.

†

Lindy returned with two keys and stepped off on the third floor to walk Angel to her room as Dawn and Candice continued to their suite.

"I'm delighted you joined us tonight, and I look forward to spending time with you," Lindy told Angel.

"It certainly feels like our paths crossed for a reason," Angel replied. "Would you like to come in for a nightcap?"

Lindy smiled. "Like to, yes, but I'll take a raincheck tonight. It has been a long day of travel and activities for us, and I'm ready for some sleep."

"Until tomorrow then." Angel smiled and leaned forward to kiss Lindy. "Rest well. It's going to be a grand day tomorrow."

"Indeed, it will." Lindy smiled. "I'll see you for breakfast."

Lindy walked back to the elevator. Her face ached from smiling so hard during the evening. She slid her key card for the Presidential Suite and leaned against the wall. "Are you ready to tumble into this adventure?" she asked, the image reflecting at her in the shiny elevator. "Why the hell not?" Lindy replied with a giggle.

†

Luna was exiting the kitchen when Lindy arrived. She held up a bottle of water. "Old habits die hard." Luna grinned.

"I understand," Lindy replied. "Are you having a good time?"

"It's been great so far. You seemed to have fun tonight." Luna smiled. "I know you didn't ask for my opinion, but you should let your hair down and have some fun."

"Opinion noted," Lindy replied. "I'm giving it serious consideration."

Luna raised her hand for a high five. "I can't think of anyone more deserving. Thank you for this wonderful trip of a lifetime."

"You are most welcome. Are you giving Marley an early Christmas present tomorrow?"

"Yes. I can't stand the thought of Marley using a disposable camera when she has a top-of-the-line camera as a gift."

"She'll love it, and we may have to drag her from the water tomorrow," Lindy said.

Luna smiled and nodded. "I'm okay with that. As long as Marley has fun, that's all that matters."

"Goodnight, Luna," Lindy said when they reached her door.

"Goodnight, boss," Luna replied.

"Luna! What did I tell you about that?" Lindy scolded.

"Old habits," Luna replied and walked on to her room.

†

"I didn't think a kitchen could smell any better than it did last night, but it does," Lindy said as she entered the kitchen and poured a cup of coffee.

"Good morning, Lindy. Are the others stirring?" Emelia asked.

"I think so. Once the aroma makes it down the hallway, I'm sure the group will appear quickly," Lindy teased.

The front door opened. Dawn and Candice arrived with Angel in tow. "See, it's working well already."

"We smelled the aroma as soon as the elevator door opened," Dawn said. "We found this one wandering the hallways, so we brought her too." Dawn nodded toward Angel.

"Welcome, everyone. Come have a seat, and I'll grab coffee or juice."

"Coffee sounds great," Angel replied.

"I hope it's jet fuel. I could use a boost this morning," Dawn said.

"The best the island has to offer," Lindy said as she began pouring.

Alex entered the kitchen, followed by Danna, Luna, and Marley. She dropped to one knee in front of Emelia. "Will you marry me and move back to the states?" Alex implored.

180

Emelia pointed a spatula at Alex. "You're already married, silly woman." She smiled brightly at Alex. "Where do you find these women?" she asked Lindy.

"We picked the cream of the crop," Lindy replied. "You have to admit they love and appreciate good food. Not a picky eater amongst them."

"I doubt there is anything you'd cook I wouldn't eat," Alex replied as she took a seat next to Danna. She leaned over and kissed her wife. "You know I love you."

"You better be careful. I might test that theory and cook you chicken feet or something odd," Emelia replied.

Alex swallowed hard. "Um, how about fish? We are having a spearfishing competition today."

Emelia turned to face them. "I hate to be the one to burst your bubble, but spearfishing is only legal for locals. There have been too many incidents of tourists getting shark bitten, not knowing the dangers of the activity."

"Well, damn," Luna said. "I guess that's smart. It could be like chumming for sharks with the fish blood. I sure don't want to fight a shark for a fish."

"I'll gladly stick to lobster and steak," Alex agreed.

Emelia laughed softly. "If you want to eat fish, we can go to the fish market, or you could charter a boat for some traditional fishing. My Uncle Henry has a boat."

"That's not a bad option either," Luna said.

Alex poured glasses of juice. "Worth considering."

Remy and Chancy were the last to arrive for breakfast. Remy had the glow about her that tipped the others off that she had received some good loving, but nobody commented.

"It smells delicious in here," Remy said.

181

"Eat well. We will burn some serious calories today," Luna replied. "No spearfishing, though," she told Chancy. "Illegal unless you're an islander."

"Too bad. I was looking forward to the money I was going to win off y'all today." Chancy grinned.

"Twenty bucks each in a pot for the biggest lobster caught today?" Marley suggested.

"You are so on." Chancy laughed. She pulled out her wallet and placed a twenty on the counter. "Who else wants to lose money today?"

Marley, Luna, Alex, and Dawn all sweetened the pot. "Anyone else?" Chancy asked.

"Nope," Lindy said. "I'll be too busy snorkeling."

Remy, Angel, and Candice all shook their heads. Danna smiled. "I'm going to be lazy and just stretch out and enjoy the sun."

"There's nothing wrong with that," Alex said. "I'll bring home the prize for us."

"Emelia, will you hold the pot for us today until we have the results?" Chancy asked.

"I surely will. Are you going by length or weight? The boat captain will clean and prepare your catches for cooking, so he needs to know how to measure," Emelia said.

"Your recommendations?" Luna asked.

"The length of the tail is the most important aspect, so I'd recommend that," Emelia answered.

"Sounds easy enough," Alex replied. "Have any of you ever gone lobster fishing before?"

"No, but the boat captain, Stephen, promised we'd watch a short video to learn on the ride out," Remy replied.

"Stephen knows all the good spots," Emelia said. "You should come home with some nice tails."

"Is that the only part worth eating?" Marley asked.

"For the meal I'm cooking tonight, yes. Stephen will make sure the heads and knuckles won't go to waste, though," Emelia assured them. "They are prepared in soups and other delicacies here on the island."

"How many will we need to catch?" Luna asked.

Emelia counted the women around the table. "Twenty will be plenty, with some potential leftovers. They are not the largest lobsters in the world, but they have the sweetest meat."

Emelia worked as she talked and began carrying dishes of breakfast meats, eggs, stacks of toast, and fried potatoes to the table. "Word of caution, go easy on the sausage if you have a sensitive stomach. It can be a bit spicy."

"The spicier, the better," Alex replied and speared two lengths for her plate.

"Is there anything we're missing from the table?" Emelia asked.

"Just you, if you'll join us," Remy said.

"I don't mind if I do," Emelia said and pulled up a seat.

†

After the delicious breakfast, the women sat around drinking coffee until it was time for the van ride to the marina.

"This is going to be so much fun," Alex said.

"Do we have five more minutes?" Luna asked. "I have something I need to do."

"Of course," Remy replied.

"I'll be right back," Luna said.

When she returned, she handed a gift bag to Marley. "Happy early Christmas. I can't wait for you to have an opportunity to use this."

Marley's eyes grew wide as she opened the bag to find a camera case, and when she pulled it from the pack, she smiled brightly.

"I couldn't stand the thought of you using one of those disposable underwater cameras."

"I can use this for underwater?" Marley exclaimed.

"It's already set, loaded, and charged for underwater use," Luna replied. "You can read up on all the land functions tonight when we return."

"Thank you, my love," Marley said and pulled Luna down for a kiss. "I will make excellent use of this today."

"Is that your way of distracting her from the competition?" Chancy asked. "Clever idea."

"Nope, I transfer my twenty to Luna, so she will have two lobsters in the competition while I photograph you all." Marley smiled. "Does anyone have a problem with that?"

"Nope, I'm still going to win," Alex replied.

"Let's go then," Luna said.

†

As promised, Captain Stephen showed them a brief video for the best technique for catching lobster, and the women felt like they had everything under control.

Captain Stephen smiled at them. "Don't be fooled by their looks. Lobsters can move very quickly. No worries

184

though, I'll have several traps for backups if we don't meet our quota."

While driving out around the island, Gregory, Stephen's son and his first mate, got the ladies set up with equipment. Luckily, everyone had some experience snorkeling, and when they reached their destination, they were all eager to hit the water.

"Remember your lessons and have fun," Stephen said as they dropped anchor. "Gregory and I will measure and process your lobsters as you bring them up to the boat."

†

Marley couldn't wait to take pictures and was the first into the water. Her camera snapped off photo after photo as Luna and the others joined her underwater. Luna posed for her underwater, with her one gloved hand giving her a thumbs-up sign while holding the menacing-looking tongs in her right. Marley took a shot, then surfaced for a breath before swimming toward the reef in the clear water. The visibility was outstanding, and she was able to focus and take pictures of colorful tropical fish as they swam lazily by her.

†

Even with a mask and mouthpiece, Luna could see the beautiful smile on Marley's face, and she realized she couldn't have selected a better gift for Marley. She swam alongside Marley for a few minutes until she saw her first prey darting between the coral. Luna took a deep breath and dove beneath the crystal clear water. Catching the elusive creatures wasn't as easy as it seemed and Luna had to return for a breath before a second attempt. She quickly figured out the escape path of the lobster, and when she made her move, her tongs captured the spiny creature. She wrapped her left hand around the body and started to the surface. She swam to the boat and offered Gregory her catch.

"You are the first," he praised. "Now go get another."

The flippers helped her glide through the water, but Luna could already feel the burn of exertion as she dove quickly in pursuit of a second lobster. She caught movement to her left and saw Marley photographing Alex as she caught a lobster. Off to her right, Luna could see the flash of Chancy's blue hair as the midmorning sun reflected on the water.

†

Marley pointed in the direction of a lobster and surfaced for a breath as Luna dove deeper. Marley realized she could use the zoom function while treading water with her head underwater. She didn't have to be in deep water to catch the action. Marley watched Luna begin her approach and took several photos as she reached for and trapped the lobster with ease this time, and then rushed to the surface.

"I think I'm going to take a short break and get some water," Luna said. "That's more physical than I thought it would be, especially when you dive quickly to catch the lobster."

"Go ahead, and I'm going to catch up with Lindy and the others to see how they are doing," Marley told her. "I think I've got some good shots of all five of you. Everyone has caught at least one so far."

"That's great news. Who has the biggest?" Luna asked.

"I have no clue. The lobsters have all looked monstrous underwater." Marley chuckled.

"Hey, remind them all to hydrate and add more sunscreen. The sun exposure is different here, especially in the water, and we don't want anyone burned," Luna said.

"Will do. Love you." Marley swam away as Luna made her way back to the boat to deliver her lobster and drink some water.

Stephen welcomed her back onto the boat. "We will need to wrap things up here by two," he said. "We have a rainstorm expected to arrive around four, and we need to dock before then."

Luna took the water he offered. "I understand and will pass the word. We will break for lunch in an hour or so and plan accordingly. How are we doing on the lobster bounty?"

"Quite well. You all have brought in some beautiful lobsters," Stephen answered.

"Who has the biggest so far?" Luna asked.

"To tell you that would be cheating." Stephen laughed a deep laugh. "You will have to wait until the harvest is complete to get that answer."

"You are no fun," Luna teased.

"The others have all asked the same question. A very competitive bunch of ladies." Stephen grinned.

"Will we make our quota in the next few hours?"

"Easily at the rate you all are catching." Stephen nodded.

"This is incredibly fun," Luna said as she drained her water.

Stephen smiled. "I am thrilled you are enjoying yourselves. Hopefully, you will come again before you depart."

"I believe we can arrange that," Luna said. She looked over at Danna, basking in the sun. "Unless you want to look like one of these lobsters, I'd recommend you turn over. At the least, cover up soon."

"Thirty more minutes, and I'll cover up," Danna replied.

"I'd hate for Alex to miss out on the fun because she's doctoring your sunburn," Luna teased.

"Oh, all right. Spoilsport." Danna grinned back.

Luna dropped her bottle in the waste can.

"Have fun," Stephen called to her, and she waved before dropping back into the water.

Marley caught up with Lindy and the others and snapped off their photos as they swam together. "Luna said to remind everyone about going back to hydrate and put on more sunscreen."

"That's a good idea," Remy said. "I feel a bit pink already."

"I'm sure Chancy will relish the opportunity to coat you down with lotion," Lindy teased.

"No doubt, but I don't want to get sunburned so soon into our adventures," Remy replied.

"Why don't we head back for a drink, maybe some lunch, and decide what we're doing from there?" Lindy suggested.

"That sounds good. Are you enjoying your new camera?" Candice asked.

"I feel like I'm getting good shots, but it's too bright out here to tell. I'll check them when we get back to the boat," Marley answered.

Luna had just arrived with another lobster when Marley and the other snorkelers arrived. She handed Gregory the lobster and helped them onboard. "Are we having fun yet?" she asked.

"Loads of fun." Remy smiled. "Have you seen my fair-haired sprite lately?"

"I see bubbles. Lots of bubbles, so hopefully, they are all on the way back to the boat," Luna replied. Three snorkelers popped up to the surface and began swimming toward the boat just as she finished. "As if right on cue." Luna laughed.

"Alex must have heard us mention lunch." Danna chuckled.

"I am getting hungry," Luna said. She handed Gregory and Stephen three more lobsters and helped Alex, Chancy, and Dawn into the boat. "How are we looking quota-wise, Stephen?

"Two more to go," he answered. "You all made some nice catches," he added.

"Let's have some lunch, and we can go back for the last two," Luna suggested. She looked at the ladies who had been snorkeling. "Have you had enough for one day? Stephen says we have some weather coming in this afternoon."

Lindy looked at her friends. "I think we'll all be sufficiently sore tomorrow and potentially sunburned, so I think we'll wait for you to catch the last two, and we can head back."

"Sounds good. Let's break out those sandwiches," Luna replied.

They sat around and ate sandwiches and chips while Marley scrolled through her camera, offering her friends a glimpse of many shots. "Not bad for my first attempt," she said and bit into a sandwich.

"You'll only get better with practice." Luna smiled at her lover. "We can hook the camera up to the television, and you can give us a slideshow tonight over drinks."

"Only if you promise to forgive me if I've cut off anyone's head," Marley replied. "I've got to get used to shooting while in the water, I was a bit bouncy at first."

"If you don't mind a suggestion, there are several companies on the island that offer basic scuba training without a need for certification, and one course they have available is underwater photography," Stephen informed them. "I'm sure Emelia could recommend the one right for you."

"I'm already certified," Luna said.

"We are, too," Dawn and Candice replied.

"How come I didn't know that about you?" Marley said.

"It's never come up before." Luna shrugged. "Would that be something you all would be interested in?"

"Heck yeah," Chancy answered.

"I'd love it," Marley replied.

"I think I'll stick to snorkeling," Lindy replied. "I can do that while you dive."

Remy, Danna, and Angel all opted for snorkeling. "I'll see who Emelia recommends and ask her to set it up for us when we get back," Luna replied. She looked at Alex, Dawn, and Chancy. "Are we ready to get the last two?"

"I'm going to sit this one out," Chancy surprised them all. "I'm not as well complected as you bronze goddesses, and I'm starting to feel a bit scorched on my shoulders."

"Okay. Hopefully, this won't take long," Luna said. "Gear up, ladies, and let's hit the water."

†

Chancy took a peek inside the cooler full of lobster tails. "Man, those look delicious," she told Gregory.

"They are nice ones," he agreed.

"Emelia has a new recipe with fresh coconut, pineapple, and a few secret ingredients she's going to try out on the grill," Remy informed them. "I'm sure it will be delicious."

"It looks like we'll get back in time for a shower and a power nap before Chancy serves more of her magic on us," Lindy said. "My legs feel like Luna worked me for hours in the gym." She chuckled.

"She has helped you sculpt a nice figure," Angel replied. "Are you sure I can't steal her away a couple of days a week?"

"Absolutely not," Lindy said with a smile. "We work her hard as it is."

"Maybe I'll just have to cough up the cash to join that fancy club of yours if there are any openings," Angel said.

"We can look into that," Lindy answered.

Luna was the first to pop back up with a lobster in hand and a massive smile on her face. She handed her catch

191

to Gregory. "Are we still okay if they both come back with lobster?"

"Yes, you're good with the number of people registered for this trip," Stephen answered.

Luna stripped off the gear and stored it on the racks before toweling off. She stepped into a pair of shorts and deck shoes and slipped in beside Marley. "Are you having fun, baby?"

"I am having a blast. Thank you for the early Christmas present, too," Marley answered.

"Just seeing that smile on your face makes it all worthwhile," Luna said. She stretched her legs out in front of her and waited for Dawn and Alex to arrive, each brandishing a giant lobster.

"I think this one's going to be the winner," Dawn said.

"I don't know. That one looks small compared to a few I brought in," Luna teased.

"Gregory will clean them and give me the winner while we head back to port," Stephen said. "It's going to be very close."

†

Luna kept an eye on the water and noted that the waves had begun to pick up. She turned to Stephen. "Anything unusual, or just your typical storm?"

Stephen nodded. "Pretty standard, but generally not this late in the season. Nothing to be concerned about, though. It will move through within a couple of hours at the most, and the sun will return."

When he made the final turn into the harbor, Gregory brought him a slip of paper. Stephen tucked the paper into his pocket until they had securely tied the boat. "I know you are all wondering who won your friendly little competition and I'll tell you it was very close. The winners, yes, I said winners, were less than an inch longer than the rest. Congratulations to Luna and Alex for tying for the longest tail."

Luna high-fived Alex.

The group all clapped for the winners. "It couldn't have gotten any closer," Stephen told Chancy and Dawn. "You all brought in some beautiful catches, and I know you'll have as much fun eating them as you did catching them."

Gregory carried a cooler full of lobster tails to the waiting van and tucked it in the back. Lindy handed them both one-hundred-dollar bills.

"Thank you both for a great day on the water," she said and stepped from the boat.

CHAPTER SIXTEEN

"Aw, Chancy, you did really well today," Remy soothed as she rubbed aloe on Chancy's shoulders.

"It was hardly a fair competition," Chancy grumbled. "Alex and Luna have orangutan arms. They're twice as long as mine."

"Why, Chancy Olsen, I didn't figure you for a sore loser." Remy chuckled. "Are you really upset that you lost the competition?"

"Nah, Alex and Luna are like Amazon women. I was never really serious competition for them. They have their talents, and I have mine." Chancy waggled her eyebrows. "Goddess, that feels divine. My lily-white skin is not made for all day in the sun."

"Neither is mine, but I kept slathering on the sunscreen. You were having too much fun playing in the water. When you finally felt your shoulders, it was too late."

Remy kissed the top of Chancy's sunburned shoulder. "Are you ready for round two tonight? Those cocktails were amazing last night. I suspect they've all had a short power nap and will be raring to go. I already hear Emelia stirring in the kitchen. The rest of the ladies will magically appear when they start to smell the food."

"True dat. By the way, did you notice the smoldering looks between Lindy and Angel? I do believe love is in the air," Chancy teased.

"It is certainly nice seeing Lindy smile again. We always have fun together, but I've hated seeing that shift in her lately. It's been hard to watch the loneliness grow. Lord knows I have no room to give advice because I stayed too long with Felix. After a while, we all just settled into our routine and seemingly expected awful marriage. You don't know what you're missing until someone comes along to show you alternatives exist."

Two quick knocks were followed by Alex's head poking inside the suite. "Hurry, hurry, put your clothes back on and stop licking each other cause we're coming in."

"Funny," Chancy deadpanned. "We just got out of the shower, and Remy was providing me with some tender, loving care." Chancy pointed to her bright red shoulders.

"Ouch. That looks painful. If I'd known you would look so much like those spiny lobsters we caught today, I would have grabbed your ass to toss into the boat for Gregory to measure, and then I would have won."

Chancy swiveled her head to look at her ass. "I do not have a big tail, do I?" Chancy looked to Remy for confirmation. "Besides, not everyone goes from one to tan in like two hours. Some of us take time, like a fine wine, to mature."

"Your butt is perfect," Remy answered.

"Although, I bet I taste as delicious as those spiny lobsters," Chancy joked.

Remy nodded, then blushed.

Danna playfully smacked Alex. "Stop teasing Chancy."

"What? As you can see, Chancy is no shrinking violet. She can definitely hold her own in a verbal spar."

"Yup, I sure can, Orangutan Arms." Chancy stuck her tongue out at Alex. "That's the only reason you and Luna won. I have Tyrannosaurus Rex arms compared to you and Luna."

"Who has Tyrannosaurus Rex arms?" Luna asked as she walked into the suite with Marley.

"Apparently, Chancy does, and we have arms like an orangutan," Alex answered.

"Let me guess, Chancy is bellyaching about our win today." Luna sniffed the air. "Mmm, Emelia must have started dinner. I'm starving."

"I was not bellyaching. Merely stating an undeniable fact," Chancy defended.

"What obvious fact?" Candice asked as the rest of their group shuffled into their private suite.

Alex started laughing. "Chancy is trying to explain why her tiny little body was never an actual threat with the great lobster challenge."

"Well, duh. I knew it was between Alex and Luna before anyone dipped their toes into the water," Dawn stated.

"What is this? The communal suite now?" Chancy asked.

"We had to get our resident mixologist moving on our evening cocktails. Some of us are way past thirsty," Alex responded.

"All right, no need to get all discombobulated. I'd like to try out a new mojito recipe on y'all. Is everyone game?" Chancy asked. "Come on, let's head to the communal area. It's getting claustrophobic in here with the Amazons taking up so much space." Chancy stood and led everyone out of their private suite.

Alex rolled her eyes.

"After last night's masterpieces, I'll drink anything you put in front of me," Angel declared.

"Not that I want to challenge your genius, but what will be different about your recipe? I didn't know there were numerous versions of a great mojito." Lindy settled herself into a chair. Chancy smiled as Angel took a seat next to her.

"Oh, there are tons of different versions, but this one is all me. I experimented earlier this year, and I think I found the perfect infused simple syrup to use in this drink. Plus, I'm going to try to use a different variety of mint. I'll let you taste my mojito and guess what might be different. Maybe we'll do another competition that isn't so lopsided. Whoever guesses correctly wins..." Chancy tapped her finger on her chin. "Hmm, let me think."

A mischievous glint formed in Angel's eyes. "How about whoever wins gets to give one task of their choice to every single participant in the competition? A dare, I suppose?"

"Is this the adult version of Truth or Dare without the truth, or can the recipient of this dare choose truth instead?" Marley asked.

"Interesting plot twist. All right, victim, or rather, participant's choice." Angel sat back in her chair and grinned.

"And will you be taking part in this challenge?" Lindy asked.

"Of course, because I plan to win. I have an especially sensitive palate. I trust in my ability to detect Chancy's special ingredients." Angel winked at Lindy.

"Let the games begin," Chancy announced.

†

Angel took another sip of her mojito and scrunched her face before stating with conviction, "Lavender."

"Hey, no fair starting already. Chancy, do not confirm or deny her guess. We should write down our guesses, and then Chancy can tell us who got all the ingredients correct. Sound fair?" Marley asked.

"Sounds good to me," Danna chimed in, then turned to Alex. "Are you getting in on this challenge?"

"Sure am. I used to taste test all of Chancy's new concoctions. I think I know what spins around in that genius brain of hers. I'll be sure to smoke the rest of you," Alex taunted.

"Don't be so sure of that. You're a mere babe in the woods. I've got at least fifteen years on you, which means I've been enjoying a variety of unique cocktails for much longer than you. Extra years on the planet give us mature women an edge over you youngsters." Lindy smoothed her shirt and grinned at Alex.

Chancy giggled. "I am so loving this. Finally, someone to put Alex in her place. The rest of you wait until I serve the last few drinks. Don't be like Angel and turn the test paper over before we officially start."

"Hey, no one explained the rules, and the drink looked so refreshing. Who can blame me for taking a tiny sip?" Angel defended.

Chancy stirred the tall glass, then walked to where Luna relaxed against Marley's legs. As she started to hand the drink to Luna, Luna waved Chancy away. "I think I'll pass. I know enough to acknowledge I am no match for the rest of these lushes."

"Okay, then, Candice is the only one left, but you're really missing out," Chancy said.

"I'll take a small sip of Marley's just to experience your brilliance," Luna answered.

"Aw, come on. Don't be a wuss, Luna. You have to participate in the challenge."

"Fine, I'll take a very small glass," Luna responded.

Chancy pumped her fist in the air and poured a small amount into a whiskey tumbler, offering it to Luna, then handed the larger glass to Candice, who eagerly accepted it.

"Let me get a writing pad, and I'll hand out slips of paper to everyone for them to mark what they believe are the special ingredients that differ from a traditional mojito. How many ingredients are we talking about?" Remy asked.

"Three. Including the different alcohol I chose. Drink up, ladies, and let's see who really has a discriminating palate." Chancy smirked.

Alex lifted the glass to her lips and moaned in appreciation. "Wow! This certainly rises to the top as one of your best creations. I think I have worked out two of the three ingredients. The third is a little harder to decipher." Sipping again, Alex grinned. "I think I know."

Chancy pointed to the pen on the table. "Write it down, and don't forget to put your name on the slip of paper."

As the other women tasted their mojito, the cacophony of appreciative noises filled the room. Lindy comically protected her paper from prying eyes as she scribbled her guesses. Alex appeared to add an exclamation point to her paper, setting the pen down with a flourish. Angel handed her paper to Chancy, displaying her supreme confidence. After five minutes, all the women had at least attempted to guess the unique ingredients, and Chancy held all the individual pieces of paper in her hands.

As Chancy began to read, she burst out in laughter. "Cointreau? Really? That's your guess? Uurnt." Chancy pantomimed pushing a buzzer. "Wrong." She tossed the paper to the side. "I disqualify Alex for such a ridiculous guess."

"You're just mad that you lost the lobster challenge," Alex taunted. "Maybe there isn't Cointreau in the drink, but something orange flavored is in there, and I know you wouldn't use orange juice. Did you infuse the simple syrup with orange?"

"You don't get more guesses, you know. That isn't how this challenge works. Let's see what Marley thinks. Hmm, so close, but no cigar for you either," Chancy announced.

As Chancy continued to read through the guesses, she tossed several more pieces of paper onto the side table. She began nodding her head and then smiled. "Good job. We have a winner. Oh wait, we might have another tie." Chancy read the last guess. "Correction. We have a three-way tie. I guess there is something to be said about our hot, mature women. Angel, Lindy, and Remy all picked out the special ingredients."

Chancy clapped her hands. "I can't believe more of you didn't get this correct. I practically spoon-fed the clues to y'all. You already knew I was using a different mint, an infused simple syrup, and different alcohol than is traditionally used. Okay, so each of you should decide between truth or dare from Lindy, Angel, and Remy."

Alex rubbed her hands together. "Since we have three winners, everyone needs to make a declaration. Angel said a task for every participant, no exclusions for winners."

Angel laughed. "Fine by me. I'm an open book. I choose truth every time."

"I'm too old for dares. Besides, isn't the saying, 'the truth will set you free,' appropriate here?" Danna asked. "I'm with Angel on this. Once you get to a certain age, you don't care what people think, and the truth is an easy pill."

"Bunch of pussies. Bring it on. I'll take the dares," Alex declared. "Who else is with me?"

"What the hell. I'll choose dare with Alex," Luna announced.

"Me too," Marley added.

Candice shared a look with her wife, who nodded. "We'll join team dare. Just don't ask me to do anything unsafe, like loop de loops with the jet while all of you are on board."

"Can we choose a mix of truth and dares?" Lindy asked.

"Sure, why not? I'm not sure we've even solidified the rules yet. We can establish whatever rules we want. Does everyone agree people can mix and match?" Angel asked.

Head nods and murmurs of assent answered Angel's question.

"I think we should also give people the option to choose truth, but only share that truth with the person asking the question. The rest of the group isn't involved," Remy suggested.

"Well, that's no fun," Luna interjected.

Chancy wagged her finger. "Hey, you don't get a vote on that. Initially, you chose not to participate. That should make your suggestions null and void."

"If someone only wants to answer their truth question to the person asking, that should be okay. Also, we should not make any of our dares dangerous. The last thing we need is to have to haul someone off to the hospital," Lindy stated. "I'm going to have to think on this a bit. Coming up with questions and fun dares may take some time."

"All right. Tomorrow morning everyone needs to present their questions and dares. Recipients can decide if they want to answer the question in front of all or only the person asking it. All dares, though, should be performed in front of everyone," Chancy announced. "I sure hope dinner is ready soon. The aroma from the kitchen is driving me mad."

Right on cue, Emelia called out, "Dinner is ready." Walking into the main area where everyone had gathered, she added, "I hope you don't mind buffet style. There are a lot of lobsters to set on the table. It might get too crowded with all the side dishes as well."

"Buffet style is perfect," Remy answered.

†

After Chancy dipped another morsel of lobster into the garlic butter sauce Emelia had prepared, she popped it into her mouth and moaned in delight as she chewed. "Fuck, that is so good." Leaning into Remy, she whispered, "If you want, I have a few ideas for dares. Especially for Alex."

Remy smiled. "Don't worry. I have something special in mind for Alex and Luna. I'm going to make them ask complete strangers if they can sniff their armpits and then sing at the top of their lungs 'We Are Family' on the beach."

Chancy roared with laughter. "Perfect. I had no idea you were so evil."

"Stop whispering over there. Chancy, you're not allowed to give Remy any ideas for possible dares." Alex narrowed her eyes and pointed to Chancy. "I'm watching you."

"Oh, don't worry, my gorgeous girlfriend doesn't need my help. You can be sure I will have a front-row seat and camera ready for when she announces your task." Chancy snickered.

Chancy continued to watch the interaction between Angel and Lindy. When Lindy dipped the succulent lobster into the decadent butter sauce, Angel watched intently as she brought the morsel to her mouth. The chemistry between the two was off the charts.

"Too bad I didn't get to take part in the challenge. I would dare Angel to suck Lindy's fingers after dipping them into the butter. Look at her. She looks like she wants to devour Lindy," Chancy whispered in Remy's ear.

"Angel chose truth," Remy responded.

"I know, but if she knew the dare, I bet she'd accept it." Chancy grinned.

"What did I say about whispering to each other in the corner?" Alex asked. "So, besides all the dares I'll need to accomplish tomorrow, what's on the agenda?"

"Parasailing? Jet skis? Sailing? Any of those sound great to me." Luna grabbed another cheddar biscuit from the basket on the table.

"I might just relax on the beach or possibly go into town and do some shopping. I'm guessing you'll want to join Luna on one of those adventures." Remy slid her hand down Chancy's arm.

"I'll come with you, Remy, if you decide to go into town," Marley said.

"Hard call. Hanging on the beach, shopping, or a fun activity on the water. What are you planning for tomorrow?" Lindy asked Angel.

"Well, I'm embarrassed to admit that I've never parasailed before. But, I would kind of like to try that," Angel answered.

"I'd love to go parasailing. It's a total kick. I've done it before. Once," Candice interjected.

"Once was enough for me. Shopping sounds more my style," Dawn added.

"Ditto. I'd love a chance at some last-minute shopping for Christmas." Danna turned to Alex. "You don't mind, do you? I know you'll probably opt for parasailing."

"Of course not. Being a happily married couple does not mean we have to do everything together," Alex answered.

Danna chuckled. "Thank goodness, because I am not nearly as fit as you, Alex. We do the important things together. I know shopping is not your thing."

"So, it sounds like parasailing it is for the more adventurous of the group, and town exploration for the rest. You're coming with us, right, Chancy?" Luna asked.

"Duh, yeah. I'm all about adventure." Chancy kissed Remy on the cheek. "Unless you want me to go shopping with you."

"Nope. I know you'd rather hang with the Amazons. Just don't try to show off and do something stupid. Alex has a way of goading you." Remy pushed her plate away. "Right now, I am so full, I'll be waddling into town at this rate. Is there such a thing as too much good food?"

"Never," Lindy and Angel declared in unison.

"Does anyone want another mojito?" Chancy asked the group.

Angel lifted her glass. "Sure, why not? By the way, you perfectly blended the orange mint, lavender-infused simple syrup, and that delicious aged spiced rum. I've only had Chairman's Reserve once before, but the flavor is distinct enough to remember."

"I suppose technically you were the only one to list the exact rum I used, versus simply saying spiced rum. But in the spirit of fair competition, I thought I shouldn't be that picky," Chancy said.

Angel shook her head. "Picky is good. But I'll be a good sport and share my win with Remy and Lindy."

Chancy stretched her hands over her head and yawned. "I'm knackered after trying to keep up with the Orangutan Twins. If y'all don't mind, I think it's time to head to bed after I make this last batch of drinks. Who else besides Angel wants one?"

Danna, Alex, Lindy, and Marley raised their hands, and the rest of the group declined.

"Okay, five more mojitos coming right up. Remy, would you like a dessert drink instead?" Chancy popped up from her chair.

"Ooh, that sounds good. Sure, I'll have a Brandy Alexander. I love the way you make that drink." A beautiful smile appeared on Remy's face, and Chancy could not imagine not having this woman in her life. Maybe someday Remy would agree to be her wife. She could certainly dream about that life.

†

Chancy had her arm wrapped around Remy as Remy's head nestled against her chest. She was absently stroking Remy's arm, making small concentric circles. "I think you should ask Angel what her intentions are toward Lindy. That would be a good truth question."

"Hmm. I suppose, as Lindy's best friend, it is up to me to find that out. It's not like her parents can fulfill that role."

"Is she close with her parents?" Chancy asked.

"Not particularly. They have deep roots in Atlanta society. I seriously doubt that either would approve of TWC nor would they be thrilled about their daughter having a sordid affair with another woman."

Chancy frowned. "Why call it sordid? You aren't having second thoughts about me..." Chancy's voice wobbled.

"Oh my, no. That was an abysmal choice of words. I'm sorry. I've never thought that what we have is anything less than beautiful and right. And that goes for the rest of our friends who have loving relationships. Lindy and Angel are both adults, and if they decide to take their friendship further, I've no doubt it would be good for both of them. It would never be a tawdry affair. I love you. We have a deep connection that is not going away anytime soon."

"I hope it never goes away. You're it for me, Remy. I know you aren't quite there yet, but I hope that someday you'll travel that road with me."

"Don't worry, I think we're pretty far on that path. Please be patient with me. My marriage ended not too long ago. I'm not ready to leap without looking around a smidgeon. I know that I love you." Remy lifted off of Chancy's chest and demonstrated her idea of a smidgeon with her thumb and forefinger.

"Patience isn't my strong suit, but for you, I'll wait as long as you need."

207

CHAPTER SEVENTEEN

"Emelia, those biscuits and gravy couldn't have been better if a true Southern Belle had made them," Remy boasted.

"I'll admit, I have been practicing them with my father," Emelia answered.

"All this time, I thought it was his new wife putting a little bit of weight on him," Remy teased.

"Oh, she's a mighty fine cook too, so I can't take all the credit," Emelia answered.

Luna looked at Marley. "How long do you anticipate this shopping trip to be today?"

Marley smiled at her. "It will be an all-day event. You'll be lucky to see us before dinner cocktails."

"No way. We can't miss out on those," Danna said.

"We have to fly home tomorrow, so we'll have to make it an early evening," Dawn replied.

"Relax, I was only jerking Luna's chain. However, I doubt we'll make it back for lunch, so you're on your own," Marley replied.

"I have egg salad and chicken salad for sandwiches in the refrigerator," Emelia told Luna. "I promise you won't go hungry."

"Are you sure you won't marry me?" Luna teased Emelia.

"While it is a tempting offer, I'm afraid I'll have to pass. It appears someone else holds your heart. I'll feed you well whenever you're here," Emelia promised.

"Okay, so that's off the table. After lunch, why don't we do some jet skiing?" Luna suggested.

"Only on one condition," Remy chimed in. "You make sure Chancy gets coated down with sunscreen. I know she won't keep a shirt on, but she's burnt bad enough already."

"I promise we'll keep her protected," Alex replied.

"For you, I'll wear a shirt." Chancy smiled and kissed Remy.

"Okay, so that's all set. We'll parasail then hit the water for some speed after we have lunch," Luna said.

"Will you be ready by one?" Remy asked. "I'll have the jet skis reserved for you."

"I believe that would be a safe bet," Luna replied.

"I'll have them loaded with snorkel gear just in case you want to do some exploring." Remy smiled.

Luna grinned. "That's perfect." She finished her juice. "Y'all have fun shopping. Let's roll." Luna stopped beside Marley and kissed her. "I miss you already."

Marley ran her hand down Luna's arm and smiled. "Have fun and be safe."

"Always." Luna smiled and followed the group out of the suite.

†

"What a beautiful day," Lindy said as they stepped into the sunshine.

"That rain yesterday has everything smelling so fresh and fragrant," Angel replied.

"Do you want to go up with me?" Luna asked Candice.

"That would be lovely," Candice replied.

"If you prefer, they have single seats," Luna said.

"Nope, I'm delighted to have a strong woman to hang on to." Candice chuckled.

"Who wants to go first?" Lindy asked.

"I think you and Angel should take the first ride," Alex said.

"I've got no problem with that," Angel said as they walked toward the boat.

Nan, the boat captain, and her deck mate, Julia, greeted them and gave them a short course on parasailing. "You are entirely safe with us, and I hope you will enjoy the experience."

"I've no doubt we will," Lindy replied.

"Let's get started then, ladies." Nan smiled. "Julia will get you geared up and ready to go. Once we clear the 'No Wake Zone,' I will speed up until we reach deeper water. Once we get there, I'll cut the speed, and Julia will set you up on the platform. When you're ready, I'll hit the throttle and gradually pick up the pace until the parachute expands. Julia will monitor the guideline once you lift off the platform until you reach the optimum observation elevation for the best view."

Both Angel and Lindy nodded.

Luna smiled at the excitement in Lindy's face as they stepped onto the platform and secured to the parachute. "Just remember to watch your feet when you descend until the back of the boat is cleared," Julia said. "Ready?"

"Yes," Lindy replied.

"Hit it, boss," Julia said and grabbed a handle as the fast boat raced forward.

Luna pulled out her camera and recorded the first take-off of the day. She smiled at how tightly Angel clung to Lindy as they rose quickly in the air. She taped them for several minutes and then turned to Alex. "I think those two look cute together."

"Yeah, they do. Angel and Lindy seem to be having fun, too," Alex said. "You two want to go next, and the kid and I will bring up the rear?" Alex slung her arm around Chancy's shoulder as Chancy puffed up.

"Who are you calling a kid?" Chancy groaned.

"You will always be the youngest of this bunch even when we hit our older years," Luna said. "You know we love ya, though."

"Yeah, I do," Chancy said, then frowned. "I'm no kid."

"Relax, smalls, you will always be like a little sister to me," Alex teased.

Chancy smiled up at Alex. "Thanks. I reckon you can get away with calling me kid, then."

They watched as Julia began retrieving Lindy and Angel. Nan slowed the boat dramatically to lower them within twenty feet of the waves before speeding forward.

Luna laughed at the excited yells escaping Lindy and Angel as they lifted higher at a rapid pace. Luna began recording again as they approached the boat and touched down perfectly.

"What a rush," Angel said.

"It's incredible how clear the water is and a bit scary to see what's in the water with you," Lindy admitted. "I hope we have time to go up again."

Nan smiled at them as Candice and Luna were preparing to soar. "You'll all get to go up three times in different spots around the island if you want."

"Oh, hell yeah," Angel replied. "That was amazing."

Julia looked at Luna and Candice. "All set?"

"Yes, ma'am. Ready to rock and roll," Luna answered.

Julia nodded to Nan, and the boat began moving as Luna started filming.

Luna was surprised by how quickly they climbed in the air and turned her phone toward the island to record the island as it shrank in the distance. Candice tapped her thigh and pointed down to the water.

"I think that must have been what Lindy was saying about what was in the water. That's a big shark," Candice said.

Luna zoomed her camera closer as they watched the shark glide effortlessly through the water. "It doesn't appear to be following the boat. I'm sure that's just one of many out here." A few seconds later, several sea turtles entered her viewfinder. "Look, sea turtles." Luna pointed out to Candice.

"The view is amazing," Candice said. "We've got to go visit that when we come back," she said, and pointed out a waterfall in the distance.

Luna turned her camera toward the fall. "We certainly will," she promised. "I wish y'all didn't have to leave tomorrow."

"We've had so much fun with you all. We will be back as soon as possible," Candice said. "I hope you're ready to dip your feet in the water. I can feel Nan slowing down."

The parachute floated even lower than before, and they were only a few feet from the crest of the waves. Then, just as quickly, they were thirty feet in the air again. "Wow, what a rush," Luna called out.

"You'll have to send me a copy of your videos. I didn't think to bring my phone," Candice said.

"No problem," Luna answered as they began approaching the boat platform and touched down smoothly.

"You are going to love this," Luna said to Chancy as she stepped onto the boat deck. "Did either of you bring your phones?"

"No," Alex said.

"I've got mine, but the camera is crappy. May I borrow yours?" Chancy asked.

Luna nodded and handed her the camera. "Enjoy." They watched as Alex and Chancy took flight.

†

"Wait until we get to the next spot," Julia said. "We will head southeast toward the convergence. We've seen a few humpback whales and dolphins out there."

"That would be awesome to see from the air," Lindy said. "I'm digging out my phone for that."

213

Julia nodded. "We will begin heading that way on this flight, and once they are back on board, we should reach there quickly."

Alex and Chancy lifted quickly in the air, and Luna laughed at Chancy's excited chatter. "I think she may have just spotted the shark," Luna said.

"It was a bit disconcerting to see the shark beneath you in the water when you are entirely relying on others to keep you safe," Angel said.

"We've been doing this for years and have only lost one passenger," Julia said calmly.

"To a shark?" Angel asked with a gulp.

"No," Julia replied. "To a young man who thought it would be fun to release his harness as he was descending. He was fine, but he quickly learned that the water wasn't as soft a landing as he thought it would be when his acrobatics ended in a face plant."

"Ouch. That was a painful lesson," Luna said.

"One I bet he never tries to repeat," Candice replied.

"He received a broken nose and a mild concussion but was still laughing when we loaded him into the ambulance," Julia said with a shake of her head.

"I bet the laughter ended when they reset his nose and the headache arrived," Candice said.

"No doubt," Julia said. "He's since been banned from all water sports on the island. That was five or so years ago."

†

As soon as Alex and Chancy were back on the boat, Nan increased the throttle as the boat powered through

214

the water. "You'll never guess what we might see on this next round," Luna said.

"I hope no more sharks," Chancy said.

"There are always sharks in the ocean," Lindy reminded her, "but these are even bigger."

"Whales?" Alex asked excitedly.

"Julia said they've been seeing humpbacks in the area we are headed to next," Luna replied.

"I've never seen a whale," Alex said.

"I haven't either," Luna said.

"Only in pictures and on television," Chancy said.

"Dawn and I took a whale-watching cruise out of Provincetown a few years ago," Candice said. "It was much colder than today, but it was an incredible experience. You don't realize just how humongous they are until you're up close and personal. We had a female swim alongside the boat, and we were eye to eye for several minutes before she breached and soaked the boat's deck."

"I've been on a few of those in the Northeast and the West Coast," Angel said.

"I saw a few on an Alaskan cruise many years ago," Lindy said.

"I bet that was beautiful. I've wanted to see Alaska for years," Angel replied.

"It's beautiful," Candice said. "We've flown many parties into Alaska."

"Do you fly over most of the United States?" Angel asked.

"For the most part. Sometimes down to the islands and a few trips to Mexico. On a rare occasion, we get a trip to Canada," Candice explained.

"If you had your choices of a romantic location, where would you go?" Luna asked.

"Without a doubt, Fairbanks, Alaska, for the northern lights," Candice said. "Late fall to spring. It's one of the best spots to view the northern lights."

"Thinking about a honeymoon?" Lindy asked.

"Yeah, but she has to say yes first," Luna replied.

"You'll know that answer day after tomorrow," Alex said.

"You're proposing to Marley on Christmas Eve?" Candice asked.

"That's the plan. I have a private dinner planned for us on the beach. I intend to ask Marley then."

"Congratulations. I have no doubt Marley will say yes," Candice replied.

"You won't be here, but if you look out your windows toward the beach at eight, I've got something special planned," Luna said.

"No other clues?" Angel asked.

"Nope, it's my special surprise." Luna grinned.

"Look," Julia said and pointed across the water.

A small group of whales was swimming south.

"Who's going first?" Julia asked.

"Same order as last time?" Luna asked.

"Sounds good." Lindy jumped up from her seat and reached for Angel's hand.

"I guess that's settled." Julia smiled. "Let's get you in the rigs."

†

All three groups had an extended flight over the whales until they swam farther out in the ocean. Nan piloted

216

them to the southern side of the island where they had a beautiful view of coconut groves, bananas, and some of the island's oldest buildings.

"I can't get over how beautiful this place is," Alex said.

Luna nodded. "The more we see, the more amazing it gets."

†

Nan got them back into the port in record time, and the group returned to the suite for lunch.

"I am starving," Alex said as she headed for the refrigerator. "Egg salad, here I come."

"I'll grab the bread and utensils if you bring the salads," Luna replied. "Chancy, will you pour us some drinks?"

"What can I do?" Lindy asked.

"Grab some chips and paper plates from the pantry," Luna directed. "We've got less than an hour before we have reservations."

"That will be plenty of time," Lindy said.

"Who wants what type of sandwiches?" Alex asked.

"I think I want one of each," Luna said.

"That sounds good," Chancy said. "I'm sure they will both be great."

"Sounds good to me too," Candice said.

Alex looked at Lindy and Angel. They nodded in agreement. "I've got the egg salad if you'll make the chicken salad," Alex said to Luna.

217

"I'm on it," Luna said and began making sandwiches.

Chancy poured drinks as Lindy and Angel set the table.

"That was so much fun," Luna said to Lindy. "Seeing the whales has been the highlight of the trip so far. I hate that Marley and the others missed them."

"If they are still in the area, we can book a whale-watching boat after Christmas when Dawn and Candice return," Lindy said.

"That would be fun," Alex said.

"Let's make it happen then," Lindy said.

"Yes, boss," Luna said with a wink.

†

Riding the jet skis was great fun, and when the group arrived at a small inlet, they decided to beach the crafts and snorkel for a while. As they geared up, Chancy started removing her shirt.

"Nuh-uh, remember your promise to Remy about keeping your shirt on so you don't get burnt," Alex reminded her.

"Dang, I was hoping you forgot that." Chancy grinned and pulled her shirt back down.

"Not on your life," Alex said.

The previous day's storm had churned up the surf, and shells and driftwood were left exposed on the shore. Lindy located a near-perfect conch shell and held it to her ear. "That sound never gets old." She grinned. "I remember the first time I heard it when I was about five, on the beach of Tybee Island," she told Angel. "It still makes me smile."

218

She placed the shell on the seat of her jet ski and slipped into her fins. "Let's get wet," she called out.

Luna looked at Alex. "We could take that so many ways," she teased.

"Come on, Romeo," Alex said as they walked awkwardly into the surf. "It was much easier to step off the boat."

Luna turned around and walked backward. "This is easier, but man, it feels odd."

"Or, you could wait to put your fins on after you reach the water," Lindy said and held up her pair.

"Where's the fun in that?" Alex grinned. She turned and dove into the surf.

They split into two groups and swam around the reefs near the shore. Chancy followed Lindy and Angel, scoping out the lobsters that darted between hiding spaces. When something shiny glimmered in the sand, she took a deep breath and dove to the bottom. The glimmer of silver caught her eye in the sunlight filtering through the rippling water. She reached for the object, realized she had missed her mark by several inches, and reached out again. With the object firmly in hand, Chancy swam to the surface for a breath. She opened her palm, hoping to see a timeless treasure, and laughed out loud when she found a silver half dollar coin resting in her palm.

Alex had surfaced and was watching Chancy. "Did you find a treasure?"

Chancy spit the mouthpiece out. "A silver half dollar." Chancy grinned.

"Well, that makes you fifty cents ahead of the rest of us." Luna smiled. "Let's keep looking."

They swam for another hour without finding other priceless objects. Luna's legs were beginning to burn from exertion, so she knew the others were probably beyond their peaks. "Are we ready to head back toward the marina?" she asked.

"If we don't, I'm not sure I can walk tomorrow," Angel said.

"The water does give you a nice workout," Candice said. "I'm ready, though, when y'all are."

When they reached the shore, Lindy picked up her shell and prepared to place it in the storage compartment. "Here, use this to cushion it a bit," Luna said and tossed Lindy her T-shirt.

"I brought a small towel too," Alex said and opened her storage to hand it to Lindy.

They observed her wrap the shell and store it away. "Go easy on the way back in," Luna said.

"I'll putter along while you guys ride some waves," Lindy replied.

"I'll stick with you," Candice said.

"Me too," Angel said.

"Let's head out then." Alex grinned at Luna, with Chancy hot on their trail.

"Those three are like little kids," Candice said. "They are having so much fun."

"Much deserved fun, too. Alex, Luna, and Chancy have worked hard to get where they are in life. I don't think any of them had an easy childhood. I'd wager this is the first real vacation they've ever experienced," Lindy said.

"I hope the first of many for them," Candice said. "You are all such a fun group."

"I'll second that. I don't think I've had this much fun in ages," Angel added.

"It has been fun. We'd better get started before Luna comes back hunting for us. I, for one, am ready for one of Chancy's drinks and to see what Emelia has planned for dinner," Lindy said.

"Definitely after a shower to get the salt and sand off," Angel said.

Lindy briefly considered offering to share a shower with Angel, then thought against it. "Let's go," she said instead. *Chicken shit. You passed on a perfect opportunity.*

CHAPTER EIGHTEEN

Angel had a fleeting thought that she should ask Lindy to join her for a cool drink and maybe activate her dare by inviting Lindy to shower with her. But, in the end, she had chickened out, deciding to save her dare for later in the evening. Perhaps she would dare Lindy to spend the night.

After their day of fun in the sun, Lindy's hair had that sexy tousled look, so opposite of her meticulous appearance at public events. It was too much for Angel, and she leaned in to kiss Lindy before opening her suite door. "I almost used up my dare just now."

Lindy quirked her eyebrow. "Oh, do tell."

"Will that be the truth question?" Angel joked.

"Nice try. No, I'm saving that for later. Asking you what dare you had in mind does not qualify as an important enough question to ask. If you were going to dare me to come in for a few minutes and have a cool drink with you, that's hardly noteworthy. I feel parched enough to invite myself inside."

Angel pulled her keycard from her bag and then tugged gently on Lindy, pulling her into the suite. "To be fair to my reputation as a master competitor, I was going to invite you into my shower as well."

"Slightly better." Lindy smiled.

Angel walked toward the mini-fridge, opening it to display Lindy's choices. "I'm afraid I don't have any wonderful cocktails to offer that would even remotely compare to Chancy's, but I do have cold water, coke, and juice."

"Water is perfect. I could fess up and let you off the hook by telling you the thought of showering with you briefly crossed my mind." Lindy winked.

"I believe you just did. Confess, that is. So, what are we to do with that bold assertion?" Angel handed Lindy the bottle of water.

"Unfortunately, we did not plan this well. I don't have any clothes to change into," Lindy answered before settling onto the loveseat in Angel's suite.

"You can borrow some of mine." Angel slowly surveyed Lindy's body, taking in every delectable curve. They were about the same size, but Lindy was clearly more fit than Angel. "We're approximately the same size."

Lindy laughed. "And give the meddlers something to tease us about? Probably not a good idea. I'm sure we'll have to contend with plenty of ribbing without adding gasoline to that fire."

Angel joined Lindy on the loveseat and mock pouted. "Well, all right, then, I suppose I'll have to stick with Plan B, which I believe is much better than Plan A, anyway."

"Intriguing. When do I get to learn about the Plan B dare?"

"Tonight, after dinner. I hope you'll join me for another walk on the beach. I have to squish in all the walks I can because when I return to Atlanta, work impedes pleasure."

"That's too bad. I had hoped we could entice you to join us for some debauchery when we return. Perhaps you'll want to take a tour of my club, among other more pleasurable adventures that I could suggest."

"Oh, I definitely want to see this famed club of yours, and I would love to join y'all in your future adventures, time permitting. Unfortunately, one of my greatest flaws is my tendency to have a laser focus on one thing. That one thing has typically been building my business, leaving little to no room for much else. Honestly, I took this trip to find more balance in my life. I've destroyed many a relationship because of that singular focus," Angel explained.

"I don't need to ask my truth question. I think you already answered it." Uncapping her water, Lindy took a healthy swig, emptying a good portion of the bottle.

Angel tilted her head to the side and crinkled her nose. "Just for grins, what was the question?"

"Why are you still single?"

"Ah, but that is a more complicated question that deserves a greater answer than, *I'm a workaholic.* I'll give you the full novel version tonight after I present my dare to you." Angel turned to Lindy. "My offer was sincere about loaning you clothes."

"Rain check? It isn't just my clothes. It's everything else that contributes to the final look." Lindy waved her hand over her body. "All my make-up, hair products, jewelry, and such are also in my suite."

Angel turned to Lindy and smiled. "I totally understand. I'm quite particular about all of that as well. I have over-the-top brand loyalty. I suppose I'm set in my ways, and it takes an act of Congress to get me to try a new product. Are you sure you wish to continue to spend time with me? I keep confessing to all my sins. It's a wonder you aren't running far and fast away from me."

Lindy took Angel's hand. "Definitely not. You are far too intriguing for me to do that. I promise, I'm not running, but I need to get back to my suite and get ready for dinner." Lindy stood and made her way to the door. "I'll see you later."

"Yes, you definitely will."

†

Lindy had just put the finishing touches on her make-up before answering the door. Lindy had long since not cared about anyone knowing how smitten she was with Angel. Although it didn't sound like there were many people milling about in the communal areas of the suite to see Angel coming to her door. Angel's smile was radiant as Lindy opened the door to her spacious suite. It was larger than Angel's, with plenty of room for another person. If Lindy were braver, she'd invite Angel to stay with her in her suite. Angel had dressed in flowing pants, a sleeveless shell, and a tailored jacket. The outfit was probably custom-fit for Angel. At least it looked like a design intended to highlight Angel's assets perfectly. Lindy's eyes were drawn to Angel's ample cleavage, which was just visible enough to tease, but not so much that most would consider tawdry. Stunning was the one word Lindy would use to describe Angel.

With an expansive gesture, Lindy invited Angel into her suite. "Please come inside. I'm almost ready. I just need to grab my bag, and then we can join the gang for dinner. Thanks for coming to collect me. How chivalrous of you. You look sensational, by the way." Lindy quickly returned to her bedroom to collect her bag.

"I could and will say the same of you. Exquisite isn't even a strong enough adjective to describe how good you look." Angel offered her arm. "Shall we?"

†

Everyone except Marley and Luna had already settled into their usual spots, waiting on the magic of Chancy and Emelia. Not even a minute later, Marley and Luna hurried into the communal area.

"Sorry we're late. Uh, we took a brief nap."

Chancy giggled. "Yeah, right. Nap. Is that what they're calling it now?"

Alex crossed her long legs in front and asked, "Does anyone know what's on the menu tonight? It smells divine."

"It's conch night. I think we're having conch fritters, conch ceviche, chowder, and some other conch dishes. Emelia wanted us to experience the different ways the locals prepare this delicacy. I went on an internet search to find the perfect drink to pair well with dinner. Of course, every site suggested rum as a base. So, I made my own version of a rum cocktail. It was hard because I've never had conch before." Chancy continued to vigorously shake the contents inside her stainless steel shaker. A row of frosted glasses lined with a colorful sugar rim sat on the counter, waiting for Chancy to fill them.

"Neither have I," Marley admitted.

"Well, it wasn't exactly a staple in Texas." Alex wrinkled her nose. "Isn't it like octopus—you know, all rubbery? I'm not sure I'll like it. Danna got me to try escargot one night. I can't say I loved it, but it wasn't as bad as I thought it would be. I suppose anything soaking in garlic butter can taste good."

Adding a dried orange slice and a cherry, Chancy handed the first drink to Alex. "Here, drink up. After a few of these, you'll be fine. And, I don't think anyone will waste their dare on something as inane as making you try the conch. This isn't Burger King, you know," Chancy teased. "You don't get to have dinner your way. Stretch your horizons. Don't judge before tasting."

Alex stuck her tongue out at Chancy. "My horizons are fine."

"I haven't had conch in years. It's delicious. I doubt there will be anything left after this ravenous crowd is done. I trust Emelia will prepare the conch in so many different ways that everyone should find a dish to their liking," Remy said.

Chancy continued to make the rum punch while Emelia performed the finishing touches on their conch extravaganza.

Wiping her hands on her apron, Emelia walked into the main area and announced, "Dinner is ready. I thought we could try buffet style again. I think I went a little crazy with the number of different dishes I prepared, and it will be easier for everyone to serve themselves. I labeled each dish so that you have a basic understanding of the different ways to prepare conch. Some you may enjoy more than others, but hopefully, you'll find at least one that you like. If not, I can prepare something else for you."

Remy shook her head. "I don't believe it will be necessary. Like sushi, many people turn their nose up until they've tried it. I have not yet failed in my ability to convert someone to diehard sushi lover."

Lindy noticed how Alex added tiny portions to her plate, while the rest were more generous with their helpings.

"What a wussy," Chancy taunted while pointing to Alex's plate.

"Mind your own damn business," Alex retorted. "I'm going to try everything, but in case there is one dish I don't care for, there is no sense in loading up my plate and wasting food. In my family, it was sacrilegious to leave food on your plate." She pointed to Chancy's heaping plate. "You better eat every morsel, you heathen."

Alex plucked the fritter off her plate and popped it into her mouth. "Mmm, okay, that's good. Maybe this conch won't be horrible after all."

"For someone who is so adventurous in bed, I'm a bit surprised by your hesitancy to try different foods," Danna whispered.

Alex shrugged. "Apples and oranges."

"So, I know I didn't participate in the challenge yesterday, but can we please know what dares Lindy and Angel assigned to Luna and Alex? If you need suggestions, I'm your girl." Chancy shot Alex a wide grin.

"Oh, no, you don't. Do not take suggestions from the little imp. Chancy's evil incarnate," Alex declared.

"Shush. Don't be a sore loser." Chancy handed Angel and Lindy their drinks. "Please, please make them do the chicken dance on the beach. I even downloaded the song on my phone. They should have to sing to it, too."

Pantomiming using a magic wand, Angel announced, "Done. Or, 'make it so,' as Jean Luc Picard would say."

Luna sat forward. "Are you serious? We have to do the chicken dance tomorrow?"

Angel laughed. "Sure, why not? It's a brilliant suggestion."

Chancy grinned again. "You could force them to ask complete strangers for condoms so they can make balloon animals. Who doesn't love balloon animals?" Chancy held her stomach as she doubled over with laughter.

"Do you want me to bury your ass in the sand?" Alex asked. "No more suggestions, please. They need to think of their own dares."

"Do we even know what we're doing tomorrow?" Marley asked.

"After today, I could use some rest and relaxation. Sipping cocktails on the beach sounds good to me," Lindy answered.

"I'm down for that, especially if we can watch Alex and Luna dance. I would not want to miss that. We can go on a whale-watching tour another day, right?" Chancy asked hopefully.

"Of course. Does anyone want to do something else besides hang on the beach tomorrow?" Remy asked.

Everyone shook their heads or responded that they were okay with relaxing on the beach.

"We can always get a beach volleyball game going if we want a little activity. Or a swim in the ocean sounds good as well. After the dares are complete. We should do the dance early in the morning. Fewer people." Luna glanced at Alex, who nodded her agreement.

"Oh, no, you don't get to decide the time," Chancy noted. "Wait until you hear what Remy has planned for you. Maybe you can do that after the Chicken Dance."

"Do I have to hogtie you and slap some duct tape over your mouth? Enough from the peanut gallery," Alex growled. Forking the small bite of conch ceviche, Alex slipped the morsel into her mouth. "Ooh, fuck me if this isn't the best ceviche I've ever tasted. So good. Okay, I am officially a conch lover."

The group laughed, and each woman continued to devour their meal. By the end of the evening, there was barely anything left.

†

Angel had vowed to enjoy her time in St. Kitts, letting go of all the pressures she placed on herself at work every day. But she hadn't prepared herself to meet a woman so utterly perfect for her. Continuing this holiday affair went against every moral principle Angel lived by. She would never knowingly enter into a relationship with a married woman. Lindy was special, though. She was the type of woman Angel could see herself growing old with. If only Lindy was free to consider something more serious with Angel.

It was now or never. When Angel and Lindy reached Lindy's door, Angel blurted, "I'd like to spend the night with you. That's my dare. Either invite me inside or come back with me to my suite."

"I thought you'd never ask."

Lindy opened her door, and Angel followed her inside. Lindy had barely shut the door when Angel had her pinned against the door, kissing her as if they only had minutes until the world ended. There was an intensity to the kiss that surprised Angel. She'd never been this spontaneous or fervent before. Yet, it felt like any minute, this would all slip away, and she'd miss her opportunity.

Leading Angel to the bedroom, Lindy kicked off her shoes before turning to Angel. Angel was already pulling off her jacket and setting it aside, leaving her silky smooth arms bare. Goosebumps appeared as Lindy ran a single finger down Angel's arm before pushing Angel's shell up and over her head. Lindy's finger returned to Angel's body, but this time Lindy drew small patterns over Angel's collarbone, dipping into the crevice between her breasts. Angel reached behind to unclasp her bra and release her ample breasts with an almost practiced move.

"Gorgeous," Lindy said with reverence.

"I believe you have some catching up to do. This feels a bit lopsided. I'm half-naked already."

Lindy chuckled and made a move to remove her linen tunic. Pleased by the desire she saw in Angel's eyes, Lindy quickly stripped down to her matching black lacy underwear. "Better?"

"Almost." Angel removed her flowing pants and then shimmied out of her lavender panties. "That set is very sexy, but I think I would prefer you naked."

"Are you sure about this?" Lindy asked.

"Yes. I've wanted you since the moment I saw you at Women Strong. I can't think of anything better than making love with you all night long. With tomorrow as a beach day, we'll have ample time to catch up on our sleep."

Lindy pushed down the covers, and both women crawled beneath the cool Egyptian cotton sheets. The exploration of each other's bodies started slowly, gathering speed and intensity as each stroke brought the other closer to orgasm. Although Angel definitely knew her way around a woman's body, this was different. It was like Angel and Lindy were perfectly in sync. Two seconds before Angel felt her own orgasm race through her body, she felt Lindy's walls contract against her fingers. Rarely had Angel had a simultaneous orgasm with a lover. That generally took years for her to learn her partner's wants and needs. But, with Lindy, it was so easy. They seemed to connect organically, anticipating exactly the correct pressure on the perfect spot. While there were definitely mysteries to unlock, apparently, bringing Lindy to an earth-shattering orgasm was not one of them.

Lindy sighed. "You are incredible. I'm not going to want to leave this island. Can we stay in this little bubble?"

Angel chuckled. "I wish. I don't want to think about reality just yet. We still have plenty of time to thoroughly enjoy one another."

"Maybe you should check out of your suite and move to mine for the rest of the vacation?" Lindy suggested.

"Are you serious?"

"I am. I'd love to have you in my bed every night. Unfortunately, it seems like we've already wasted two nights. I'd rather not fritter away the remainder of the time we have together in this paradise."

"I'd love to," Angel answered. "But I insist on paying half."

"Well, half of zero is nothing. Remember, Remy owns this resort," Lindy reminded.

"I guess I will have to think of some way to thank Remy. But right now, I believe there may be a spot or two I missed when earlier worshipping your body. We can't have that, now can we?"

"Certainly not."

†

Chancy skipped along the beach and set down the Bose speaker Remy had found to use for Alex and Luna's dare. Syncing her phone with the speaker, The Chicken Dance blared from the surprisingly powerful speaker.

The spattering of beachgoers turned their attention to the music, and a cacophony of laughter filled the air as Luna and Alex flapped their elbows, mimicking a chicken. Chancy fell on the sand and rolled around, holding her stomach and laughing loudly. "That is by far the funniest thing I've ever seen. Come on, you stud muffins, more flapping."

"Shut it, pipsqueak," Alex yelled.

"More hip action. You two are way too stiff. Just think, strap on. I know y'all have the moves," Chancy taunted.

With Chancy's heckling, more people had gathered to watch the spectacle on the beach. A few joined in the dance, and before too long, there was a line of people doing the chicken dance with Luna and Alex.

Once the music stopped, a young man approached Alex and Luna. "Is this the afternoon entertainment? Will you lead another dance? How about the Macarena?"

"Sorry, little dude, we aren't part of the entertainment crew. We lost a challenge the other day, and this is our punishment. We have very evil friends," Alex explained. "But we could use you on our team when we challenge those losers to a game of beach volleyball."

"Nuh uh. You two do not get to be on the same team. This isn't the Amazons versus the pygmies," Chancy argued. "Luna is on one team, and Alex has to be on the other team."

"Fine, but you're joining Luna's team, and when my team kicks your ass, I'm making you do a dare."

Luna laughed. "Marley's with us."

"Angel, want to join the winning team?" Alex asked.

"Sure. Let's recruit Lindy, too. I have a feeling she's a competitor."

"I better get my wife to join our team as well. Babe, you up for some beach volleyball?" Alex asked.

Danna crossed her arms over her chest. "Just like in high school. I'm the last one picked. I suppose I don't blame you. Before TWC, sweat was not in my repertoire. But I'll have you know I was actually on the women's volleyball team in high school."

Alex pumped her fist in the air. "Score. We have a ringer on our team."

Chancy squatted next to Remy. "You up for a game?"

"Maybe just one," Remy answered. "I didn't play in high school, but I believe I can hold my own. I might have gone through a phase in college. Beach volleyball is far different from high school volleyball. We'll wipe their butts all over this sand."

"That's my girl," Chancy crowed.

"I guess that means I'm joining Alex's team," Lindy said.

"Okay, we need to recruit at least one more person for Luna's team since our new friend here wants to play." Alex pointed to the young man who had approached Alex.

The young man started running toward his family and called over his shoulder, "I'll get my little brother to join us."

†

After an hour of back-and-forth play, Alex's team finally managed to eke out a win with a decisive spike from Alex, who had taken advantage of the perfect pass Danna made to Angel, who set the ball high enough for Alex to put her whole body into the kill shot.

"Yes! We won. Smoked your asses," Alex cheered.

"I'd hardly call two points a landslide win. Just for the record, I never agreed to a dare if we lost," Chancy interjected. "But, since I am such a good sport, I'll do one. You better make it good because you aren't likely to get a second chance."

"I'm going to have to ponder this." Alex scratched her chin.

Danna grabbed Alex and pulled her to an empty lounge chair. "Okay, you two. Enough goading each other. Can we relax for the rest of the afternoon, minus the competitions?"

"Is it noon yet?" Angel asked.

"Close enough," Lindy answered.

"Wonderful. I think we deserve some cocktails after our riveting volleyball tournament. Shall I go to the bar and ask for a pitcher of Pina Coladas?" Angel asked.

"Probably a good idea to order drinks. You might need a drink or two once you hear Remy's dare." Chancy cackled. "The Chicken Dance was merely a warm-up."

Alex and Luna groaned in unison.

"I think the server is heading our way. We can order from him," Remy said.

"Sounds like a plan. We should also order some water. After all the exercise, we need to hydrate. Heat exhaustion is no fun," Lindy warned.

"No, it's not," Luna agreed.

CHAPTER NINETEEN

Alex noted Luna was as nervous as a cat on a hot tin roof as the afternoon wore on. The volleyball match was a great idea and helped settle Luna by keeping her occupied. Once the games were over, they ordered pitchers of Pina Coladas and bottles of water. Luna downed the water almost immediately and reached for a cocktail. Luna wasn't much of a drinker, so it surprised Alex by how big a drink Luna had taken.

"Let's go cool off in the surf for a few minutes," Alex suggested to Luna.

Luna nodded. "Are you coming, squirt?" Luna teased Chancy.

"That depends," Chancy answered. "Are you going to drown me for making y'all do the chicken dance?"

Luna looked at Alex. "I hadn't considered that, but it isn't a bad idea."

"Bring her back before it's too late for mouth to mouth," Remy said to join in on the teasing. "I'll gladly volunteer."

Chancy raised her hand to her forehead. "I believe I'm feeling faint already."

"You don't get off that easy," Alex said and grabbed Chancy's hand.

Luna took Chancy's other hand. "Should we swing her between us like our lovechild?"

Alex broke out laughing. "Our lovechild? I like that, but no. Our child would be bigger and darker," Alex replied.

"Yeah, you're probably right." Luna winked.

"You feeling okay? You've been jittery all afternoon," Alex asked as they waded into the water.

"My nerves are on edge. I believe Marley will say yes, but until I hear it from her mouth, I can't relax," Luna said.

"Marley can't tell you no," Chancy said. "She loves every adorable ounce of you."

"What's not to love?" Luna joked. "This will be the most important night of my life, and I don't want to screw it up."

†

"They sure seem to be having a serious conversation out there," Remy said as she lowered her sunglasses.

"Alex and Luna are probably contemplating the next challenge or payback for the chicken dance scandal,"

Marley said. "I have to admit, it was hilarious to see those two dancing."

Danna nodded with a chuckle. "I need to send you all a copy of that video. I'm afraid it will disappear from mine once Alex realizes I have video evidence."

"That's a smart move," Lindy said. "Are you excited about your special date tonight?"

"I can't wait to go on the sunset and dinner cruise," Marley replied.

"Oh, we should have thought about that," Angel replied.

"You could probably still make reservations," Marley said.

"No, not tonight. You two deserve a romantic night apart from the rest of us," Lindy said. "We'll all have opportunities to spend private time apart from the group. Tonight is your night." She turned to smile at Angel. "We'll take the dinner cruise after Christmas, or we can go dolphin watching instead.

"Do you still think the whales are in the area?" Remy asked. "Chancy was so excited to tell me about them."

"No clue, but I bet Emelia can probably find out for us," Marley said. "She seems to know everyone on the island."

"That's probably not much of an exaggeration," Remy said. "Between her and Marcus, there are probably not many folks they don't know on this side of the island."

"Did y'all see the glass-bottomed kayaks for rent at the marina?" Danna asked.

"No, but that sounds like fun, too. Single or doubles?" Marley asked.

"Both," Danna said.

"Chancy has mentioned visiting the coconut and banana plantations to make some purchases for fresh drinks," Remy said. "I didn't have the heart to tell her she could buy all she wanted at the open-air market."

"A banana daiquiri sounds delicious," Marley said.

"Yes, it does. Maybe we should make that our next round of drinks," Lindy suggested.

"I'm game," Angel replied.

†

"What did you tell Marley to get her out of the suite?" Chancy asked.

"I told her we were taking a sunset and dinner cruise," Luna said. "The sunset part is true. I plan to take her on a walk to the marina to watch the sunset, but we have a private dinner set up for us on the beach that she doesn't know about."

"I'm excited for y'all," Alex said. "I know you two are inseparable now, but making it official takes it to a whole new level. Never in my wildest dreams did I think I would find such a love as I have with Danna."

"I know. It's an incredible feeling," Luna replied.

Chancy scowled, shielding her eyes from the sun. "I hope Remy and I get there one day."

"You will. Remy has had so many drastic changes in her life over the last few months. She probably just needs time for her heart to catch up," Luna said and ruffled Chancy's spiked hair.

"Hey, watch the do. It took me twenty minutes to look this good," Chancy exclaimed.

"Really?" Luna replied and grinned at Alex. "Let's see what we can do about that."

They both grabbed an arm and a leg and tossed Chancy five feet ahead of them as she squealed with laughter.

†

"I was wondering how long that would take," Marley said as they looked toward the sound of Chancy laughing.

Remy smiled. "I can't think of two better idols for Chancy to have than those two. They do treat her like a baby sister."

Marley crossed her arms and deepened her voice. "I pity the fool that tried to mess with Chancy. They would have hell to pay from her two Amazon friends."

"There's no doubt about that," Danna said.

†

Alex, Luna, and Chancy returned to their chairs and were toweling themselves dry when the next round of drinks arrived. Marley quickly grabbed a banana daiquiri and took a long sip, causing brain freeze. "Oh, damn," she cried out, scrunching up her face. "I forgot how lousy brain freeze hurts. The taste makes it worth the pain, though." She looked at Chancy. "You need to make some of these after we go on an adventure for fresh bananas and coconuts."

Chancy's face lit with excitement. "I'll make you the best daiquiri you've had in your life."

"You are so on." Marley returned her smile.

After finishing the drinks, Luna looked at her watch. "We'd better head inside and get ready for our night out," she told Marley.

"Will you stay for one drink before you head out?" Chancy asked.

"Time permitting. It depends on how long it takes us to get dolled up." Luna chuckled.

"I'm betting you both will be incredibly handsome." Lindy smiled. "Go ahead on up. We'll head up that way and have one of Chancy's potions while we wait for y'all. We can shower for dinner after you leave."

"We'll see you all soon then," Luna said and reached for Marley's hand.

Alex looked at Lindy. "Luna's about to jump out of her skin with nerves, afraid Marley will say no."

Lindy shook her head. "That will never happen. Nope. No way, no how."

"You have to remember how nervous you were when you approached me," Danna reminded Alex. "For a moment, I thought you would turn green on me."

"It's a big commitment," Remy said. "Not one to be taken lightly."

Alex glanced at Chancy and would later swear her pale skin turned whiter after hearing Remy's comment.

†

Luna had a towel wrapped around her waist when she heard the front door to the suite open, and the room filled with laughter as the group walked to the patio. "The posse has arrived," she informed Marley, who was brushing her teeth.

Marley rinsed her mouth. "This has been such a wonderful trip. I can't imagine how it could be any better."

I hope you change that opinion in a couple of hours, Luna thought. "It's been a load of fun so far, and we still have another week. I believe you made Chancy's trip by asking her to make you banana daiquiris. Did you see her face light up when you asked?"

"Yes, I did, but I am sincere. That young woman makes some delicious drinks." Marley spun around and kissed Luna. "We better get a move on if we're going to share one with them before we leave."

"It won't take me long." Luna grinned. "Especially if you stop hogging the sink."

"I'm out," Marley said and slipped her robe off as she walked into the bedroom.

"Damn. That body makes me wanna skip the cruise and have you for dinner, drinks, and dessert," Luna said as she prepped her toothbrush.

"You can have seconds on dessert later," Marley promised as she began dressing.

†

"Oh, my Lord," Angel said as she was the first to see Luna and Marley arrive. "Would you look at the two goddesses who just fell from the heavens?"

"Damn, my friend. You clean up nice," Alex teased Luna. "Marley, you are even more beautiful than ever."

Marley spun around so Alex could have the full view.

"You both look fantastic," Lindy said. "I love those outfits on you. We may have to have more open social nights at the club if you're going to look this good. The hormone levels will skyrocket," Lindy teased.

"I know mine just did," Angel replied with a smile to Lindy.

"See, it's paying off for me already." Lindy giggled.

Chancy brought two small drink glasses. "We thought we'd go small since y'all are probably in a rush to leave."

Marley took a sip. "Mmm, coconut rum and soda?"

"Light, but sweet," Chancy said. "A lot like me."

"That is tasty," Luna replied.

"A lot like you, too." Remy laughed with a wink at Chancy.

"Two questions," Lindy said. "What time will you bring her home, and do you both have your good underwear on?"

"You'll see us when you see us, and that's not your business, mama," Luna teased. "You know she's in good hands with me."

"Oh, I know that. I just wonder who's going to beat the women off of the two of you?" Lindy asked.

"I think we'll survive," Marley answered.

"I don't know. I think a cruise ship has arrived, so there's probably a ton of horny women on board," Alex informed them.

"We'll do our best to dodge the tourists," Luna replied. She looked at Marley with complete adoration. "Are you ready?"

"Yes, my handsome protector," Marley answered.

"We'll see you all later." Luna smiled. "Much later."

"Have fun, you two," Lindy called out.

†

Luna placed Marley's hand on her elbow as they left the resort and started toward the marina just as the sun was beginning to sink toward the horizon. When they reached the marina, Marley frowned when she saw the slip for the sunset cruise boat empty.

"Oh, no," she said as she pointed at the ship in the distance. "We're too late. I'm sorry, I didn't realize we had taken so long."

Luna felt bad that Marley thought she was the cause of making them miss the boat. "We're not late. I have a confession to make."

"We're not going on the sunset cruise and dinner boat?" Marley asked, confused.

"We are, but not for a few days until Dawn and Candice return, so technically, we're several days early. I used the cruise to get you all to myself tonight," Luna said.

"Aw, all you had to do was ask, sweetie," Marley said.

"I know, but this was much more fun. We will have a nice dinner in a little while, but I wanted us to enjoy the sunset first." She took Marley's hand and led her down the pier to watch the beautiful sunset.

†

"Okay, ladies. Time to spring into action. We need to dress, have eaten, and be back out here by eight," Lindy said. "Emelia said dinner in thirty minutes, so don't get sidetracked." Lindy looked specifically at Chancy. "Especially you," she teased.

"Aww, that hurts." Chancy grabbed at her chest. "I'll be quick."

"Let's go then," Alex said. "I've still got to get the camera set up on the tripod."

"Do you want to do that while I get a head start?" Danna asked.

"That's probably a great idea." Alex kissed Danna and returned inside to get the camera and tripod.

†

"That was an incredible sunset," Marley said as she leaned against Luna's chest.

"Yes, it was, and even the glare of lights from that big cruise ship doesn't interfere with the twinkling of lights on the island," Luna said as she pointed across the marina. "Are you getting hungry?"

"I'm getting there," Marley replied.

"Let's go then," Luna said and took Marley's hand. "I've got reservations for us in fifteen minutes."

They walked down steps at the end of the pier to a boardwalk leading down to the beach. Marley looked up at Luna. "There's no restaurant on the beach."

"There is tonight. Just for the two of us," Luna replied as she pointed to a table surrounded by tiki torches.

"Are you kidding me?" Marley asked in shock.

"No, ma'am, this is for us." Luna led Marley to the table, and the server held the seat for her.

"Good evening, ladies. I am Merita, and I will be your server tonight. Would you like me to pour the wine?"

"Thanks, Merita. I am Luna, and this lovely lady is Marley."

"It is my pleasure to serve you both tonight," Merita said as she poured glasses of wine. "Should I bring out the salads and fresh bread for you now?"

Marley nodded. "Yes, please. We worked up a bit of an appetite today."

Luna nodded.

"That is no problem. I will guarantee you won't leave this table hungry tonight," Merita replied. "I shall return shortly."

"Luna, what can I say? Tonight, has to be the most beautiful, romantic thing that's ever happened to me," Marley replied.

Luna saw the tears shining in Marley's eyes. "We deserve something special, particularly while we're on vacation," Luna replied.

"Wow, this is just, wow," Marley stammered.

"Let's enjoy this beautiful night together," Luna said.

Marley took a sip of her wine. "Look at that. Even the moon is smiling down on us tonight."

"I can't take credit for that, so we'll have to thank Mother Nature," Luna replied. "Thank you for a beautiful night. Cheers."

Merita delivered two salads and a large basket of sliced bread. "Would you care for butter?" she asked.

"Yes, please," Marley replied. "These salads are huge."

"Don't fill up on it. You won't want to miss the main course. Or dessert," Luna teased.

They both ate a portion of the salads. "Would you like me to pack these to go?"

"Yes, please, Merita," Luna answered.

Merita cleared the salads and carried out two large stainless steel-covered platters. "Enjoy, and I will check on you in a few minutes. Would you like something different to drink with your meal? We have sweet tea, just as you asked."

"Yes, please," Marley said, and Luna nodded in agreement.

Marley's eyes grew wide as Merita removed the cover from her platter. A filet mignon, still sizzling was surrounded by a lobster tail and fresh steamed vegetables. A dish of drawn butter sat on the side of her plate. "Oh, my word. That's almost too beautiful to eat," she proclaimed.

"You can gawk all you'd like, but I can't wait to try this. It all looks and smells divine," Luna said.

"I'll be right back with your drinks," Merita said.

Marley took a bite of lobster she had dredged through the butter. "Don't tell Emelia, but this is almost as good as hers."

Merita walked up with their drinks. "It is hers. Emelia cooked this wonderful meal for you," she told Marley.

"No wonder it's so good. Thank you, Merita."

"Is there anything else you need at this moment?"

"I think we're good for a few minutes, Merita," Luna replied.

Merita nodded and disappeared from view.

†

"These shrimp are fantastic, Emelia," Lindy praised.

"I am so happy you are enjoying them. The shrimp came fresh off the boat this morning," Emelia said.

"I love this place, but I swear I'd gain fifty pounds if I lived here," Alex said, then popped another shrimp in her mouth.

"Not as hard as you work," Danna said. "You eat so healthy and never gain an ounce unless it's more muscle."

"Me too," Chancy said and flexed her smaller arms.

"There is absolutely nothing wrong with your body. I love every inch of it," Remy said.

Chancy nearly bounced from her seat, laughing so hard. "I am so glad you do because try as I might, I will never look like the Amazons."

"It doesn't have to be an Amazon to be a beautiful body," Lindy replied. "Even if they are nice to look at."

"I don't mean to rush anyone, but it's getting close to eight. Do you want to wait on coffee and key lime pie?"

"I think so," Lindy replied.

"I'll help with the last of these shrimp, so you don't have leftovers," Alex said.

"That is so very kind of you, Alex." Emelia chuckled. "We have a surprise for you tomorrow."

"Yes, we do. Remy and I have decided to cook breakfast and our Christmas dinner," Lindy said. "Emelia has promised to bring a traditional dessert that we can share with her and Marcus as we watch the Carnival Events from the balcony tomorrow afternoon."

"Carnival?" Chancy asked.

"Parades, music, and dancing to celebrate our African and island heritage. We are the only island in the Caribbean that celebrates a traditional Christmas," Emelia explained.

"That will be so neat. So, what are you cooking for breakfast?" Chancy waggled her eyebrows at Remy.

Remy smiled. "We're going light, with French toast and bacon. We don't want anyone to miss out on the feast."

"I hope I can help," Angel said. "I can be handy in the kitchen."

"Your assistance would be greatly appreciated, but the rest of you," Lindy shook her fork, "the kitchen is strictly off-limits for y'all."

"You're going to make us sit on the couch and watch Christmas movies and melt, smelling the feast you have planned?" Alex inquired.

"That's about it." Lindy grinned.

"It's time, ladies," Emelia said and walked out to the patio with them.

"I better start the camera," Alex said.

†

Luna and Marley had finished most of the meal but saved room for the key lime pie and coffee. "I am so stuffed." Marley groaned.

"You have just a bit more wine to finish," Merita said as she refilled their glasses and cleared the plates. "It has

250

been a joy serving you tonight. Stay as long as you wish, and I hope you've had a lovely experience."

"It was fantastic, Merita," Luna said. "Thank you for everything."

Merita winked at Luna and carried the dishes and empty wine bottle from the table.

"This has been the best night," Marley said.

"There is something I'd love to share with you before we waddle back up to the suite."

"No more food, I hope." Marley groaned.

"No, ma'am. No more food," Luna replied as she stood and removed a box from her pants, and bent down on one knee. She looked into Marley's wet eyes. "Will you do me the honor of becoming my wife?" Luna opened the box to show Marley the ring.

"It's so beautiful," Marley said. She watched Luna remove the ring with trembling fingers. "Yes," she said. "I would love to spend the rest of my life with you."

Luna smiled with relief and slipped the ring on her finger. "There is just one more thing I have to do."

"What's that?" Marley asked.

"This," she said and returned to her feet. She walked over to one of the tiki torches and pulled it from the ground. She walked a few steps into the darkness and lit a small fuse. She turned back to watch the look on Marley's face as the fuse traveled quickly and lit up the words 'She said yes,' in the night.

Cheer's erupted from their patio and several other balconies as other people were sitting outside enjoying the beautiful night.

Marley clapped. "That is so amazing."

Luna sat down at the table and picked up her wineglass. "Thank you for saying yes."

"I would love to be your wife," Marley answered and touched her glass to Luna's.

When they finished their wine and stood to leave, Merita approached. "Congratulations," she said

"Thank you," Marley said.

"Thank you for making it the perfect evening." Luna held out a fifty-dollar bill for a tip.

"Oh, no." Merita waved her off. "My gift to you. Spend it on your beautiful bride-to-be."

Luna pulled the woman into a hug. "Thank you so much."

"My pleasure. Now go have some fun and celebrate for real," Merita said.

Luna reached for Marley's hand. "Let's go. We got some explaining to do." She grinned.

†

Chancy began pouring drinks to celebrate the proposal. Dessert and coffee became a distant memory. The group partied until midnight. "Merry Christmas, everyone," Lindy said and took Angel by the hand. "We have food to prepare in the morning. Breakfast at nine?"

"That sounds great. I'll see you earlier," Remy said.

"I will see you all around two," Emelia replied. "Congratulations again, Luna and Marley. That was beautiful. Goodnight, my friends," she said.

"Goodnight, Emelia," they answered in chorus.

"I guess we all should head off to bed," Luna said. "We have a fun day planned tomorrow, from what I hear." She took Marley's hand, and they all returned inside.

Alex slapped Luna on the back as she walked by. "That was epic, my friend. I'm proud for you and of you."

"Thanks, Alex. We'll see you in the morning." She turned around, scooped Marley into her arms, and carried her into the room.

"Isn't that a bit premature?" Marley laughed.

"What? I can't practice?" Luna said and kicked the door gently closed as she kissed her fiancée.

CHAPTER TWENTY

"Whoa." Chancy grabbed the edge of the door jamb after swaying slightly. "One too many banana daiquiris."

Remy snickered. "I don't believe sprites can handle as much as Amazons."

Chancy quickly changed into her comfortable sleep shorts and T-shirt, haphazardly tossing her other clothes on the chair. "But they were so damn good. I think I like rum more and more every day. I'm so happy for Marley and Luna. They're perfect together."

Remy began undressing, carefully hanging her clothes in the closet while Chancy sprawled her body across the bed, watching. "Hmm, yes, they are."

"Can I ask you something? I'll probably regret asking, but I have to know. At least the daiquiris have given me liquid courage."

Remy pulled a nightshirt over her head and sat on the bed next to Chancy, taking her hand and stroking the palm lightly. "Oh, Chancy, you know you can ask anything. You should never be afraid to broach any topic."

Chancy sucked in a big breath and began, "Would you ever consider getting married again?"

Remy furrowed her brow. "I don't know. I was so young when I married Felix. Making a lifelong commitment should never be done cavalierly. I won't make that same mistake again."

Chancy fluffed the pillow on the bed and leaned against the headboard. She wasn't sure about Remy's answer. It certainly wasn't a rousing indictment of the joys of marriage. Chancy's vision of a wife and maybe even a child dissipated more quickly than a winter fog in Atlanta.

"Oh, I guess that means you don't want to get married again." Chancy tried to keep the disappointment from her voice, but it oozed its way into the room, all gooey and dark like thick black tar. It would have been impossible for Remy not to notice.

Remy gently lifted Chancy's face to hers. "Hey, I love you. A piece of paper won't change that."

"I suppose you're right. Although, that little piece of paper signifies something important. Sometimes little pieces of paper can be the ultimate representations of love. At least I hope so because otherwise your Christmas present will be a total bust." Chancy began to pluck on the threads of her worn-out T-shirt.

Remy laid her hand on top of Chancy's to settle her fidgeting. "You're around happily married couples like Alex and Danna or Candice and Dawn. Now you see Marley and Luna getting engaged. I can understand why this topic rose to the surface. But Chancy, you're so young. You have plenty of time to find the perfect woman. Maybe it's me, but perhaps it's someone else. Regardless, marriage doesn't always equate to happiness. I should know. Lindy knows that as well. Frankly, I'm not sure why she stays with Jaydub. Did you say Christmas present?" Remy grinned.

"Yes. I couldn't very well bring her to the island with me, so a picture will have to do."

"Her?" Remy lifted her eyebrow.

"Yes, and you'll have to wait until tomorrow morning to find out. Can we exchange gifts before you make breakfast?" Chancy pushed the marriage topic to the back and replaced it with a vision of Remy opening her gift and squealing with delight. At least Chancy hoped the new mare would delight Remy.

"Sure. I'm not too embarrassed to admit that I'm a little excited about Christmas. Your gift sounds intriguing. I haven't been energized for Christmas in many years. But, now I'm afraid that your gift will be this wonderful romantic gesture, and all I could think up was something practical. We should get some sleep. The morning will come quickly." Remy leaned into Chancy and offered her a sweet kiss before walking to the sink to brush her teeth and remove her make-up.

Chancy popped up from the bed and joined Remy. She wanted to brush away the conversation about marriage and the subsequent disappointment. If only a vigorous tooth brushing would do that. Chancy wished she had met Remy before Remy married that A-hole and soured on the whole institution of marriage. But Chancy was only a toddler when they'd married, definitely not old enough to steal her away from her ex. Chancy thought that her age did not adequately represent her maturity. Chancy still had that youthful optimism, mainly because that was just who she was. But Chancy's early life experiences had shaped her and forced a kind of early maturity that other women her age did not possess. She hoped that, given time, Remy's perspective on marriage would change. One thing Chancy knew for a fact was that she wanted to spend the rest of her life with Remy. If Remy didn't want to marry, that was one thing, but she hoped Remy wanted to make a life with her as much as she wanted that with Remy.

†

Remy was on the verge of waking when she felt Chancy's youthful energy. She opened her eyes to a grinning Chancy who sat cross-legged on the bed with a flat silver box sporting an enormous red silk bow in her lap. Her megawatt smile was on view, looking like an extravagant cinema marquee. She wiggled on the bed in what Remy thought was a valiant attempt to keep her excitement in check. She was surprised Chancy had waited until her eyes opened. Remy wasn't that patient when she was a young child. She used to run into her parents' bedroom before the sun rose on Christmas morning. Remy never waited until they woke, and instead would shake her father's shoulder to get him to rouse from a deep sleep. Of course, Chancy wasn't a child, and Remy suspected she hadn't had the same happy childhood as Remy. Now Remy was second-guessing her gift. Would Chancy view it as too impersonal? She would definitely believe it was too much and raise a fuss about that.

"Someone is eager to exchange gifts. Merry Christmas, my love." Remy yawned and stretched in bed before sitting and relaxing against the pillows.

Chancy thrust the package in front of Remy. "You still have a little time, but that window is quickly closing. I wasn't sure if I should wake you or not."

Remy yawned again. "What time is it?"

"A little past eight-thirty," Chancy answered.

"Shoot, Lindy and Angel are probably going to make their way into the kitchen any minute. I suppose I can forego a shower until after breakfast." Remy reached for her phone on the bedside table. "I'm going to text her and ask her if we can start the day a little later. She can also let the others know that we'll have breakfast around 9:30 instead of 9:00. I'm sure they won't be too disappointed to have a little more time to relax this morning." She thumbed her message to Lindy.

"Will we still have time to see the parade and enjoy the other festivities?"

"Plenty of time. It's Island Time. It won't surprise me if everything is a tad bit later than scheduled today." Remy tossed the covers aside and walked to the closet to retrieve a small box wrapped beautifully in silver and gold paper with a fancy lace bow. She set the gift in front of Chancy. "If you don't like it, we can exchange it for something else."

"Don't be ridiculous. It's from you. I'm sure I will love it. Um, I wrapped it myself. It isn't as pretty as yours, but..." Chancy pointed to the box. "Go ahead and open it."

"All right. I must admit to being curious about your mysterious gift." Remy gingerly lifted the top of the box to reveal a picture of a beautiful black Arabian horse.

"Until I have your stables built, I've arranged for her boarding at this ranch. It was nice. I checked it out myself. I remembered when you said your favorite thing to do as a child was ride horses. They were like your special friends. I always wondered why you didn't have any because you have plenty of land..." Chancy stopped rambling when Remy placed her hand on Chancy's thigh.

Remy swallowed hard and choked back the tears that threatened to fall. This gift was the most thoughtful gift anyone had ever given to her. Felix always bought jewelry for her. Expensive, but somehow from him, it always felt impersonal. The necklaces or bracelets were always gaudy pieces with precious stones far too large for her personal taste.

"Oh, Chancy, I don't know what to say. This is so...but I can't let you spend more money having stables built on my land."

Chancy frowned. "You don't like it? We'll get another horse soon to keep her company."

"I love it, but I know how much stables cost..."

"Don't worry. I have that covered. Or at least I will when I get Alex to help and take more shifts at TWC. I know we haven't really talked a lot about the possibility of me offering the special services, but if I can do that, I'll easily be able to pay for the stables."

Remy shifted uncomfortably on the bed. She wanted to be honest with Chancy, but if she really loved Chancy, she wouldn't want to influence her decision regarding TWC. Remy knew that Marley, Luna, Alex, and Danna had all navigated the issue with ease, but none of them were minus their breasts. She didn't want to feel insecure about her body, but she feared the comparison to the women who had club membership and participated in the upstairs activities. Thanks to Luna's individualized workout plans, Chancy offering intimate services at TWC would expose her to women with sculpted bodies. Older, mature women were exactly Chancy's type.

"That's probably a discussion we need to save for later." Remy hoped her neutral suggestion would not give away her feelings.

"You don't want me to work at TWC, do you?"

"I want you to pursue whatever career fits for you. And, of course, I love Club Nights. It would not be the same without your tasty concoctions. You are a truly gifted mixologist."

"I'm talking about the sex stuff upstairs. That's where the women make most of their money. Like ten times what their primary job pays."

Remy nodded. "Yes, I'm aware of that." Handing Chancy a silver and gold box, Remy hoped to steer her from the conversation she was not prepared to have. This was worse than the discussion they'd had about marriage last night. She knew she'd hurt Chancy and was not ready to upset her again so soon, especially after the very thoughtful gift she'd given to Remy. "Your turn to open your present. And, given how expensive your gift to me was, I don't believe you have a leg to stand on regarding the cost of my gift."

"Uh oh. Already making your arguments before I even open this beautiful package. I think I am not going to like how much you spent. We should have established spending limits." Chancy chuckled as she opened her gift. Her brows rose in confusion as she looked at the key fob inside the box and a folded piece of paper nestled underneath the key. Chancy hesitantly plucked the paper from the box and opened it.

Remy watched carefully for Chancy's reaction. She knew the pieces had clicked in her brain when her eyes widened in surprise.

"You bought me a Tesla?" Chancy asked.

"I had them come pick up the Ford. I remembered you going on a mini-rant about climate change and thought an electric car would be more suited to your personal tastes than a gas-guzzling SUV. Although, I think you enjoyed the Edge."

"I did. This is way too much. You know I can't accept this."

"Oh, you most certainly can. If I can graciously say thank you for my beautiful horse, you will not raise one single fuss about my gift. You need a car. You haven't even replaced your bike yet. Besides, it is too far from my house to the bar. Not to mention TWC is even farther away."

"But, a Tesla! You know there are electric hybrids that are like half the cost of a Tesla," Chancy grumbled.

Remy smiled. "But not nearly as cool as a Tesla. That thing goes from zero to sixty in five seconds."

Remy was thankful to hear a stirring in the large kitchen. She hoped that, given a bit of time, Chancy wouldn't continue to raise a fuss about the car.

Chancy hopped off the bed to greet whoever was tooling around in the kitchen. Her head swiveled to where Remy had gathered the silver and gold Christmas paper from the bed and the two boxes. "Saved by the breakfast fairy, but we haven't quite finished this discussion," Chancy warned.

"It's Christmas. Where's that Christmas spirit?" Remy teased.

Chancy strolled into the kitchen and greeted a grinning Lindy and Angel. "And what have you two been up to this morning? A bit of a late start, huh?" Lindy asked.

Remy made her way into the kitchen. "I'm ready to rock and roll. We have a lot of hungry people to feed this morning before we go to the parade," Remy said.

†

The rest of the women slowly shuffled into the large kitchen as Remy and Lindy prepared breakfast. Chancy made her version of a mimosa, adding a few extra ingredients to give the drink a bit more panache.

Marley sipped her mimosa, then asked, "So, what did Santa Claus bring you?"

"Danna and I decided that instead of exchanging gifts for one another, we would sponsor Christmas for a deserving family. So we bought gifts, food for their dinner, and decorations," Alex answered.

"Wow, that's like really nice of you guys. Maybe next year. I feel like I won the lottery this past year. It's probably time for me to pay it forward like you two." Chancy smiled.

"You already know what Santa brought me," Luna answered with a wink.

"I mostly wanted to hear about Remy and Chancy's gifts. Alex said she knows what Chancy got Remy, and I'm sure Remy told Lindy what she got Chancy, but the rest of us want in on those secrets," Marley stated.

"We're still negotiating," Chancy began. "Remy bought me a Tesla. A Tesla! Which is way too much."

"Says the woman who bought me an Arabian and plans to have stables built," Remy countered from the kitchen.

"You both need to learn to be gracious recipients of incredible gifts. By the way, nice job of selecting them," Lindy added. "Okay, people, breakfast is ready. If you don't mind dishing up your own plates, we can have breakfast, then head to the parade and other festivities."

"Not that I'm angling to get out of building those stables, but what about if we organized a stable-raising party? Kind of like a barn raising. That way, we can have those stables built in record time. Of course, the adult beverages will need to be served after completion because I don't want those rafters crashing down on our skulls or that beautiful Arabian. Chancy showed me pictures of him. He's a beaut," Alex said, before grabbing a plate and heading to the table completely filled with various breakfast foods. "You don't have to ask me twice. This looks incredible."

"He's a she," Remy corrected. "I'd love a stable-raising party."

"I'm in." Marley raised her hand.

"Me too," Luna added. "I can't let Marley have all the fun. Speaking of people hogging stuff. We better load up our plates before Alex cleans out the buffet."

"Can outsiders get in on the action?" Angel grabbed a plate and followed Marley and Luna to where Remy and Lindy had laid out the food.

"You're not an outsider anymore. Consider yourself one of the gang. Be prepared for many more invites." Lindy turned toward Angel and smiled.

"Well, I'm not letting the rest of you have all the fun. I might not have the brawn or engineering skills of my lovely wife, but I can hammer a nail. I mean, how hard can it be?" Danna asked.

Alex chuckled. "I'll buy you a pink tool belt. You definitely rock that accessory."

"Don't make fun of me. I take instruction really well. You know that." Danna winked at Alex before kissing her.

"Well, then, that's settled. We'll let Chancy decide on when to do this barn raising. Oh, I mean stable raising. That sounds so funny to me," Lindy said.

"It won't be for a little while." Chancy's face flushed. She wasn't about to confess to the group that she needed to save up more money to afford the supplies. "I, uh, need to order the supplies after Alex tells me what I need to get."

Lindy's eyes narrowed at Chancy, and she was sure that Lindy knew she was short of cash. Chancy fully expected Lindy to approach her later to offer her a loan. Not much got by Lindy. She would probably ask her about the special services TWC offered. Chancy wasn't sure how she would answer. Maybe Lindy would be the best person to talk to about her dilemma. Eventually, she would have enough to pay for the new stables, but it would take her ten times as long to save that much than if she agreed to service some of the women who had approached her on Club Night.

"Hey, Chancy, want to give me a hand with something I forgot in my room?" Lindy asked.

Angel shot Lindy a strange look but continued to fill her plate with food.

"Um, sure," Chancy answered and followed Lindy out of the suite. *Well, that didn't take long*, Chancy thought.

✝

"What's going on?" Lindy asked as soon as they were far enough away from Remy and Chancy's room.

"I don't have enough cash to buy the supplies yet. And before you go offering me another loan, I don't want to do that. I'd rather work more doubles or pick up more work at TWC. If I agree to the special services, I'll have the money in no time. Can I ask you a question?"

"You can ask," Lindy teased.

"Do you think Remy would have an issue with me providing those services to the women at the club?" Chancy asked before following Lindy into her suite.

"Have you talked with Remy about your plans? It really isn't my place to get in the middle of this."

"But you're her best friend. I know Remy doesn't lie, but she hasn't really opened up about her thoughts on this. Kind of like our discussions on marriage. It's like she's holding back from telling me what she really thinks."

"I'm not so sure Remy is holding back. She's always been tactful and gracious in her approach."

"Yeah, I know that, but this time, I believe she feels like she needs to sugarcoat her answers or something. She hates the idea of marriage and probably equally despises the idea of me having sex with other women. But, just like when I gave blowjobs to those disgusting men, I don't even consider it sex. It was a way to survive on the streets, and I'll likely view it as a way to make easy money if I join the TWC special services team."

"Remy has also gone through a lot in the last year. I don't think she quite knows where she lands on several issues, another marriage included. Patience might not be your strong suit, but I'm afraid the best advice I can give is to allow Remy time to work through things. She needs more time than you or I to process most major events in her life. And she's had more than her fair share of items to handle this past year. In the meantime, a loan is simply that. If it makes you feel better, I could charge you interest. A modest amount, of course."

"I'll think about it. Now, did you really have something you need help with?" Chancy asked.

"As a matter of fact, I do. I bought everyone gag gifts for Christmas. All with a sex theme." Lindy grabbed a large red bag and handed it to Chancy. "You can be Santa for us."

"What? No gag gift for me?" Chancy mock pouted.

"Now, what do you think? How could I forget my favorite mixologist? Your gift is in the bag. You can simply set it aside to open later if you like." Lindy waggled her eyebrows.

"Fair enough. Thanks, Lindy. I'll give some more thought to the loan. We'll see. How much interest are we talking?"

"One percent."

"Too low. How about three percent?"

"Two, and that is my last and final offer."

Chancy stuck out her hand. "Deal."

"Tell Alex I want to operate the nail gun. That sounds fun to me."

"I don't think Alex uses a nail gun. She's like old school. I don't think she or her papa had the money for expensive tools."

"Darn. Oh well, it was worth a try. Maybe I'll buy one and donate it to Alex after we raise the rafters of this epic stable we're going to build. Come on, we better head back before Remy thinks I've cornered you for nefarious reasons."

CHAPTER TWENTY-ONE

"That was one heck of a celebration," Lindy said when they arrived back at the suite. "I know it's late, but I think I need another slice of rum cake."

"I was thinking about a turkey sandwich," Luna replied with a slightly tipsy grin. "I think I need something to help soak up some of the alcohol we consumed tonight."

"I'm with you there, my friend," Alex said. "They were so tasty, but I didn't realize how much rum was in them." She grinned.

"It wouldn't be a bad idea for us all to take a dose of Tylenol before we go to bed. I'd hate for any of us to wake up to a hangover tomorrow," Chancy said.

"I think we may all choose to have a day of leisure tomorrow," Marley said. "Most of us are up way later than we are used to, or at least Luna and me are. It's been a long time since we've seen two in the morning."

"I agree. We should just have a lazy day, and when Dawn and Candice return, we will be ready to go again. Maybe we can plan some activities tomorrow," Lindy suggested.

"I vote for one of those glass-bottom kayak trips and maybe a whale-watching cruise. I do believe someone owes me a trip." Marley winked at Luna.

"That I do, my love," Luna replied.

"I'd like to get more snorkeling in, too," Lindy said.

"Another lobster trip?" Alex asked Luna.

"I'm sure that could be arranged," Luna said as she began making sandwiches.

"Right now, all that sounds good is that comfortable bed that's been calling my name," Remy replied. "I'll see you all for breakfast later today." She smiled at Chancy. "Don't rush to bed. Stay and have a sandwich and some fun if you'd like, but I'm exhausted."

"I won't be long," Chancy said and kissed Remy. "I'll try to be quiet when I arrive."

"I think I could sleep through a tornado right now," Remy said. "I'll see you all later."

Lindy cut a slice of cake. "Does anyone else want a piece?"

"No more rum," Luna said and made a face.

"Do you want water, juice, or milk to drink?" Marley asked Luna.

"I think I'd better stick with water," Luna said.

Angel walked into the room and shook a bottle of Tylenol. "Any takers?"

"Oh yeah," Marley said, took four for her and Luna, and passed the bottle to Alex.

†

Luna flopped down on the bed after changing into a T-shirt. "Is the room spinning?" She giggled.

Marley stretched out beside her. "Nope, I think it's just your world. Maybe that last drink wasn't such a good idea."

"I thought the sandwich might help," Luna said with a goofy grin on her face.

"I don't think so. Did you take the Tylenol?"

Luna nodded her head. "Yeah, I did. I brought a glass of water to bed with me, too."

"I'll be right back," Marley said and walked into the bathroom to brush her teeth. When she returned, Luna was asleep. She lay down beside her and admired the beautiful woman who would soon be her wife. Marley saw the strong pulse beating in Luna's neck and kissed her softly. "Goodnight, my love." Marley smiled and turned off the lamp.

†

Luna was still asleep the following morning when Marley climbed from the bed and slipped into sweatpants and flip-flops. She smelled the wonderful aroma of French roast coffee as she closed the door quietly behind her. Thank goodness someone had made coffee.

Angel was at the counter sipping coffee when Marley arrived and walked to the coffeepot. "Are we the only ones awake?"

"Yeah, it's all quiet." Angel smiled.

"What time is it, anyhow?" Marley asked.

Angel turned her wrist to see her watch. "Nearly ten," Angel replied. "Emelia arrived to cook breakfast, and I told her we could handle breakfast and lunch once everyone began stirring. She said she'd be back to prepare dinner."

"I don't think anyone is going to starve in the meantime." Marley smiled. "How do you feel this morning?"

"I'm glad we took Tylenol last night. After a hot shower, I feel good to go again."

"I think we may be the only two," Marley said. "Or maybe three," she said as she nodded to Chancy, walking into the kitchen. "I hope you don't feel as bad as your hair looks," Marley teased.

"I'm in serious need of some caffeine to stop the pounding between my ears. I'll worry about hair later." Chancy groaned.

"Take a seat, and I'll grab some coffee for you." Marley grinned.

Marley poured a cup and set it in front of Chancy.

"Thanks, but can you tone down the brightness of your smile this morning? It's like a bolt of lightning shooting through my brain. I take some pleasure knowing that I beat the Amazons awake this morning." Chancy forced a weak smile.

"Luna was sawing logs when I left the room," Marley said. She began opening cabinets and the pantry to survey the contents. "Grits or oatmeal and toast might be a good idea this morning."

"As much as I love bacon, I don't think my stomach could handle the grease," Chancy said.

"Grits do have a certain appeal this morning," Angel said. "Do you want me to put some on?"

271

"I'll make them," Marley replied. "You can do toast and juice for us."

"I'm going to step outside for some fresh air," Chancy said.

"If it's nice out, we could eat out there," Marley suggested.

Chancy nodded and took her coffee onto the patio.

†

It didn't take long for Chancy to realize her mistake. The sunlight was viciously bright, and the humidity she'd never felt before clung to her skin like a wet blanket. "Oh hell no," she said, reversed her path, and returned inside.

Marley was stirring grits into the boiling water when she heard Chancy return. "That didn't take long," she said and shot a wink at Angel.

"The sun felt like missiles, and the humidity threatened to make me melt. Not in a good way either," Chancy grumbled as she took her seat at the counter. "Is there anything I can help with?"

"Do you need more Tylenol?" Angel asked.

"That's not a bad idea," Chancy said.

"Come finish your toast, and I'll go get Tylenol for you," Angel suggested.

"Thanks," Chancy replied.

†

Angel snuck back into the room and found the bed empty. Lindy was in the bathroom when she entered for the Tylenol. "Good morning," Angel said as she planted a kiss

272

on Lindy's shoulder and hugged her from behind as she brushed her teeth.

Lindy spat and rinsed her mouth before turning in Angel's arms for a proper kiss. "Mmm, coffee. Tastes good."

"Marley and I are making grits and toast for Chancy and us. Nobody else is up yet. I came for Tylenol for Chancy's headache."

"She's moving a bit slow this morning, huh?" Lindy asked.

Angel smiled. "You could say that. Do you want me to bring you a cup of coffee?"

"No, I'll throw something comfy on and be there in a minute. Ask Marley to save me a bowl of grits." Lindy smiled.

"Butter, salt, and pepper?" Angel asked.

Lindy nodded. "Just a splash of milk, too, please."

"You got it. Butter on your toast?"

"Most definitely. My stomach feels fine this morning," Lindy answered.

"There is oatmeal if you'd rather have that," Angel suggested.

"Grits are fine with me. Thanks for asking, though." Lindy kissed Angel as she left the bathroom.

Marley was chopping some leftover ham to add to the grits as desired when Angel returned. "Our numbers are going up by one," she announced.

"Lindy?" Marley asked. "Is she okay with grits?"

Angel took a sip of coffee and nodded. "Said they sounded perfect." She topped off her coffee and poured a cup for Lindy. "Anyone ready for a refill?"

"I'll take one, please," Chancy said.

Marley slid her cup over to Angel and turned to Chancy. "Go easy on the coffee until you have something in your stomach to soak up the acid."

Chancy nodded. "I will. Can I sneak a slice of toast?"

"No, but I'll bring you one," Angel said.

When Lindy arrived in the kitchen, Angel handed her a cup of coffee. "I hope you don't mind, but I sent Emelia home until dinner. I told her we were moving slow today and could handle breakfast and lunch."

"That's fine. I don't think any of us will be running a marathon today." Lindy chuckled.

"The bartenders on the island sure know how to pour on the rum," Chancy said.

"They are much more used to drinking it than we are," Lindy reminded her.

"That's true. I feel like I've been kicked by a mule." Chancy groaned.

"The Tylenol should help soon," Angel said as she took a bowl of grits from Marley and placed it in front of Chancy. "Do you want some ham bits to go in them?"

"No, I think I'll pass," Chancy answered.

†

Marley ate, then took a cup of coffee to Luna. She sat on the edge of the bed. "It's time to wake up, sleeping beauty," she whispered.

"I didn't die and go to heaven? A beautiful angel is sitting on the bed holding a fantastic-smelling cup of coffee," Luna said as she opened her eyes.

"Good morning, my love," Marley said and leaned down to kiss Luna. "I made some grits, but there is also oatmeal when you're ready to eat."

"Oatmeal sounds nice," Luna said. "Sorry I crashed on you last night."

"It was a fun night. Angel and I were the first ones up. Lindy and Chancy have joined us, but Chancy is moving a bit slow this morning."

"Those rum drinks kicked our ass, but they sure tasted good going down," Luna said.

"Chancy said the bartenders were heavy-handed with the rum. Do you need these?" Marley opened her hand and showed Luna the Tylenol.

"Probably not a bad idea," she said. She picked up the water and downed the tablets.

"Go slow with the coffee until you get something in your stomach. I'll go start your oatmeal if you're ready," Marley said.

"Thank you," Luna replied. "Let me freshen up, and I'll be right there."

†

"I don't think I can stand the sunlight today," Alex said as she finished her oatmeal.

"Let's just chill inside in the air conditioning today and make plans for the next few days," Lindy suggested. "I got a text from Dawn that they would return by three today."

Angel turned to Lindy. "I know you want to do more snorkeling. Why don't we rent the glass-bottomed kayaks in the morning, and then we can snorkel in the afternoon?"

"Would we have time to harvest more lobsters for dinner?" Alex asked.

"With steaks," Luna added.

"For someone hesitant to put red meat in your body, you sure have turned into a carnivore," Marley teased.

"I've got catching up to do," Luna said.

"I think we can probably arrange that," Lindy said. "I'm sure Emelia won't mind repeating that meal. It was delicious the first time."

"I'll get Marcus to call and make our reservations," Remy said. "Do we still want to do the whale-watching cruise?"

"Yes, if they are still in the area," Lindy said.

"I'm feeling better already," Luna said.

"Enough for a walk on the beach?" Marley asked.

Luna nodded. "Yeah, I think I can do that. Anyone else?"

"I'll be your Huckleberry." Alex laughed. Danna nodded.

"If nobody objects, I think we should pass on cocktail hour tonight," Chancy said.

"Not a bad idea," Danna replied. "After last night, I think we all need a break."

"Let me go find my sunglasses," Luna said.

"I think we'll continue to relax and wait on you all here," Lindy said.

"Hang on. I'll need my glasses too," Alex said, and rushed to catch up with Luna.

CHAPTER TWENTY-TWO

"I almost feel human again. Of course, as a mixologist, I shouldn't advocate for 'dry days.' But, damn, did we need one yesterday. I don't think I've ever been so hung-over." Chancy yawned and rolled to her side to face Remy, who stirred next to her.

"What time is it?" Remy's rough, sleep-addled voice asked.

"Early. Aren't you excited about going out on the glass-bottomed kayaks? I had never even heard of them before this trip. Sure, I've heard of glass-bottom boats, but not kayaks." Chancy tossed the covers aside and jumped from the bed. She grabbed her swimsuit and quickly dressed, excited to start this newest adventure.

"How early?" Remy asked with a smidgeon of irritation.

"Um, about six-thirtyish."

"You do know that most of our gang will not be ready to head out for at least another couple of hours? Some of us need more beauty sleep. I can barely remember the days where I only needed four or five hours of sleep."

"I'm sorry. I was just so excited. I didn't realize how early it was. Can you go back to sleep?" Chancy asked.

"Not with a gorgeous little sprite bouncing around the suite like it's still Christmas morn. I might as well get up with you. We can start the coffee at least, and then when we hear people stirring, I'm roping you into preparing breakfast."

"I make an exceptionally tasty omelet. Or, I could try my hand at eggs benedict, but I heard the hollandaise sauce is a bitch to get right." Chancy ran her hand through her spiked hair, shaking her head when she looked into the mirror and found her blue locks in complete disarray. "Only problem with short hair is the awful bedhead in the morning. I should just shave it, and then I wouldn't have to worry."

Remy slowly emerged from the bed and pushed a lock of hair aside. "While I am quite sure you have a beautiful head and could definitely own the look, I like your morning hair. It's adorable."

"I'd rather be considered sexy," Chancy grumbled.

"Oh, you are sexy. Both sexy and adorable. Nothing wrong with that."

†

"I don't think I've ever had a better omelet. Good idea to add goat cheese and smoked salmon." Lindy set her fork down, then wrapped her hands around her coffee mug, lifting it to her lips for a sip. "Thanks for making breakfast."

Murmurs of appreciation filled the room as the rest of the gang finished their breakfast.

Chancy bounced in her chair. "Do you think we'll see dolphins or whales today? Seeing those sharks while we were up in the air during our parasailing adventure was a little unsettling. I'd rather not run into any while in the kayaks. I'm not even sure I want a marine mammal as large as a whale cozying up to my kayak, either."

"Wimp," Alex teased.

"Maybe, but I'm sending them your way if we come across any. You can send the dolphins my way." Chancy grabbed her tablet. "I've been doing a little research on dolphins. I think they are my new favorite animal." She turned the screen toward the group. "Look here. I found this article that says dolphins are very sexual. Lots of lesbian sex, too."

"Shut the front door. You're making that shit up," Alex said.

"No, I'm not. They, like, get each other off with their flippers or their nose. The snouts are like sleek little dildos. I wonder if they penetrate each other." Chancy handed the tablet to Alex.

"Stop. Stop. The visual is killing me." Marley began laughing.

"Oh my Goddess, she isn't kidding. Apparently, dolphins masturbate, too. I'm not sure I want to see a dolphin porn show today." Alex handed the tablet back to Chancy.

"Well, I do," Angel interjected. "I'm far too curious about how they go about masturbating. Do you think they are flexible enough to reach their pleasure spots with their noses? Now that would be something fascinating to watch."

Lindy smiled. "I had no idea you were such a voyeur. Good to know."

"Actually, I think I read something about that on social media. Researchers discovered that a dolphin's clitoris was very similar to humans. I'll bet they didn't have to endure lectures about the sins of the flesh. No wonder they have a ton of lesbian sex and masturbate all the time. No Catholic guilt to sway them from pleasure." Danna snickered.

Chancy continued to wiggle in her chair, excited about the possibility of seeing dolphins having sex. "Well, I want to see this with my own eyes."

"I hope you won't think less of me, honey, but I kind of want to see this, too," Luna said.

"Nope. Whatever floats your little kayak," Marley answered.

†

"These are the coolest things I've ever seen," Chancy gushed. "I thought there would be a small area that was glass at the bottom of the kayak, but the whole thing is clear. So fucking awesome."

Remy lazily dipped the paddle into the crystal cobalt water as they paddled farther from the shore. "Do you want to stop paddling for a bit to see if the fish and other wildlife approaches?"

"Sounds great. I need to drink some water and reapply sunscreen, too. Should we call the others over and daisy-chain our kayaks together?" Chancy asked.

Alex, Danna, Luna, and Marley had ventured even farther away from the rest of the group, and Chancy frantically gestured for them to paddle back to where Candice, Dawn, Chancy, Remy, Lindy, and Angel clustered close to a large reef. Chancy squinted when she saw Alex gesture farther out to sea.

"I think Alex is trying to point something out," Remy said. "Maybe we should paddle a little closer and find out what's got her so excited."

"Okay, but can we return to the reef? I'll bet there are tons of tropical fish to see." Chancy cupped her hands against her mouth and shouted. "We're coming. Don't get your britches in a bunch."

"Let's hurry to catch up and see what's happening out there." Remy dug deeper into the warm water with a powerful stroke, sending a small twinge into the area where the doctors had removed her breast tissue. She hoped that Chancy wouldn't notice when she flinched, but luck was not in her favor today.

Chancy scrunched her face. "I saw that. We have all day to catch up to them, don't do anything to cause unnecessary pain. I'm sure that whatever has them all excited will still be there when we reach them."

"I thought you might want to get there in a hurry. I saw a dorsal fin breach the surface just now."

Chancy's grin widened before a sober expression took over. "Big fin or little fin. Black or gray?"

Remy laughed. "I don't think it was a shark fin. Too small."

"Dolphins?" Chancy declared excitedly.

"I think so. I'm sure when we get closer, we'll know for sure."

"You let me do the heavy lifting. I may be small, but I'm mighty." Chancy laid the paddle across her thighs and flexed her biceps. When the kayak started to wobble, the paddle slipped from her lap, and Chancy grabbed for it, causing her to plop into the sea with a large splash.

"Cold, cold, cold. So fucking cold. I thought the Caribbean was warm water," Chancy spluttered.

Remy was happy when Alex and the rest of the group quickly made their way to Remy and Chancy's boat because she wasn't sure she had enough strength to pull Chancy into the kayak by herself. Alex's powerful strokes made quick work of closing the considerable distance. Since the others were closer, they had already surrounded the kayak, stabilizing the boat, so Remy didn't join Chancy in the water.

As Alex approached, she teased, "Did you get a little hot there? Decide to go for a swim? Find any lobsters while you were bathing? I suppose you would need to cheat to get a leg up on me with lobster hunting."

"Funny, but I'm not laughing." Chancy grabbed onto the edge and tried to wiggle her way into the boat, nearly tipping it over.

Alex pushed on her ass while Lindy, Angel, Candice, and Dawn held onto the kayak to keep it from completely tipping over. Marley and Luna held onto Remy to keep her firmly inside the boat. Finally, Chancy was back inside the kayak. Alex had plucked the paddle from the sea and handed it to Chancy.

"Forget it takes a village. I'm changing that to it takes a fleet. Thanks for helping out. Now, what the hell were you pointing at?" Chancy asked.

"Dolphins. But the real question is, what the heck were you trying to do? Did I really see you flex your puny muscles?" Alex joked.

"They're not puny. I've been working out. Lifting cases of beer every chance I get. I figured it would help speed up my healing after I broke my arm," Chancy defended. "Can we paddle to where you guys were? I want to see the dolphins."

"Sure thing, Mighty Mouse. I don't think they plan on swimming away. They were playing around our boat. I might have even seen two of them in the throes of passion," Alex answered.

"You did not. Quit fucking with me." Chancy flicked water onto Alex.

"Careful, pipsqueak. You're gonna end up in that cold water again. You do know that the farther out you go, the colder the water gets. You'll be like a human popsicle for the sharks." Alex snickered.

"Don't let her goad you," Marley said. "There weren't any sharks, only dolphins."

The group carefully made their way to the location that Alex and Danna had just come from. Luna tied the cluster of boats together to allow the women to visit with one another as they watched the antics of the dolphins at play. Chancy would swear that she saw two dolphins making love as her eyes tracked the two beneath her boat. Remy wasn't positive she saw the same thing as Chancy, but the two dolphins looked cozy together. After the group had their fill of the sleek marine mammals, they traversed slowly back to the reef to take in the sight of the colorful fish who lazily swam around the coral.

†

As the group approached the shore to return their kayaks, Lindy suggested, "We were out there a lot longer than I thought we would be. It's getting late, so how about we bypass catching our own lobsters and buy them from the locals?"

Remy raised her hand. "I vote for that. Besides, Chancy's shoulders are looking scarlet again. I wonder if this sports screen really works like they say it does."

Chancy poked her shoulder with her finger. "Yup, they're toasty again. I'll put on a shirt. I guess I won't have time to rechallenge Alex and Luna."

"Not today, but maybe another day. We still have time," Lindy answered. "I think I might be ready for a cocktail, though. Chancy, are you up for mixing us something special before dinner?"

"You bet. I have just the drinks for y'all. No rum today. I'm breaking out the tequila or vodka." Chancy handed the rope to the young man on the beach. He proceeded to pull the kayak farther onto the sand, away from the tide.

"I need to stretch my legs a little. Does anyone want to join me for a walk on the beach before we head back?" Luna asked.

"Always." Marley leaned in and placed her head on Luna's shoulder.

"Yeah, I'll bet you Amazons need to unfurl those long limbs of yours. You probably felt like a sardine in the small kayak. How did those legs of yours fit?" Chancy teased.

"A longer or single might have been better, sure, but I prefer the cramped version with the love of my life versus a solo journey." Luna kissed Marley on the cheek.

"Agreed," Alex added. "Hey, Chancy, did you pick up any pointers from the dolphins?"

Chancy laughed. "Maybe. I thought you said you also saw them getting down and dirty in the water. I could ask the same thing about you."

Alex grinned. "But I don't need any pointers."

"Neither do I," Chancy retorted.

"No, you certainly do not," Remy whispered in Chancy's ear.

Alex laughed and pointed at Remy and Chancy. "I think Remy is talking dirty to Chancy. Hmm, do you think that when the dolphins chirp at one another, they're saying, 'Oh, yes, right there, give me all of your enormous snout.' Maybe that's why they seem to have a perpetual smile."

"Wow, you're more obsessed than I am. And, you need to keep your enormous snout out of our whispers," Chancy taunted.

"Fine. You two are adorable together."

"We are, aren't we?" Chancy pulled Remy in for a passionate kiss.

CHAPTER TWENTY-THREE

Lindy pointed in the distance as they approached a pod of whales. "We're in luck," she cried out as everyone raced to the railing to get their first glimpses of the humpback whales.

Marley and Luna glanced in the direction Lindy was pointing.

"I see them," Marley said, looking through her camera's viewfinder. "Not just whales. We have dolphins, too."

The engine's sound churning through the water attracted the dolphins' attention, and they came in for a closer inspection.

"Would you look at them," Luna said as they swam effortlessly beside the fast-moving boat? "They make it look easy to keep up with us."

One of the dolphins breached, performing a flip in the air, and Marley was quick enough to capture the image. "Hey, I think I got that," she squealed with excitement.

"I only managed the reentry into the water," Danna said.

"They are beautiful," Lindy replied. "Such graceful creatures."

"Unlike me," Angel joked, waddling like a penguin.

"I don't know. That looked pretty cute," Lindy said with a soft laugh.

The dolphins continued to race the boat and peeled off just before they reached the pod of whales. The captain reduced the speed as they moved parallel to the whales.

"Holy cow, they are huge," Alex said. "Almost as long as this boat, if not longer."

"There's a baby," Dawn cried out.

Marley's lens spun to find the smaller creature as it swam close to its mother. "That is adorable," Marley said after snapping dozens of shots. "Call me crazy, but those eyes seem so full of intelligence and caring."

"They are smart creatures, and they nurture their young for years," Candice replied. Several heads turned to look at her. Candice shrugged. "My degree is in marine biology," she said. "I don't get to use it much at thirty thousand feet, but I have so much more fun."

Marley grew nearly hypnotized by the whales' movement through the water and the sound of them exhaling through their blowholes. In the excitement of the sighting, she had forgotten about the ache in her lower abdomen.

When the captain announced they had weather moving in and needed to return to the port, the group groaned in protest.

"I don't think any of us want to be caught out here in rough seas," Dawn said. "If you think turbulence is bad, it's nothing compared to twenty-foot swells."

The group moved into the small cabin and took seats away from the spraying water and the rain droplets that had begun to fall. Luna sat next to Marley as she scanned through the photos she had taken. They oohed and aahed over several of the shots. Luna noticed Marley rubbing at her side and frowning. "Are you okay?"

"I've got this pain in my lower abdomen," Marley whispered. "It's too early for my monthly, but it feels like an intense cramp. I'm a bit nauseous, too."

"Why don't we get you checked out when we get back into port?" Luna said.

"No, I'm sure everything is fine," Marley said. "I'll take some Tylenol and relax. I don't want to dampen anyone's fun."

"You won't dampen anything. I prefer you get checked out if you're not feeling better. Do you want me to see if Angel has her Tylenol?"

"Yes, please," Marley replied.

Luna walked over to Angel and Lindy. "Sorry to interrupt, but did you bring the Tylenol with you?" she asked Angel.

"I never travel without it," Angel said. "Do you have a headache?" she asked as she pulled the bottle out of her bag.

"No, it's Marley. She's having a pain in her side. Maybe early menstrual cramps."

Luna's tone wasn't convincing. "What side?" Lindy asked.

"Her right," Luna said, feeling worried by the look on Lindy's face.

"Any nausea?" Lindy asked.

"Yes, some. What are you thinking, Lindy?" Luna inquired.

"Is it time for her cycle?" Angel asked.

"No, Marley says it's too early," Luna said, her panic rising when she saw a look pass between Lindy and Angel. "Will you tell me what you're worried about?"

Lindy sighed. "It could be her appendix if she still has one. Do you know if she does?"

"She doesn't have a scar, but that doesn't mean much these days," Luna said.

Lindy nodded. "We probably should have her checked out."

Luna looked back in horror as she saw Marley rush out of the cabin and vomit over the railing. She raced outside to Marley. "Do you have your appendix?" she asked.

"Yeah, I do. Do you think that may be what's causing the pain?" Marley asked.

"That may be a good possibility," Angel said when she heard Marley's question.

Lindy slipped into the wheelhouse and located the captain. "May I help you, Mrs. Freemont?"

"I think we have a medical emergency developing. How much longer until we get back to port?"

"Twenty minutes. What's going on?" the captain asked. "I just assumed seasickness since the water has become rougher."

"We think she may have appendicitis, and it can become serious if it ruptures," Lindy replied. "Does the hospital have a helicopter?"

"Yes, I believe it does. I will give emergency services a call. At worst, I'll arrange to have an ambulance waiting for us."

"Thank you, captain. Please keep us informed," Lindy replied.

The captain nodded. "Please help yourselves to any ginger ale or anything in the pantry you think might help."

Lindy nodded and stormed back to the cabin. Marley was pale and in noticeable pain. "The captain is putting a call into emergency services. We are twenty minutes out from the port," she told them. "Hold on, Marley. Can we get you something to drink or anything?"

Marley winced in pain. "Some water and a cold rag for my face. I feel like I'm on fire all of a sudden."

Luna raced into action, Alex hot on her heels. "What can I do?" Alex asked.

"Take her a bottle of water, but make sure she takes small sips only," Luna replied. "I'll get an icy rag for her face."

"On it," Alex said then grabbed a bottle from the ice chest, and ran back to Marley.

"Dear God, let Marley be okay," Luna said, with tears running down her cheeks. She looked around for a towel and, finding none, pulled off her T-shirt and dunked it into the icy water.

She knelt beside Marley and began stroking her face with the cold fabric.

Marley managed a smile. "It smells like you."

"Sorry, babe, I couldn't find a towel," Luna apologized.

"I'd rather have something with your scent on it any day," Marley said. Her stomach churned as another wave of nausea left her void of any stomach contents.

Luna wiped her face. "Try to take it easy," Luna told her.

"I'm sorry for ruining our trip," Marley said with tears filling her eyes.

"Oh, Marley, you haven't ruined anything," Lindy said.

The captain rushed out to them. "The helicopter is on the way and will be here in five minutes. They can't land, but they will lower a basket to us."

"We'll be ready," Luna said. "You can help me carry her to the basket," she said to Alex.

"Damn straight," Alex said.

"I'm calling Marcus to send a van for us to go to the hospital," Remy said and stepped inside to make the call.

Luna's heart beat wildly in her chest as she held Marley close. "You're going to be okay, baby. Just hang tight. I can hear the helicopter."

The helicopter arrived, and a man lowered a basket. Alex and Luna carried Marley as gently as possible and placed her inside. "Can I go with her?" Luna asked.

The man saw the panicked look on Marley and Luna's faces. He nodded. "I'll send a ladder down as soon as we get up. You'll have to climb while we get her stabilized," he told her. "Climb as fast as you can."

"Just send it," Luna said.

He nodded, and the basket lifted off the deck.

Luna pulled her wet shirt back over her head as she waited for the ladder.

"We'll meet you at the hospital," Lindy said. "Give us a report when you can."

Luna nodded, and when the ladder dropped, she climbed it with incredible speed and disappeared inside the craft as the pilot turned for land.

"I hope she's going to be fine," Danna said.

"Have faith she will be," Alex said and slung an arm around her shoulders.

Lindy breathed a sigh of relief when she saw the resort's van waiting at the end of the dock and Marcus waiting for them to depart.

†

Luna watched as the medical crew began to examine Marley and somehow managed to get an IV started in mid-flight with fluids and anti-nausea medicine.

"I know you're in pain, but we cannot give you anything until we get you to the hospital and the doctors can examine you. You still have your appendix, right?"

Marley nodded. She reached for Luna's hand.

Luna gripped it firmly. "I'm right here."

"Is she your partner?" he asked Marley.

Marley nodded. "Soon to be wife." She smiled through a grimace.

"I've never known anyone to climb that ladder so fast. Congratulations on the engagement." The medic smiled. "Wait? Christmas Eve proposal on the beach?"

Luna looked at him, a bit confused. "Yes, that's when I proposed after a great dinner."

"Your fireworks were the talk of the ER for a good hour. Brilliant idea," he said with a smile.

"Thanks," Luna replied as she watched him continue to work.

She could feel the helicopter begin to lower and glanced out to see a team with a gurney ready to transport Marley.

"When we get inside, they will ask you to wait in the waiting room while they examine Marley. I promise as soon as permitted; I will bring you back to see her."

"I don't want to leave her," Luna protested.

"I know, but it's necessary for a few minutes. You'll only be in the way and delay her getting the care she needs. My name is Tito, and I promise I will come for you."

Luna's jaws clenched in frustration, the muscles taut, but Luna managed a nod. She would never do anything to harm Marley.

When the helicopter touched down, the crew lowered Marley onto the gurney. Luna jumped down beside her. "I will see you soon," she promised.

"I'm going to be okay," Marley spoke loudly over the sound of the helicopter.

"Room three," a nurse told Tito.

"I'll be in just as soon as I get Luna settled."

Tito and Luna raced ahead of the gurney, and he led her to a private waiting room. "I'll let the desk know to send your friends back here," Tito said and disappeared before Luna could thank him.

Luna began pacing the room, the clock ticking louder with each passing minute. Ten minutes passed before the door opened, and Lindy and the crew rushed in. "Any word yet?"

"No, I was hoping you were Tito coming to get me. He promised he would come as soon as possible."

Tito was the next person through the door. "Sorry it took so long, but we had to get an x-ray and some blood work. If you want to come back, the doctor will give you the report."

Luna followed him down the hall. She was surprised to enter the hallway to find Marcus outside the door.

"Ms. Luna, this is Dr. Ricco Samuels, a good friend of mine and the best surgeon on the island," Marcus said.

Luna shook his hand. "What's going on?"

"She's having an acute case of appendicitis, but you were able to get her here before it ruptured. We are getting her prepped for emergency surgery. I'll make a tiny incision," Ricco said, pointing to his side, "remove the damaged organ and have her superglued and in a room in no time."

"Will she have to stay in the hospital long?" Luna asked.

"A day, two tops unless there's an infection," he said. "Then five days' rest, and she'll be almost as good as new."

"Can I see her?" Luna asked.

"Yes, but just quickly. I'm going to prepare for surgery, but I'll come to see you after with a report."

"Thank you, Dr. Samuels," Luna said and stepped inside. "I can't stay, but I wanted to tell you I love you, and I'll be waiting for you." Luna leaned down and kissed Marley's lips.

"You're going to catch your death of cold in that wet shirt," Marley said.

"No, she won't," Tito said. "I've already got her a scrub shirt to change into."

"Thanks, Tito," Luna said. "Stop worrying about me and do everything these doctors and nurses say."

Tito cleared his throat.

"Tito too." Luna smiled.

"That's better. Now get out of here so we can take Marley to the operating room," Tito teased Luna.

Luna placed a hand on his shoulder. "Thanks for everything."

"My pleasure," Tito replied.

Luna stopped in the restroom and peeled off her wet T-shirt and damp sports bra. The scrub top fit her loosely and was still warm from the dryer.

All eyes were on Luna as she walked into the waiting room. "They are taking her back to surgery, but the appendix has not ruptured. Dr. Samuels assures me she will be fine. She will be here for a day or two at most and then needs to take it easy for five days after that."

"Dr. Samuels is a great surgeon," Marcus said. He looked at Remy. "Thanks to you. He would never have made it to medical school without your help."

"I wasn't sure if that was the same Ricco or not," Remy replied. "I'm glad he came back here to practice."

Marcus smiled. "He beat it back here as soon as he could."

"How long did he say the surgery would take?" Lindy asked.

Luna shrugged. "He didn't give a specific time but said it was an easy surgery and she wouldn't even need staples or stitches. A small incision and then some super glue, and she'd be all better."

"That's great news," Angel replied. "I'm happy she got here in time before it ruptured."

Luna walked to the coffeepot and poured a cup before sitting next to Alex.

"Would you eat something light if we bring something back from the cafeteria?" Lindy asked.

"I'll try," Luna replied. "Just no turkey sandwich. I'm on turkey overload." She grinned.

"Let's go then," Lindy said to Angel. "Remy, will you and Chancy help, and we'll bring something back for everyone? Burgers and fries good?"

"We'll come help too," Dawn said and took Candice's hand.

"I need to get back to the resort, but call me when you're ready to return," Marcus said.

"Thank you for getting us here so quickly," Remy said and placed a hand on his shoulder. "You sure you won't stay for a bite?"

"No, Emelia will have something waiting for me," Marcus said. "I'll also let her know you may be late for dinner."

"We can manage dinner if we need to," Lindy said.

Marcus threw up his hands. "I will not tell my daughter that. She'll wait however long you need."

Marcus followed them out of the room.

Alex laid a hand on Luna's arm. "You okay?"

"Scared to death, but at least she's where she needs to be right now," Luna answered.

"She's in great hands, so have faith she will be out of surgery and on the mend in no time." Danna smiled.

"I'll rest easy when she's back in our room, and we can all fuss over her for a few days," Luna said with a forced smile.

Alex smiled. "Marley will receive the royal treatment."

Danna chuckled. "Lindy has already set arrangements for Dawn and Candice to fly back down to bring you home once Marley is clear to travel. She's going to handle re-opening the TWC until you make it back."

"That should be interesting." Luna smiled. "She'll be ready for us to return quickly."

"I think it will be eye-opening for her to see how much the two of you perform in running the club," Alex said.

"I agree. Marcus is getting you a suite on a lower floor once we leave, and Emelia will keep you well-fed," Danna added.

Luna shook her head. "Marley was worried it would ruin everyone's trip."

"I'm just sad she ended up in here. I think we'd all agree that it's been a fantastic trip," Alex said. "The best vacation I've ever had."

"Me too, and I'll leave here an engaged woman." Luna smiled.

"I promise you both, this is the first of many great experiences we'll share," Danna said. "We all deserve more than what we have allowed ourselves, and it's time to change that."

"Amen to that," Alex said.

†

The group kept her engaged while they ate, and Luna was surprised to find she had eaten almost the whole meal. A few minutes later, Dr. Samuels arrived.

He smiled and sat across from Luna. "Marley did fantastic in surgery and is in recovery now. In an hour or so, we'll admit her to a private room for the night. Barring any complications, I think she can go home tomorrow afternoon if you promise to keep a close eye on her." He winked at Remy. "Looking around this room, I think Marley will receive better monitoring there than we can do here. Any objections to that?"

"None whatsoever. May I see Marley?" Luna asked.

Dr. Samuel nodded. "Yes, but you'll need to wait back here once they get a room ready for her, and the nurses will call you up. Just don't wear her out and try not to make her laugh. She'll be sore for a while."

"I guess that means you have to stay down here," Alex said and ruffled Chancy's hair.

"What? Why me?" Chancy said.

"Because you're the biggest clown among us," Alex replied.

"I promise to be good if you let me see Marley," Chancy told Luna.

"That, I have to see. I'll be back soon," Luna said, and followed the doctor out of the room.

†

Luna walked into the recovery room and found Marley sleeping soundly from the anesthesia. Linens were tucked tightly around her to keep her warm. She looked pale and angelic to Luna at that moment, missing the bright glow that graced her cheeks when she was awake. Luna's heart ached for the pain Marley had suffered, and she worried that even though lessened, it would still affect her.

"You can sit beside her, and I bet she would enjoy you holding her hand. She asked for Luna as soon as she arrived, and I bet that's you."

Luna looked up to the warmest brown eyes she had ever seen. She nodded. "Yes, I'm Luna. When will she be awake?"

"She will wake soon. I am Anise, her nurse. Just call for me if you need anything while I make arrangements for her room transfer."

"Thanks, Anise," Luna said as she maneuvered her hand beneath the linens to take Marley's. Her hand felt cool against Luna's as she caressed it with her thumb. She looked into Marley's face when she heard a sigh as their hands touched. A few moments later, Marley's eyes fluttered open.

"Hello, my angel," Marley replied in a whisper.

"Hey, baby, how are you feeling?" Luna asked.

Anise heard them talking and stepped into the room.

"Thirsty, and my throat is on fire," Marley whispered.

Anise nodded. "During surgery, you were intubated, so your throat will be sore for a day or so. I can't give you anything to drink until you are fully awake. Once we get you into a room, this handsome lady can begin giving you some ice chips. Those will help."

"No steak and lobster?" Marley asked.

"Not tonight, dear." Luna smiled. "As soon as you can, you will have all you can eat. I promise."

"I need to get in on this deal somehow," Anise teased. "Let me go see if your room is ready."

†

Anise sent Luna back to the waiting room with orders to answer the phone when it rang that Marley was ready for visitors. "She'll be in room 202, but only a few visitors at a time, please."

"Thanks, Anise," Luna said.

"Oh, here, I almost forgot." She handed Luna a container of Marley's jewelry. "Congratulations too on your engagement."

"Thank you, Anise. For everything," Luna said. She bent down to kiss Marley. "I'll see you upstairs in a few minutes."

Marley lifted her hand. "My ring?"

"Is it okay to put it back on?" Luna asked.

Anise nodded. "Yes, go ahead."

Luna slipped the ring back on Marley's hand and kissed it. "Love you. I'll see you soon."

Marley smiled and nodded. Her throat was so dry it hurt even to whisper.

†

Lindy was happy to see the smile on Luna's face when she walked back into the room. "How is she?"

"I'd say she's doing pretty good. She asked the nurse about steak and lobster," Luna said. "She's struggling to talk from the breathing tube from surgery, and is dying for something chilled to drink to cool off her throat."

300

"Should I go make her a banana daiquiri?" Chancy asked.

"No," Luna and Lindy answered together, then broke out laughing. "No more alcohol until she's cleared by the doctor," Lindy instructed.

"I'll drink one for her," Luna replied. "They will call us when she gets to her room. She's going to be in 202, and we can visit in small groups once she's settled."

"Marley will need her rest," Lindy said. "We won't stay long. Just enough to see for ourselves that she's okay, and we'll go back to the resort. Do you need us to pack a bag for you?"

Luna nodded. "A clean outfit, something warm to sleep in, and hygiene stuff. For both of us, please. I know she won't be able to shower, but Marley will insist on brushing her teeth and hair as soon as she's able. Marley will also need clothes to wear home tomorrow."

"I'll bring them back up," Alex volunteered.

"Thanks," Luna said. She settled in next to Alex until the phone rang. "Okay, we'll be right up. Thank you." She turned back to the group. "We can all go up. There's a waiting room on the second floor."

"What are we waiting on, then?" Lindy said.

†

"Hey, baby," Luna said as she, Lindy, Angel, Remy, and Chancy entered the room.

"Hey, gang," Marley said.

"You sound better already," Luna said.

"I never thought ice chips could taste so good," Marley said. "I've got ice cream coming too."

301

"That's great news," Lindy said.

"Chocolate?" Luna asked. "I know that's your favorite next to mint chocolate chip."

Remy laughed and then covered her mouth.

"What?" Lindy asked.

"I remember Luna being my ice cream Goddess when I was in the hospital," Remy said.

"That's right. Maybe we should return the favor. Are you up for some mint chocolate chip?" Lindy asked.

"I don't want you to go to that trouble," Marley said. "Anything they have here will be perfect as long as it's cold."

"I'll be right back," Chancy said.

Chancy walked back to the waiting area. "Alex, will you go down to the cafeteria and see if they have mint chocolate chip ice cream?"

"I'm on it," Alex said and rushed to the elevator.

"Thanks," Chancy said and walked back to Marley's room.

"Where'd you go?" Remy asked.

Chancy grinned. "To put an Amazon to work."

Luna shot a glare at her. "You promised to be good, remember?"

Chancy threw up her hands. "Sorry, it just comes so naturally out of my mouth."

"You better come with me before we get tossed out a window," Remy said.

"Sorry, Marley," Chancy said and hung her head.

Marley smiled. "Hey, Chancy."

"Yes, Marley?"

"You did well. Thank you," Marley said.

Chancy's smile lit the room, and before the temptation to stick her tongue out at Luna overwhelmed her, Remy escorted her from the room.

Dawn and Candice came in next. "You know, if I knew you wanted a helicopter ride, I would have brought you one," Dawn teased.

"Dawn," Candice elbowed her wife. "Stop it. It hurts to laugh."

"It's okay. Chancy's already broken the ice. The pillow technique works," Marley said.

"We'll have a recliner with a dozen pillows ready when you come home tomorrow," Candice promised.

"I can't wait," Marley replied.

The door cracked open, and Alex and Danna walked in. "I got you covered, girlfriend," Alex said and handed her a pint of her preferred ice cream.

Marley smiled. "Thank you, Alex. Thank Chancy for asking you to find some, too. She kind of got rushed out of here."

"So we heard," Danna said. "We won't stay, so you can enjoy your ice cream. Alex and I are bringing some clothes and hygiene stuff up later. Anything in particular you want?"

"Sweatpants and a baggy T-shirt to wear home tomorrow." Marley looked around the room. "Are my clothes here?"

"Yes, in a bag over by the sink," Alex answered.

"Please leave my flip-flops, but you can take the rest," Marley said. She watched Luna remove the lid to the ice cream and scooped out a spoon for her. "I love you, baby, but my hands are fine. You don't need to feed me."

"What if I want to?" Luna asked.

"Chirp, chirp," Marley said and opened her mouth and held the pillow tight to her stomach as she laughed.

Lindy looked at Luna. "We'll head out and let you two rest. Call if you need anything."

"You are not sleeping up here tonight," Marley said.

"Yes, dear, I am, so don't argue with me, or I'll go get Chancy to clown around for you," Luna warned.

"That chair is going to be so uncomfortable. We have a perfect bed for you at the resort," Marley replied.

"It's not perfect unless you're in it with me," Luna said.

"Give it up, Marley. Luna will survive one night," Alex said.

Marley nodded. "I'm not up to fighting."

"We will see you tomorrow. Do you think you'll be ready for steak and lobster for New Year's Eve?" Lindy asked.

"I'm ready now," Marley said.

"Sorry, babe, but liquids for you tonight," Luna said.

"What will you eat?" Marley frowned.

"I'll bring her something when we bring the clothes," Alex said. "A couple of turkey sandwiches?" she teased.

"That would be fine," Luna said. "Thank you."

Lindy sent Marcus a text, and they left the room. Lindy stopped at the door and turned back. "Get some rest. You are my two most important people."

Luna nodded. "We will, Lindy. Thank you." She turned back to Marley. "Open wide."

"Damn, that tastes good. Even better when you feed it to me." Marley smiled. "I'm sorry I scared you today."

"You had no control over that," Luna said. "I'm relieved you're going to be okay. That's all that matters."

CHAPTER TWENTY-FOUR

Luna had wrapped a fluffy white comforter around Marley, who lounged on the love seat. She had barely left Marley's side since she'd awoken from her surgery. Although Marley's recovery was going well, Remy noted the worried look on her face.

"Y'all don't need to stay in on New Year's Eve just because my appendix decided to divorce me without notice," Marley lamented.

"Shush. If you can't come out and party with us, we'll bring the party to you. Besides, we have everything we need in this awesome suite. An exceptional mixologist"— Chancy dramatically pointed to her chest with her index finger—"with a fully stocked bar and Emelia's perfect hors d'oeuvres to ring in the New Year. Not that 2021 was so awful because this year brought me the love of my life, but I am looking forward to 2022."

"I prefer staying in on New Year's Eve, anyway. Too many drunken fools out there. I am quite content hanging out with all my favorite people and watching the ball drop with Anderson and Andy. It's honestly been years since I ventured out on New Year's," Remy noted.

"You should at least venture out onto the balcony to watch the fireworks. I hear they are truly incredible." Marley sighed. "I feel like I am ruining everyone's New Year's."

Luna leaned into Marley to gently kiss her. "You are doing no such thing. All the partying we've been doing is more than enough for me. I'm looking forward to a more relaxed evening, even if it is New Year's and we're supposed to be wearing stupid hats, drinking too much, and blowing on silly noisemakers. We've never been the type to follow the crowd. So why should we start now?"

"Oh, we'll be wearing ridiculous hats and blowing hard on these little gems that I bought from a local on the beach." Chancy grabbed a large bag and began handing out the party favors.

Alex groaned. "The only hat that looks good on me is a baseball hat."

"Maybe I got you one. Don't be so grumpy," Chancy chastised. "Come on. Everyone has to wear them, or it's no fun."

Angel held out her hand. "I look great in hats. Lay it on me. I think I should have been born in an earlier era when hats were all the rage for women. But, then again, a Boston marriage is not really my cup of tea. I suppose there is an advantage to living in these times."

Chancy grinned as she handed over a hat with a large feather and a kazoo. "That's the spirit."

Angel promptly placed the hat on her head, stood, and twirled for everyone. A chorus of laughter followed, but each woman held out their hands for Chancy to distribute the goods.

Luna glanced at the gaudy hat in her hands, complete with plastic flowers. "How come I don't get a normal baseball hat or that cool top hat that you gave to Candice?"

"Because that long silky hair of yours is just begging for something like what Chancy gave you." Marley snickered.

Luna smiled. "You must be feeling a lot better. I'll take the compliment and be a good sport. But remember that payback is a bitch. I see you also found a cool top hat for yourself, Chancy."

"It goes with my outfit." Chancy grinned and ran her hands along her front, preening for the crowd.

†

Angel wasn't sure if this was the best time to talk with Lindy about where she saw things heading after they returned to Atlanta, but the anxiety of the unknown was getting the best of her. Before she had a chance to lead Lindy to the balcony, Chancy spoke up.

"Hey everyone, it's a couple of minutes before midnight. Do we want to watch the ball drop or go on the balcony and catch the fireworks?" Chancy asked.

Luna caught Marley's eye, then answered, "I think we'll stay and watch the ball drop, but can you leave the drapes open for us?"

"Of course," Remy answered.

308

Lindy leaned into Angel. "I've seen the ball drop in person. The television version pales in comparison to watching it live. Do you want to join me on the balcony?"

Angel grinned. "I thought you'd never ask." She looped her arm with Lindy and announced, "We're heading to the balcony."

"Is it okay if we join you?" Chancy asked. "I can never get enough of fireworks."

"We'll join you after we have our midnight kiss. I want to time it perfectly. You know, the kiss sets the stage for the entire year. Supposedly, according to English and German folklore, the first person you encounter in the new year and the nature of that encounter establishes the tone. A kiss is supposed to strengthen the ties with the person you kiss. Not that our marriage needs strengthening, but I am not taking any chances. Besides, I make it a point to outdo my kiss from the previous year," Alex explained.

"We'll also join you later," Candice said.

After everyone had declared their intentions, Angel found a corner on the balcony and glanced at her watch. They had less than a minute before midnight.

"Ten, nine, eight, seven, six, five, four, three, two, one." The chant reverberated from inside the suite, followed by "Happy New Year" and multiple noisemakers blaring in the background of the already noisy television.

Angel captured Lindy's lips, and instead of a quick kiss at midnight, she took her time to explore the outer edges, nibbling until her tongue gently sought entrance into Lindy's mouth. Lindy, for her part, eagerly accepted Angel's silky tongue, which was causing all kinds of fireworks inside her body.

When they broke apart, Angel sighed. "I don't want this vacation to end. I'm afraid that my feelings for you trump moral ambiguity. I'm not willing to let what we have developed so far go. Please tell me you feel the same."

"Mm, I do. What are you suggesting?" Lindy asked.

"I'm not asking you to divorce your husband and move in with me. I know how ridiculous that sounds, but I would like to play this out and see where it takes us. Maybe, down the road, we'll have a better idea of what to do about what is certainly bound to be a complicated relationship."

"Lately, I've been taking stock of my life and my marriage. It's brought a lot of uncomfortable feelings to the surface, but I don't know that I'm ready to make major changes. The fact that you are willing to sidestep your personal rules on relationships means a lot. Thank you. I need a little time to unravel my knotted feelings on everything, not just you."

"I understand. As long as I get to spend more time with you, I think I can be patient and wait until you've worked everything out. In the meantime, we can get to know one another a little better. Perhaps we can simply forego a specific label."

"I'd like that."

Angel captured Lindy's lips again to seal the deal.

†

After the countdown to midnight, Chancy put all her love into the kiss, earning a satisfying moan from Remy.

"Wow, that was some kiss. I don't believe I've ever kissed anyone like that on New Year's," Remy breathlessly noted.

"I wanted to make sure you know I don't just want to spend the next year with you. I want us to be together for a very long time."

"Oh, Chancy—"

Chancy placed her index finger on Remy's lips. "I know, I know. You aren't ready for marriage, a white picket fence, and two-point-five kids with me. Besides, you already have the white picket fence, and I don't bring a whole hell of a lot to the table."

"You bring plenty to the table. You still have so much of life ahead of you..."

"It won't be much of a life without you in it. I won't apologize for wanting a long future with you. I will apologize for pressuring you into something you're not ready for. But I can't help myself. I'm so in love with you, it's probably unhealthy. Obsessed is probably what everyone is thinking, and it isn't that far from the truth, but my feelings are real and deep."

"As are mine," Remy answered. "I would never ask anyone to move in with me. Just because I am not running to the altar for a second time does not mean that I don't see a future for us. I also need to come clean about a few things. Sometimes it takes me a bit of time to process my feelings."

Chancy scrunched her nose. "Come clean?"

"I need to tell you that my insecurities over my new and not improved body get the best of me. Anytime I imagine you providing special services to anyone, but especially Helena, causes a mini panic attack."

"Okay. I guess I kind of sensed that. You know it's just a job. To me, it would be no different from mixing a special drink and serving it to strangers. There aren't any feelings attached."

"Helena is not a stranger. She's your former lover." Remy pointed to her head. "In my head, I understand, but even Lindy, who takes part in those services, has feelings for Luna and Marley. Maybe it's not the same kind of love, but it is love. It's hard not to be worried."

"Well, then I won't do it. I'll find another way to make money that doesn't involve licking a stranger's or ex's pussy."

Remy chuckled. "Chancy, you can do anything you put your mind to. If you want to become a famous television mixologist, I know you can do that. I have faith in you. There is that television producer who comes to the club. I'll bet you can pitch her. She raved over your drinks at the last Club Night."

Chancy grinned. "She did, didn't she? Do you really think she might be interested? I'm not sure I can be mean like that Ramsey dude, but I was thinking something along the lines of that show, where up-and-coming mixologists can compete with one another. It would be novel."

"Yes, it would. I think the show would be a colossal hit. I'd watch it."

"I love you so much." Chancy kissed Remy again.

"Me too. You know, it's not only that I am making myself vulnerable again by having you move in with me, but I have actually thought about marriage again. My stance has softened over the last couple of weeks. You're a hard person to resist. Don't give up on me."

312

"Never. Even if you hold me off for thirty years, I'm going to make it my mission to marry you." Chancy's eyes traveled to Lindy and Angel. "Do you think those two will keep seeing each other after we return to Atlanta?"

"That's a bet I would definitely take. I need to have a heart-to-heart with my bestie. She's been so lonely lately. I've worried about her. The connection between her and Marley or Luna is not a replacement for deep and respectful love. I'm rooting for Angel and hoping Lindy will finally kick Jaydub to the curb. I'd never push her into a decision she's not ready for because, Goddess knows, I take eons to process things and make necessary changes for my personal well-being, but I can be a good listener and reinforce any decision she might lean toward."

"I don't have your filter, so I can be the blunt friend who tells her to dump the bastard. I like Angel, and even more, I like who Lindy has blossomed into when she's with Angel."

Angel turned her head in Chancy's direction. "Are you whispering about us? I think I heard my name. Do tell. What salacious things are you saying about me?" she teased.

"All good. Go back to lovingly looking into each other's eyes. We approve," Chancy responded.

"Well, in that case, we better listen to the sprite. I suspect under all her fun and frivolity, Chancy is an old soul with excellent love advice for us." Lindy winked.

†

"Hey, you four, quit having sex on the balcony," Alex called. "The fireworks are over. Come join us, and Chancy can make another round of drinks."

313

Chancy strolled inside with Remy by her side. "You're just jealous that I have enough stamina to last past midnight. I see how you are. I'm only useful when I can make your cocktails."

"Not true. You're also the perfect person to tease. Nobody else even comes close." Alex laughed.

Danna poked Alex playfully. "Stop ribbing Chancy. I can make us some drinks."

"No offense, honey, because you are skilled at many things, but nobody comes close to Chancy in the drink territory."

Candice lifted her empty glass in the air. "Totally agree."

Dawn turned her head to her wife. "Hey, I thought you loved my margaritas."

"I do, but Chancy's are a whole new level of yummy," Candice answered.

"All right, already. Another batch of my special champagne cocktail coming right up." Chancy walked to the bar and began mixing.

Remy settled on a chair and stretched her legs in front of her. "I hope it's okay that I arranged a different suite for you two. I already booked the Presidential suite for after the rest of us leave."

"Of course it is. This place would be way too much for two people," Marley answered. "You aren't displacing anyone, are you?"

"No, no, nothing like that. There's a special suite they held for me, just in case we wanted to go crazy and extend our vacation. It's always tempting, but I had to factor Chancy into the equation, and I think Janice and Selene would murder me if I kept her here for another week," Remy explained.

"Damn. One more week would have been glorious, but I really need to get back to work and make some money. Besides, we have a stable raising to attend to. I don't want your new baby to think we abandoned her. The sooner we build the stables, the better."

"Stables? As in plural?" Remy asked.

"Well, yeah. I'd like to know what all the fuss is about. I thought maybe you could teach me to ride, and then I'll buy the other horse I have my eyes on."

Remy's eyes brightened. "You'd want to ride with me?"

"I'd go anywhere with you. I love animals. Hopefully, I'll be able to charm another horse. Raven took a shining to me. Just call me the horse whisperer."

"Raven, huh? What if I wanted to name her something else?" Remy joked.

"You can't. Raven and I already talked about it, and she likes her name." Chancy grinned.

"Um, not to put a wet blanket over your plans, but do you really think it's a good idea to have a stable raising during the cold and wet season in Atlanta?" Alex asked.

Chancy snickered. "Why, Alex, I didn't take you for such a wussy. I'll buy you rain gear. Come on. It doesn't rain every day."

"Fine. We'll build your stable in the shitty weather. But you're so going to owe me," Alex retorted. "And you better never call me a wussy again, pipsqueak."

"Can we please start as soon as we get back?" Chancy batted her eyes. "Please, pretty please with rum on top."

"No rum. No more rum. Ever," Luna lamented.

"I echo that sentiment." Alex grabbed her head. "That hangover the other day was wicked."

"Everything in moderation. Y'all seemed to forget that," Chancy chanted.

"Shut it, you little alcohol pusher," Alex responded.

"Just saying, you seem to be a wussy in more ways than one. Maybe we should start calling you Princess Alex. Did you feel that pea I put under your mattress?"

"Careful, or I will shove an entire bag of peas up your ass." Alex shook her finger. "I warned you about calling me a wussy. You're just small enough to shove into my suitcase and have the bag handlers lose my luggage."

"I'm not afraid of you, even if you are bigger than me. It isn't the size that counts, but what you do with the assets you have." Chancy stuck her tongue out at Alex.

"Um, I beg to differ. Alex's long fingers are definitely a huge plus," Danna interjected, then blushed. "Shoot, why did I just say that?"

"Because we're all family here. I've never understood why talking about sex is such a big taboo," Lindy noted.

"Me neither," Marley added. "In fact, I've learned a few new techniques from my gorgeous Amazon, which I think others would definitely benefit from. Remember when Alex taught us about Yoni massage? The clients love that."

"Hmm, maybe we should sponsor a class on different sexual techniques? Alex, Marley, and Luna, are you up for something like that?" Lindy asked.

"Absolutely, sure, and hell yeah," the three women answered.

"Can anyone attend those classes?" Chancy shyly asked.

"Of course, and as a member of the TWC family, they'll be free for you, but we'll charge our clients an arm and a leg. This could be another great revenue source." Lindy nodded her head.

"Where can I sign up?" Angel asked.

Danna raised her hand. "Put me on the list, too."

Lindy smiled. "Perfect. We can do a dress rehearsal and invite all the TWC family. That way, we can work out the bugs before we start to charge club members."

"Okay, no more business talk. I want one more drink before heading to bed. It's so sad that our time here on the island is ending. Gotta sneak in that last little bit of fun before we have to leave," Luna said.

"I second that," Alex added.

CHAPTER TWENTY-FIVE

"Are you ready?" Luna asked. "It's time to head back to the hospital."

Marley nodded. "I'm torn, though."

"Over what?" Luna asked.

Marley leaned into Luna. "I've enjoyed the last three days of sleeping in and snuggling with you all day, but I know we need to get back to Atlanta." Marley smiled. "I'm a bit worried Lindy hasn't called, and what kind of mess we are going to walk back into at the club."

"I think she'll do okay. Lindy is a brilliant businesswoman, after all," Luna replied.

"Yes, but if she knew how to run the club, she wouldn't need us," Marley joked.

"That's not true. Lindy hired us because we are the best at what we do. She's taught both of us a bunch about running a business," Luna reminded her.

"That's true. I guess I've just become spoiled having you all to myself," Marley said. "Let's go face the music."

Marcus drove them to the hospital. "Text me when you're ready to be picked up," he said.

"Thanks, Marcus," Luna replied and closed the door.

Luna found the suite for Dr. Samuels, and he didn't keep them waiting long.

"You are certainly looking better," Dr. Samuels said when he entered the room. "Has she been a good patient?" he asked Luna.

Luna smiled. "She's followed your orders implicitly."

"Good. Let's take a look at the incision," Dr. Marcus said and lifted Marley's shirt. "You must have had a fantastic surgeon. The scar you will have won't look like more than a small scratch." He smiled. "Any pain?"

"No, just a bit itchy," Marley replied. "I assume that means it's healing."

He nodded. "You would be correct, my dear. Do you feel well enough to travel?"

"I'd love to spend a month here, but it's time to get back to reality," Marley replied.

"Plan to take it easy for at least three more weeks. Resume activities as tolerated. You're a massage therapist, correct?"

"Yes, I am," Marley answered.

"If possible, don't spend more than two hours in a row on your feet and no lifting anything over twenty pounds. If you feel tired, rest. Listen to your body, and don't hesitate to ask Luna for help."

319

Marley smiled at Luna. "I will. She's been a rock for me."

He held out his hand. "I hope the next time you visit, you will stop by to say hello."

"We will," Marley promised. "Thank you for everything."

"There is no way I can ever repay Ms. Remy for her support that allowed me to follow my dream. Helping one of her friends in an emergency is my pleasure."

Marley stood and pulled him into a hug. "Will you tell Tito thank you for me when you see him next?"

"I assuredly will. Enjoy your trip home."

†

Luna sent Lindy a text with the news Marley had clearance for travel. Lindy replied she would make arrangements with Dawn and text her with details. Luna sent Marcus a message, and they walked downstairs to wait for him.

Marcus dropped them off at the front of the resort. "Are you up to a walk down to the marina for one last sunset?" Luna asked.

"That sounds perfect." Marley smiled.

Luna reached for her hand, and they strolled down the boardwalk to find the perfect spot. Luna gently lifted Marley to sit on the seawall and then hopped up beside her. "We sure won't have this view in Atlanta." Luna sighed.

"Maybe we should convince Lindy to open a club here," Marley said.

"Beautiful in theory, but I don't think the economy would support the special services," Luna said. "Maybe when we are ready to retire, we can get Remy and Marcus to hire us to give massages and personal training for the resort guests."

"You wouldn't miss the special services?" Marley asked.

"No, you have always met my needs, and I'll never have the emotional connection with anyone but you."

"I feel the same. Maybe we can slowly back off those services and bring in some new talent in a couple of years. Get Angel to do some investing for us, and maybe returning here would be possible."

"I could live in the Caribbean," Luna said. She smiled as a flock of seagulls fought as they trailed a fishing boat, begging for handouts from the crew. "Noisy buggers, aren't they?"

"Yeah, they are." Marley smiled and laid her head on Luna's shoulder as the sun sank into the horizon. "Are you ready to see what Emelia has planned for dinner? Then we can pack our bags for the trip home."

"I'll pack while you relax on the bed. It won't take long," Luna said. "We don't have much left."

Marley asked. "Have you gotten a text from Lindy with the arrangements yet?"

Luna pulled out her phone. "They will be here by ten, and we should be home no later than three," she answered.

†

They walked into the room to find candles lit and covered plates sitting on the table. A bottle of wine was uncorked and breathing on the counter. Luna smiled when she opened a note on the table. "Emelia has prepared dinner for us and will be here in the morning to prepare breakfast before we leave."

Marley lifted the lid on a plate and chuckled. "I love that woman."

Luna saw Emelia had prepared steak and lobster for them. "Me too. I wish we could kidnap her," Luna said as she held a chair for Marley. "Can you handle some wine?"

"I think so," Marley replied.

Luna retrieved the bottle from the counter and poured two glasses. She lifted her glass. "What a wonderful trip this has been. I can't wait for our next adventure. I love you."

Marley tapped her glass with Luna's. "I love you too. The first of many we will share."

Luna sent Marley into the bedroom to rest while rinsing the dishes from dinner and placing them in the dishwasher. Luna took glasses of water and joined her.

Marley had opened a drawer and placed folded clothes on the bed when Luna arrived.

"What are you doing?"

"Getting you a head start, so you can come to cuddle with me," Marley replied.

Luna sighed. "I can't argue with that. Did you leave an outfit for tomorrow?"

"I did. The rest you can pack," Marley said as she changed into a nightshirt and slipped underneath the covers.

Luna made short work of packing and took the large suitcases into the foyer. They both had one small bag left in the room to pack hygiene and sleepwear. She stripped down to a T-shirt and panties, then climbed in beside Marley. "Do you have enough pillows?"

"Yes, I just need your warm body next to me," Marley said.

Luna stretched out next to Marley and held her in her arms until Marley drifted off to sleep. Then she slipped from the bed and wrote Emelia a note of thanks. Marley had turned on her side, away from her, so Luna snuggled into her back and joined Marley in slumber.

†

Marcus sent a porter for their bags as they said goodbye to Emelia. "Thank you both for everything. You have made this trip unforgettable for all of us," Luna said.

"It's been a pleasure, and I hope you return as soon as you can," Emelia said.

"It's going to take months to burn off all the calories you fed us, but your meals made it worthwhile. Thank you for all your special touches."

"Good luck to you both, and I hope the wedding will be as beautiful as you." Emelia hugged Marley and then Luna. "Now go before you make me cry."

Marcus walked them out to the van. "Safe travels, my friends."

They hugged Marcus and made the quick trip to the airport. Dawn and Candice met them at customs and supervised the loading of the bags after inspection. "Are you ready to go home?" Candice asked as they settled in.

"Yes, and no," Marley answered with a smile.

"I understand that completely. Once we're in the air, you can recline those seats back and relax until we arrive," Dawn said. "Lindy is picking you up from the airport."

323

"I bet she's ready for us to get back," Luna said.

"I think Lindy has a new appreciation for all that you do at the club, but I think she's managed," Dawn replied. "All set?"

Luna nodded. "Let's go home."

They watched the islands disappear from the window and then reclined the seats as they chatted with Candice until Marley drifted off to sleep. "Do you need anything?" Candice whispered to Luna.

"I'm good," Luna said.

"I'll go harass Dawn and let y'all relax. Call me if you need anything. How about a blanket?"

"Yeah, I think that would be fine," Luna replied.

Candice spread one over Marley. "Do you want one?"

Luna shook her head. "I'm good."

†

The lowering of the landing gear woke Luna, and she found Marley and Candice making arrangements to meet for dinner over the weekend. "I guess we'd better belt up before the captain growls at us," Candice teased. "We'll be on the ground in a few minutes. Dawn and I will handle the luggage and meet you at customs."

"How long have you been awake?" Luna asked.

"Not long. You were sleeping soundly, so I didn't wake you. I know you've worked hard tending to me lately."

"I'm ready to be back in our bed," Luna said as she stretched and fastened her seat belt.

"Me too," Marley agreed.

†

Lindy met them in customs with Angel by her side. "Am I ever glad to see you two," she said as she hugged them and kissed their cheeks.

"I believe she missed us," Marley told Luna.

Luna winked at Marley. "It would appear so, even though it's only been a few days."

"How are you feeling?" Angel asked.

"Pretty good. Glad to be home and ready to get back to work," Marley said.

"With a few restrictions," Luna reminded her.

"I know." Marley groaned.

"After seeing how much the two of you do in running the club, I think I need to give you a raise," Lindy said. "It was a good experience for me, but I'm glad you're back. I'll be around the next few weeks until you're back to one hundred percent."

"You don't need to do that. I have to limit the number of massages I do and can't lift over twenty pounds for a few weeks." She bumped into Luna. "I have plenty of muscle for any lifting I need."

"Who's going to keep an eye on you when she's busy?" Lindy asked.

"I promise to be good," Marley replied.

"I distinctly remember the classic fail from the last person who promised that," Angel said.

"Well, that was Chancy. You can't expect her to be good for long," Luna teased.

"That's true, but I insist," Lindy said.

Marley raised her hands in surrender. "You're the boss," Marley replied, conceding to Lindy.

"The bags are loaded, and you're ready to go," Dawn instructed. "We'll see you this weekend."

"Yes, you will." Marley smiled.

"I hope it's for the stable build on Saturday," Lindy said.

"We had planned on dinner, but we can do that another time," Dawn stated. "We've got stables to build. Text me an address and a time," she told Lindy.

"I will. Remy is in charge of supervising you, so don't get any wild notions," Lindy told Marley. "She plans on using you for a gopher while she cooks for us."

"That, I can do," Marley said with a smile.

"Let's get y'all home," Lindy suggested.

CHAPTER TWENTY-SIX

Chancy twirled the hammer in her hand, almost like a baton in a marching band, and pranced around. Although there was a slight chill in the air, at least the sun was shining. The light breeze caused her blue bangs to flutter. Chancy was in a good mood. Alex had researched do-it-yourself kits versus building a stable from scratch and chose the latter when she came across a video with step-by-step instructions.

Chancy had tossed the hammer in the air one too many times when the hammer landed on her foot. She'd been showing off for the last five minutes, awaiting the rest of the crew to arrive, by throwing the hammer into the air, then slipping the tool into her belt like a gunfighter preparing for a shootout.

Jumping up and down on one foot, Chancy exclaimed, "Fuck, that hurt."

"Serves you right for clowning around. I'm rethinking my decision to loan you that hammer and tool belt. Maybe you should stick to being water girl," Alex reprimanded.

"No, please don't sideline me. I'll be good. I promise," Chancy begged. "Besides, Remy thinks I look sexy in this tool belt."

"Yeah, like you adhere so well to your promises." Alex shook her head. "At least let me show you how to properly hit the head of a nail."

"Pcht," Chancy scoffed. "How hard can that be? I think I can handle hammering a few nails. By the way. How come you don't have a nail gun? That'd be a lot easier and more fun."

Alex pointed to Chancy's foot. "Because I'm working with amateurs and clowns. You would be the first to nail your hand to the board. No way am I going to tempt fate."

"Give me a little credit," Chancy countered.

"Seriously, there's some spare wood I brought to demonstrate a few simple techniques that will make this job a whole lot easier. So put that hammer back in your tool belt, and when the others arrive, we're going to have a short class before we begin. I expect you to give me your full attention."

Chancy saluted Alex. "Yes, ma'am."

Remy walked toward Alex and Chancy. "Did I see you hopping on your foot just now?"

"Um, yeah. I sort of dropped the hammer on my toe."

"Because she was fucking around," Alex interjected.

Chancy stuck her tongue out. "Tattletale."

"Infant," Alex retorted.

Remy sighed. "While I love your youthful energy and that sprite charm of yours, please be careful. I came to let you know that coffee is ready, along with a simple breakfast. Danna also brought those wonderful scones you love. Lindy and Angel just arrived, and I think I saw another car arriving as well. I would imagine the rest will be here shortly."

"I'm going to hold a mini-class before we begin. I know you and Marley won't participate in the heavy lifting or the more strenuous activities, but I thought I would invite everyone. Learning how to do basic maintenance and easy builds might interest you. Thanks for making the food for us," Alex said.

Remy walked to the house, and Alex and Chancy followed. "I won't be making all the food. I figure calling for takeout will be just as good. So that's what I'll do for lunch if that's okay with everyone."

"Fine with me, babe." Chancy caught up to Remy and grabbed her hand as she walked alongside.

"I'm not picky," Alex added.

†

Luna leaned back in her chair and patted her stomach. "Damn, that was good. I should have plenty of energy to dig those holes while you teach the newbies a few things. So glad you bought that power auger. I can't even imagine digging those by hand. Although, when I was younger, we didn't have a fancy power auger. I got my fair share of blisters using a manual post-hole digger."

"I didn't buy it. I borrowed it from a friend. It didn't seem worth it to buy one for just a few holes. I suppose if I built fences for a living, having one would make sense, but that is not my primary business. This whole stable-raising thing is new to me. But the basic principles for safety and tool-use are the same. I know you don't need a refresher, Luna, but I expect everyone else to attend my demonstration. Y'all ready?" Alex asked.

A chorus of affirmations reverberated in Remy's large kitchen. Everyone filed out and followed Alex to where the lumber yard had dropped off supplies.

Alex picked up a weathered piece of wood and placed it on the ground. She pointed to her safety glasses. "Everyone gets their own fashionable eyewear, and I insist you wear them at all times. I debated having y'all wear hard hats because some of you have a tendency to clown around." Alex glared at Chancy. "But I am trusting you to follow directions and be safe without the added security of a hard hat. Besides, Chancy appears to have a pretty hard head already," she teased.

Chancy shot Alex her middle finger.

Alex pulled the hammer from her tool belt. "Always hold the handle at the bottom rather than at the top. You'll have more power to drive the nail. Like this." She pulled a small nail from her pouch and, after a slight tap to settle the nail on the wood, drove it into the old wood with one strike of her hammer.

"Okay. I admit that was kind of badass. Can I try?" Chancy asked.

Alex nodded and handed Chancy a larger nail, smirking. "Have at it."

Chancy held the nail and swung with all her might, making solid contact with her thumb. Shaking her hand, she yelled, "Fuck that hurt!"

"Here, let me look at your thumb," Remy directed.

"Nah, it's fine. Nothing broken. I'll just have a nasty bruise."

"I didn't think I had to spell out that the nail needs to be firmly in the wood before you swing away." Alex covered her mouth, apparently trying hard not to laugh at Chancy. "Don't try to drive in the nail like I did with one swing. Remember, I've been doing this for years. Try again." She handed Chancy another nail.

Chancy gingerly accepted the nail and correctly tapped it into place. Concentrating on the nail, she drove it in with two powerful swings. Beaming at the group, she announced, "I did it. Okay, I admit holding the hammer the way you showed us is much better than when I used to choke up on it."

"Yeah, this isn't softball," Alex answered.

Alex continued for the next fifteen minutes, giving the group tricks of the trade and pointers on remaining safe. It took most of the morning to set the posts in cement and put together the framing pieces for the roof. The group seemed disappointed they would need to wait for the cement to set before beginning the bulk of the work to finish the framing and then build the sides of the stable.

†

Chancy danced around in the kitchen, vibrating with energy as she sipped her coffee. "We get to build the sides today. I can't wait for Raven to see her new home."

"Will you let me buy your horse?"

Chancy shook her head. "No, I already have her picked out. The breeder promised he wouldn't sell her until I was ready. She's a pretty little American Quarter Pony, considerably smaller than Raven. Just my size."

"No showing off today, okay?" Remy brushed her hand down Chancy's arm.

"Knock, knock," Alex called before entering the kitchen. "Ready to get to work?"

"Is everyone else here already?" Chancy asked.

"Yeah, I think they are as excited as you to get the job done. After we raise the stable, the electrical won't take too long. I won't need everyone to help with that, but I can teach you a few things if you want to be my helper," Alex said.

Chancy punched her fist in the air. "Yes. I would love to learn. Maybe that will increase my butch creds."

Alex laughed. "Doubtful. You're too cute and little to be a proper hard-core butch."

Remy stepped between Chancy and Alex. "Do not start anything this early. You two love and respect each other. So act like it."

Alex punched Chancy playfully in the arm. "Yeah, act your age today."

†

By two in the afternoon, the temperature had reached a balmy fifty-one, and Chancy was hard at work on top of the ladder, reaching for the nail she had just tapped. Unfortunately, the angle was slightly off for her, making it incredibly challenging to drive in the nail.

Right before Chancy was about to swing the hammer, Alex yelled, "Don't reach. Let me take care of the high areas."

332

Chancy ignored Alex and swung, hitting the nail but losing her balance in the process.

Thump Chancy landed on the hard earth, rolling slightly and groaning, holding her arm. "Fuck."

Remy caught the whole disaster when she came out to bring the group freshly made sweet tea and lemonade. She quickly set the pitchers she carried on the ground, and ran to Chancy while she writhed on the dirt in obvious pain. "Oh no. Does anyone have their cell phone? Call an ambulance."

Alex nodded. "On it."

"Don't move, okay. The ambulance is on the way."

Chancy began to cry. "I'm so sorry. I've ruined everything."

"Shh, shh." Remy brushed a lock of Chancy's hair aside. "You have not. I'm sure the gang can finish the stables without you. Everything is going to be fine. Can you tell me where it hurts?"

"Besides my pride. I think I may have broken my arm again. Not sure what else I managed to break. But this time, it's all my fault, not some douchebag in a car sideswiping me on my bike. How am I gonna make money now at Club Night if I can't make my signature cocktails?"

"That should be the least of your worries right now," Remy answered.

"Are you mad at me?" Chancy's voice came out in a pitiful whisper. "I wouldn't blame you one bit. Alex is right. I need to grow the fuck up. No wonder you don't want to marry an immature clown."

"Shh. I'm not angry. I'm worried. There's a big difference. And, just for the record, I have not crossed out the

333

possibility of marrying again. And you better listen hard to what I'm about to say. If I do marry again, the only person I would ever consider making that level of commitment to is you, silly. I love you. Your clowning around is all part of your charm. I wish it wouldn't result in harm to you, but I don't want you to change, Chancy. You bring out the playful side of me, and I wouldn't want to lose that. I need you in my life. To quote one of my favorite movies, you complete me, Chancy Olsen."

"You mean that?"

"Of course I do. Every single word."

A small smile formed on Chancy's lips, and she attempted to move closer to Remy to kiss her, but the pain overwhelmed her, and she laid back down, grimacing. Her pain did not stop Chancy from asking, "So, do you prefer summer or winter weddings?"

"What happened to fall or spring? Always the extremes with you," Remy joked.

Remy breathed a sigh of relief when she heard the sirens in the distance. Kissing Chancy's forehead, she announced, "Hear that? They're almost here. Just hang on for a few more minutes."

The medics made quick work of attaching a neck brace and putting Chancy on a gurney as they began assessing her injuries. The female medic raised her eyes to Remy, seeming to assess her mental state, and asked, "Did you want to ride in the ambulance with her?"

"Yes, please. Thank you."

†

By the time the rest of the crew reached the hospital, Remy had nearly created a rut in the carpet. When Lindy walked into the waiting room and opened her arms to Remy, she stopped pacing and accepted the hug.

"How is she?" Lindy asked.

Remy swiped at her tears. "I don't know yet. Nobody has come out to tell me anything. Believe me, I've tried. What good is being connected in this damn community if I can't use my influence to get information?"

"Hon, relax. They probably don't have much to tell you yet. Want me to see what I can find out?" Lindy asked.

"Please," Remy said as water filled her eyes again. "I love her so much. It was tough to see her in pain again."

"I'm sure it's been just as challenging for Chancy. She might have covered it up with her joviality, but she was pretty worried about you, too. Cancer is a scary thing. She'll be fine. She was talking to you, right? A few broken bones won't stop her. You know that."

Remy nodded. "Thanks, Lindy. I needed someone to talk me off the cliff."

"Absolutely. I take my best friend duties seriously. Let me see what I can find out. Go and sit with the rest of our friends." Lindy pointed to where Alex, Danna, Candice, Dawn, Marley, Luna, and Angel milled about on the far side of the waiting room.

Remy couldn't hear what Lindy was saying to the emergency department clerk, but it seemed to work because the young woman's eyes went wide, and she hopped from her seat to push open the doors into the patient care area. The gang surrounded Remy and performed their version of a protective circle as Lindy leaned against the desk, waiting for the clerk to return.

Remy kept looking toward the desk, where Lindy waited patiently and watched as the clerk had a brief conversation with Lindy. Lindy nodded several times then made her way to the group.

"So, they're taking films right now. Someone will be out in a few minutes after they've had a chance to review the X-rays. They suspect multiple fractures," Lindy informed the group.

"Shit," Alex bemoaned. "I should never have let her climb that ladder. I'm at fault here."

Remy touched Alex's arm. "Stop berating yourself. No one is to blame for this. It was an accident. They happen."

"She's right, honey. You gave us all excellent lessons," Danna added.

Luna shrugged. "Shit happens. Chancy is one tough girl. Have you forgotten she survived on the street for a long time? She'll shrug this off like every other challenge she's already faced in her young life. She'll be giving you shit again in no time."

Alex's lips curled slightly. "Yeah. No doubt she will, but not before I give her a really long lecture on the importance of listening to a crew boss. I'll let her heal first," she added.

A nurse strolled out to the waiting room and asked, "Which one of you is Remy?" She nodded once to Lindy.

Remy raised her hand. "I am."

"The doctor is in with Ms. Olsen right now. The arm is a clean break at almost the same spot as before. Our main concern is her hip, which will probably require surgery.

336

We're contacting the on-call orthopedist right now. She should be in surgery within the hour, barring any unforeseen issues."

"Can I see her before she goes into surgery?" Remy asked.

The nurse briskly nodded. "This way. Follow me. Don't worry. Chancy will get the five-star treatment. Lindy Fremont is a big donor to this hospital. I won't even try to deny that having friends in high places helps."

Remy smiled. So that's how she got the clerk to act.

†

"They gave me the good stuff," Chancy slurred. "I guess I royally fucked up this time. I've never had surgery before. Will you think poorly of me if I say I'm scared? Sometimes people don't wake from anesthesia. The doctor told me everything that could go wrong with the surgery."

Remy stroked Chancy's face. "They have to tell you about all the risks, but I'm sure everything will go well. The nurse says because Lindy is a big-time donor, you're about to get the imperial treatment. I wouldn't be surprised if they placed the red carpet underneath the surgery table for you. The nurse assured me the orthopedist is the best in the state. I'll be here waiting for you when you wake. I'm not letting you wiggle out of a proper marriage proposal."

That earned Remy a sloppy smile. "I love you."

"I love you, too," Remy answered as she grabbed Chancy's hand and squeezed.

The nurses pushed aside the curtain. "You ready?" she asked Chancy.

Chancy weakly nodded. The nurse disconnected the wires and rolled Chancy out of the room. Remy reluctantly let go of Chancy's hand and returned to the waiting room.

"How's she doing?" Lindy asked.

"She's scared. I think she believes she might not wake from anesthesia. The doctor shared all the risks of surgery. I wish they wouldn't do that. She's never been under the knife, so she doesn't know the risk is low for young, healthy people. I tried to reassure her, but it broke my heart to see her so distraught. Even with the amount of drugs they pumped into her, I could see her distress."

Lindy returned to her seat and patted the chair next to her. "Come. Sit. We're going to be here for a while."

CHAPTER TWENTY-SEVEN

The hours crept by like molasses in the winter before the surgery waiting room door opened, and Dr. Andrews walked inside. "Mrs. Fremont, it's good to see you again." He smiled. "Is our patient a friend of yours?"

"She is a dear young friend. How is she?" Lindy asked.

"The surgery was a success, and she is in recovery now. The break was clean, and with her age and good health, she will make a full and quick recuperation."

"Will she be in pain?" Remy asked.

"With the medications we have scheduled, she won't feel much pain for the next two days," he promised. "She will feel discomfort, but we don't want her to experience pain. She will likely sleep through the night." He saw the look of relief on Remy's face. "Tomorrow will be tough as the physical therapist will get her up to stand, and if she weight bears well, take a few steps."

"So soon?" Remy asked.

"The sooner, the better, to keep that joint working. It will take a few days to transition Chancy to oral pain medications and get her strong enough to go home. I assume she will be going home and not into rehab," he said.

"Yes, she will come home to me," Remy replied. "Do I need to arrange for a private nurse or aide?"

"Nurse, no, but an aide wouldn't be a bad idea to help her with dressing and other self-care activities. I will ask the physical therapist to give you a list of equipment that will help." Dr. Andrews smiled. "She will need physical therapy for a few weeks, but we can arrange for that in-home as well. Do promise me one thing," he said. "Keep her away from ladders for at least six months."

Remy smiled. "Maybe six years. How will she walk with a broken arm to do her therapy?"

"Normally, she would use a walker, but she'll have to use a one-sided walker and support from the therapist. Once her cast comes off, she should already be using a cane for several more months. Does she have any history of addictions or sensitivity to opioids?" Dr. Andrews asked.

Remy shook her head. "She's rarely taken Tylenol. She says she doesn't like medications. Why?"

"She's on some pretty strong pain medications, and sometimes it can be difficult to wean a patient from pain medications. We don't want her on them any longer than is medically necessary."

Alex stepped into the conversation. "Chancy has a high level of pain tolerance and will be the first to request medications to be stopped, even if she's still in pain."

"We don't need that either," Dr. Andrews replied. "I will bring her down as quickly as possible, but I don't want her fear of pain to interfere with her therapy."

"We will make sure she does the therapy," Luna said. "She will get the best care this family can give her."

Dr. Andrews smiled. "I do not doubt that. I'll be in the hospital for several more hours and will check in on her before I leave for the day. The nursing staff has my number if any complications arise."

"When can we see her?" Lindy asked.

"The nurses will come for you when she's transferred to a private room."

"Thank you, Dr. Andrews," Lindy said.

They settled back into their seats when he left the room. "I think we need to make some plans," Marley said. She looked at Remy. "I know you won't want to leave Chancy tonight, but since I'm still on limited activity, I should be the one to come relieve you in the morning. I can sit with her during the day while you get some rest. I've got the rest of the crew I can call on to help until she gets discharged."

"I can help you, too," Danna replied.

Alex looked at Luna. "Will you help me finish the stables? If possible, we can work tomorrow and maybe a few nights next week. I'd like to have them done before she comes home so we can have Raven delivered."

"I can pay to have a contractor come finish the job," Remy replied.

"Excuse me, but you are talking to a contractor," Alex reminded her.

"You know what I mean. I know you have other contracts to complete, and I don't want it to interfere with your schedule," Remy said.

"I always finish a job I've started. You worry about Chancy, and I'll take care of the stables."

"Candice and I can help again tomorrow, too," Dawn said. "We don't fly again until Tuesday."

"See, I've got help. Do you want me to talk with Janice and Selene? It's going to be a while before she can return to Sisters."

"Wasn't Chancy talking about someone named Kelly who wanted some experience as a bartender?" Marley asked.

"Yeah, she was. Maybe we can find out who she was talking about and see if Janice would hire her," Luna said.

"I know who she is," Alex said. "I'll suggest her to Janice."

†

The waiting room door opened, and the nurse stopped short when she saw the size of the group eager for news on Chancy. "Um, Ms. Olsen has been transferred to room 645. If you follow me, I'll take you up. Only two visitors at a time, though, but there's a waiting room upstairs."

"Can Alex and I go see what else we can get done before it gets too dark out?" Luna asked.

Marley nodded. "I'll get a ride back to the club."

"May Dawn and I help?" Candice asked.

"Me too," Angel said. "I was having a great time."

342

"Are you okay if we leave you?" Alex asked Remy.

Remy nodded. "That's fine. We'll only be watching Chancy sleep, I'm afraid."

Marley smiled at Luna. "Lindy and I will keep her company until they boot us out."

"Let's go then. Call if you need anything," Luna told Marley. "Love you."

"I love you too. Be safe and don't work too late," Marley said.

"Let's try to get the rest of these walls up today if we can. The rafters and roofing will require full daylight. If you can help with the roof tomorrow, I can do the electrical work on my own Monday."

Luna pulled her tool belt on. "Daylight's burning, boss."

†

Alex hammered the final nail three hours later, and they stored the tools in Alex's truck. "We did good tonight," Alex said. "I'd hire you all as a crew if I could afford you," she teased. "I'll leave my truck here and ride home with Danna. Can we meet by nine in the morning?"

"Would eight be better?" Angel asked. "Lindy and I will bring breakfast for an early start."

"If that's not too much to ask," Alex said.

"Eight it is then," Luna said.

"Will we be able to finish tomorrow?" Luna asked Alex after the others left.

They were walking toward Danna's car as they talked. "If we can get the roof on, I can do the electrical and interior work as time permits. A tack room and feed storage should be easy enough to do solo."

"I will take some time off and be your extra pair of hands," Danna replied.

Luna nodded. "If the schedule is light at TWC, I can help, too. Angel's right, this has been fun, except for Chancy's injury."

"I hope our little sprite recuperates well," Alex said. "I know she's tough, but that was scary as hell."

"I know what her next year's Christmas present is going to be from me," Luna said. "Human size bubble wrap," she said with a chuckle.

"I shiver at the thought of her wanting to learn to ride a horse," Alex added.

"Thank goodness she's young and healthy," Danna said.

Luna reached her Jeep. "I'll see you in the morning."

†

Marley was in the kitchen preparing a salad when Luna entered. Marley took Luna in her arms and kissed her deeply. "Please don't ever get hurt."

"I try my best not to. How are Chancy and Remy?"

"Chancy was resting peacefully. I don't think Remy will sleep a wink tonight. Lindy is meeting me at the hospital at seven to take Remy home for some rest."

Luna smiled at Marley. "I'll get up with you and meet Alex early. We aren't supposed to start until eight, but I know she'll be there when the sun rises."

"That sounds like a plan. I'll have a salad ready in a few, so take a shower. What do you want to drink?"

Luna kissed her again. "Tea will be fine. I'll be right back."

†

Marley placed the salad in the freezer to chill and entered the bathroom when she heard the water stop. She handed Luna a towel. "How far did y'all make it on the stables?"

Luna ran the towel through her hair. "We got all the walls in place. The roof supports are ready to go up tomorrow. If we're lucky, we'll finish the roof. Alex will do the electrical and interior work this week. I'll try to help her when I can."

Marley leaned against the sink and watched her lover dry her body. "Are you still considering getting a haircut?"

"I was. Why do you ask?" Luna inquired and cocked her head.

"Because it's so beautiful," Marley said. "I know you plan to donate it to cancer patients."

"If you don't want me to cut it, I won't," Luna said.

"No, that's selfish of me," Marley said. "You promise it will grow back fast?"

"It will, especially if you run your hands through it every night," Luna teased. "I'll even let you tug on it to help it grow." Luna reached for a robe and slipped it over her body. "Is the salad ready? I'm starving."

345

"I've got it chilling. I put in extra eggs, meat, and cheese, so you'll get your protein." Marley smiled.

"I do love you and your salads," Luna said. "Let's eat and get ready for bed. I'm exhausted."

†

Marley reached for Luna's hand. "I know Lindy is bringing breakfast out to you, but do you want something now?"

Luna took a seat at the bar. "Maybe I'll make us some ham and egg sandwiches before we go. Don't forget to dress warmly. Hospital rooms stay cold."

"With cheese?" Marley asked.

"With anything you want, my love," Luna replied.

†

Luna arrived at Remy's at a quarter to seven, and Alex was already at work digging a trench. Danna was busy gluing sections of PVC pipe. "I figured you'd be out early. What can I help with?"

"Grab another shovel. You can dig a smaller trench next to this one for the electric line. I'm glad you arrived early," Alex said. "We need to work hard to get the roof on today. I had the tin cut to specs, but we still need to get the rafters and plywood installed first. I think we can get it done, though."

"I'm here until we finish. Do you have lights we can hook up if we lose daylight?" Luna asked.

346

Alex nodded. "Yes, but I'm not risking anyone on a ladder after dark. We can't afford to have anyone else in the hospital right now."

"That's for sure." Luna slipped on her gloves and began digging. "How deep?"

"A good six inches deep, but it doesn't have to be wide," Alex said. "Just deep enough to bury the conduit." She pointed to her trench. "Waterlines have to run deeper to prevent freezing."

Luna looked up at the swimming pool enclosure. "I'm glad we didn't put the stables at the back of the property."

"Me too," Alex said and dumped another shovel of soil. "At least it's a pretty easy soil to dig into."

They had barely finished digging the trenches when Dawn, Candice, Angel, and Lindy arrived carrying bags of food. "You've been busy already," Dawn said.

"Just a bit," Luna said. "Did you convince Remy to come home to rest?" she asked Lindy.

"It wasn't easy, but yes. Remy's taking a shower. I'm sure she'll come out before she lays down. Are you at a stopping point to break for some food?"

Alex nodded. "I'm starving. Luna's working me hard."

"She's good for that," Lindy replied. "Can we use your tailgate for a buffet?"

"Yes, ma'am," Alex said and hopped down.

†

While they ate, Alex explained the process of raising the rafters and gave each of the group assignments.

Remy arrived as they finished eating. Lindy handed her a biscuit.

"You've got a lot done already," Remy said as she inspected the stables.

Alex smiled. "I'm aiming to have the roof up by the end of the day. I can work on the interior, water, and electric this week."

"How did Chancy do last night?" Luna asked.

"She woke up a few times, but just briefly, to give me a drunken smile," Remy said. "I feel bad for leaving her."

"Marley will keep a good eye on her today," Luna said.

"I know, but the first days of therapy are going to be painful," Remy said.

"Probably best that you aren't there then," Alex said. "Chancy will try to do too much trying to impress you. She needs to follow instructions. Marley will be tough and make sure that happens." She smiled. "You need to be there when she starts getting bored at the hospital. She won't care where she is if you're there with her."

Lindy chuckled. "You offer a strong point there, Alex."

†

"Daylight's burning. Are we ready to start rafters?" Luna asked.

"Please, be careful," Remy said.

"We will. Lindy, will you make sure she gets in the bed for some sleep?" Alex said.

"You heard the boss," Lindy said. "Let's go."

"Thank you all," Remy said.

†

There were only two more rafters to set when Alex looked at Luna. "We need a break."

"I won't argue with that," Luna said. She looked at her watch. "We're making good progress, aren't we?"

"Yes, you ladies are impressive," Alex said. "If you ever need a job, I'll hire you in an instant."

"You're a good teacher," Angel said. "Lindy and I aren't tall enough to be much help in the decking. Is there something else we can do?"

Alex nodded toward a roll of conduit. "You can unroll and stretch that the length of the narrow trench. Once you get it stretched, I'll cut it, and you can start threading electrical wires through it for me."

"That sounds easy enough," Lindy said.

"That will save me a lot of time," Alex told them. She looked at Luna. "Ready to knock these last two out?"

Luna refilled her nail pouch. "I am now."

†

"Holy hell, that hurts," Chancy said when the therapist helped her stand.

"It will get easier every day," Sue, the therapist, promised. "The first few days aren't easy, but you have to get started to heal and regain strength."

"It feels, I dunno, so foreign," Chancy complained.

"You will get used to that, too. Are you ready to try a few steps?"

"How many?" Chancy asked.

349

"To the door and back," Sue replied. "For now."

"What do you mean, for now?" Chancy growled.

"You will have therapy three times a day while you're here, so get used to seeing me," Sue teased.

"Fucking A." Chancy groaned when she took her first step.

"You're doing good," Marley said. "Keep coming."

"I will never climb another ladder," Chancy said.

"Right," Marley said. "Sure you will. Whenever the Amazon sisters do another project, you'll be right there in the middle of the action."

Chancy smiled at Marley, and then the smile disappeared when she took the next step.

"Maybe we should put one of those safety harnesses on you like we used ziplining," Marley said.

"That's probably not a bad idea. Where did you zipline?" Sue asked.

Chancy took another step. "Over the rain forest in St. Kitts during a Christmas vacation."

"That sounds like it would be a lot of fun," Sue said.

"Much more fun than this," Chancy said.

"You're doing good. Let's turn slowly, and we'll walk back to your bed," Sue promised.

†

Danna left midafternoon and returned with bags filled with burgers and fries. "Time for a food break," she hollered as she placed bags on the tailgate.

"One more sheet of decking, and we'll be down," Alex called to her. "Let's knock it out. At least two of those burgers are calling my name," she told Luna.

"I think we're ready for you to cut the conduit, too," Angel said. "We started threading from the open end and have gone as far as we can."

"Good job," Alex said. "Do you want to lay the water pipe in the trench next? I think there is enough glued already."

"If not, I'll glue some more," Danna said.

Luna looked at Lindy. "Have you checked on Remy?"

"Sleeping like a baby." Lindy smiled. "I checked in with Marley, too. Chancy made it through her first round of therapy. She didn't waste time hitting her medication pump when she got back into the bed, and she's sleeping too."

"Thanks," Luna said.

"I sent her pics of her two favorite Amazons working on the roof, too," Lindy said. "Her answer, 'swoon.'"

†

Alex secured the last section of tin as the sun was sinking. She looked over at Luna. "We did it."

Luna stepped off the ladder. "Good job, everyone. Raven now has a home."

"When do you think she'll be delivered?" Angel asked.

"I'll get the information from Remy and see what we can do," Lindy said. "I may need some muscle to get supplies picked up."

Luna flexed. "Have muscle, will travel."

"What about sawdust and tack?" Alex asked.

Lindy hopped up on the tailgate. "I'll get Remy to pick it out and have the tack delivered with a truckload of sawdust or shavings. I think Remy wants to go ahead and have Chancy's horse delivered too, even though it will be a while before she can ride."

"It may be some good incentive for Chancy to finish her therapy to be able to ride with Remy," Alex said. She looked back at the stables. "Good job, everyone. These stables wouldn't be possible without your hard work."

"I've already snapped a few photos to show Chancy," Lindy said.

"Are you taking Remy up tonight?" Luna asked.

"No, she's going to drive, but Angel and I will go up to relieve Marley so she can go home." Lindy looked around at her group of friends. "Cookout here next weekend to celebrate Chancy coming home and all the hard work we've done? Maybe we'll even have horses to watch."

"That sounds good," Luna said.

"We have to fly Sunday," Dawn said.

"We'll do it Saturday then," Lindy said. "Everyone good for Saturday?"

"Count us in," Alex and Danna said. "Make it a potluck, and we can bring something."

Lindy smiled. "I'll coordinate that this week. Let's go home," she said. "Thanks again, everyone."

"Please tell Remy I'll be out a couple of days this week to finish the rest of the work," Alex said.

†

Luna helped Alex load the tools and equipment into her truck. They sat on the tailgate as darkness surrounded them. "We did good, didn't we?" Luna said.

"Yeah, we did." Alex grinned. "Nothing we can't do when we need something done."

"Roger that, my friend. Let's go home." Luna hopped down and walked to her Jeep.

EPILOGUE

Two months passed quickly. Chancy still used a cane to keep her balance stable, but she didn't let that keep her from walking and starting back part-time at Sisters. Remy had made her promise to take frequent breaks to rest her hip, and Chancy kept that promise.

Raven and her new stablemate, Spryte, settled into their new home, and Remy was happy to take Raven on rides around the field. Chancy was excited for Remy to teach her how to ride but would have to wait for her six-month clearance from Dr. Andrews before she could climb into a saddle.

†

When that day finally arrived, Chancy was eager to give up her cane for a set of reins. Remy taught her how to saddle Spryte and then asked Chancy to go to the tack room for a bridle. When Chancy returned, she was surprised to see her friends gathered around Spryte, Raven, and Remy.

"What's going on?" she asked.

"Do you honestly think we'd miss your first ride?" Alex asked.

"Well, at least I'll have two Amazons here to pick me up if I fall," Chancy joked.

"Spryte won't let you fall, and neither will I, but there's something I need to ask before we mount our horses," Remy said.

"Yes, my insurance is paid..." Chancy stopped in mid-sentence when she saw Remy down on one knee. "What?"

Remy smiled. "I thought it would be safer for me to get down on one knee, and besides, I'm the one that's been hesitant. Chancy, will you marry me?"

"I thought you'd never ask," Chancy said. "Hell, yes," she hollered, and Spryte twitched her ears but didn't flinch.

"Um, honey, don't yell around horses," Remy joked.

Chancy offered Remy her hand and lifted her to her feet. She pulled her into a kiss. "I've waited for this moment all my life. Yes, I will marry you."

"Finally," Alex cheered, and the group clapped.

"Congratulations, you two," Danna said.

"We still have much to discuss, but I want you to know you are the one I want to spend the rest of my life with. No more excuses," Remy promised.

†

Later, as they rode home, Luna took Marley's hand in hers and kissed it. "It feels so good for everything to be working out so well. Chancy and Remy finally engaged."

"I have a sneaking suspicion Lindy and Angel will be the next to make a commitment," Marley said. "Lindy and Jaydub have agreed it's in everyone's best interest to divorce." She sighed. "He's already got a young woman pregnant in DC, so he'll be moving there."

"Good riddance," Luna said.

"Amen," Marley said.

"I guess we'd better get busy planning our celebration," Luna replied.

Marley smiled. "I'm on it, babe."

ABOUT THE AUTHOR

Annette Mori

Annette is an award-winning author, published by Affinity Rainbow Publications, who lives in the beautiful Pacific Northwest with her wife and their four furry kids. With twenty-six published novels, three Lesfic Bard Awards, and one Goldie Award for her fourth novel, *Locked Inside*, she finally feels like a real author. Annette is as much a reader as a writer and is always looking for the next sapphic novel to queue up. She came up with the One Fan at a Time tagline, because it rolled off the tongue much better than One Reader at a Time. After pondering who she was at her core, she feels it was all about connecting to each reader on a personal level. Annette would be the first to admit she doesn't do well with the masses. If someone picks up her book and it touches them, she believes she has achieved what she wants with her writing by reaching each reader. It is who she is at her core. Drop her a line. She loves to hear from readers.

Email: annettemori0859@gmail.com.

Sign up for her mailing list:http://eepurl.com/cS7nr9

Check out her blog: Everyday Occurrences: https://annettemori0859.wordpress.com/

Visit the Affinity Rainbow Publications website for her books and many other outstanding authors: www.affinityebooks.com

Ali Spooner

Ali Spooner lives in beautiful northwest Florida with several fur babies. Ali's writing began as a hobby, and with the assistance of the Affinity Rainbow Publishing team has advanced her love of storytelling to a new level.

Ali's characters are primarily everyday people, from cowgirls to psychics. Ali also has created a few supernatural characters in her paranormal series. Several of her twenty-plus books have been Amazon-rated number one choices, and always include a happily ever after. Ali's hobbies include photography, reading, travel, college sports, and spending time with family and friends.

OTHER AFFINITY BOOKS

<u>Georgetown Glen</u> by Annette Mori

Lucy Manetti is positively euphoric over her recent purchase of an old ghost town. Unfortunately, she failed to consult with her wife, Bea, before buying the abandoned village. Predictably, Bea is not as enamored with transforming the ghost town into a sapphic retirement community, but Bea's love for her wife trumps her displeasure over Lucy's impulsiveness. The mature couple hires Fiona, an expert at restoring old houses, and Saville, a certified electrician, to bring the ghost town back to its glory days.

According to the adorable real estate agent who recommended the pair, Fiona and Saville have *history*. Lucy detects a spark between the two young women and decides, against the advice of her wife, to play matchmaker, bringing her beautiful niece into the mix. As the ragtag team begins their work on the old saloon, they discover a lot more than they bargained for, including ghosts, long-buried secrets, an abused golden retriever, and maybe even love.

Serenity by K Belmar
After Kirby MacLennan had lost her partner and her
only sibling in a horrific accident, all she wanted to do was
move from the city and live the rest of her life alone in a
small mountain village. When she meets Samantha Parker,
the village sheriff, they soon become friends. Samantha's
cousin Jackie, and her wife Beth, along with their children,
moved into the old farmhouse next door to Kirby. Something
makes Kirby uneasy about the couple's relationship and she
finds herself drawn to Beth, and her silent plea for help.
Can Kirby overcome her own trauma of the past to help
a neighbor in need? Will she finally accept love back into her
life, enough to move out of the shadows and into the light?

Along Came Sally by JM Dragon
Angela Barossa is content with her life as the local
realtor in the small town of Whistler. Until a request to
see a property that can only be sold to a local or ex-local
disturbs her.
The name of the potential client…Sally Maguire. Why
on earth would her childhood nemesis want to return to
Whistler? Angela needs to be dispassionate in her dealings
with Sally, but can she?
Simply a timeless romance.

Artist Free Zone by Annette Mori
Melissa just moved to a conservative part of Washington
State. A move designed to set her and her longtime partner
up for early retirement. But best laid plans go awry when her
partner, Colette decides, out of the blue, their relationship
isn't working for her. The only thing left to do is sob all over

her beloved kitties. Vowing never to get involved, ever again, with another artist.

Colette is torn up about hurting Melissa. She hasn't been entirely honest about her reasons for leaving and that tears her up even further. She keeps calling to make sure Melissa is okay. Life is exciting and wonderful for her because she's met her soulmate and plans on moving to Alaska. But will Karma exact its revenge?

This is a raw and honest portrayal of love lost and love found again.

Not to mention the soothing influence of a beloved feline.

Finding her Heart by Samantha Hicks

Ellis Davis's self-imposed isolation is blown apart when a new neighbour moves in next door. Having spent the last five years working from home, shutting herself away from the world she once knew. The last thing Ellis wants, or needs, is the woman next door challenging her beliefs about herself and bringing out feelings Ellis has never experienced before.

Melissa Cole moves into her new home as a recently divorced woman, raising her young son as a single parent with the help of her parents. Melissa is instantly intrigued by her mysterious neighbour next door.

Forever Home by Ali Spooner

Nat, Marissa and Maggie survived their first winter by the ocean. Spring brings new growth, friends and unwelcome visitors to the homestead. Find out how Nat and Marissa's tiny community deal with the hazards and rewards before them, as their homestead continues to grow and prosper. Expect romance, adventure, danger, good fortune, and the odd meal or two, in this sequel to The Bee Charmer.

<u>Disconnected</u> by Annette Mori

Vanna has always felt like something was off with her parents, leaving her feeling oddly disconnected. She decides to move across the country and establish a new and independent life after college. On the way to her new position in Flagstaff, Arizona, Vanna meets out and proud Trey, who loves to flirt.

Trey has never forgotten the beautiful young woman she met briefly and is determined to ensure their paths cross again.

Thousands of miles from home, Vanna finds out more about herself, but not her feeling of being disconnected from her parents. Will Vanna ever form the connection she desperately seeks? Does Trey's determination work out?

Affinity
Rainbow Publications

eBooks, Print, Free eBooks

Visit our website for more publications available online.

www.affinityrainbowpublications.com

Published by Affinity Rainbow Publications
A Division of Affinity eBook Press NZ LTD
Canterbury, New Zealand

Registered Company 2517228

www.ingramcontent.com/pod-product-compliance
Lightning Source LLC
Chambersburg PA
CBHW070401260626
47161CB00001B/233